THE URANIUM DRIVE-IN

SETH CAGIN

The Uranium Drive In

Copyright © 2024 by Seth Cagin

First edition—July 2024

ISBN: 979-8-9901095-2-0 (Paperback)
ISBN: 979-8-9901095-3-7 (eBook)
ISBN: 979-8-9901095-5-1 (Hardcover)

*This book is dedicated to everyone who worked at
The Watch newspaper, serving Telluride and the
surrounding region between 1996, the year it was founded,
and 2014, when it was sold and subsequently folded.*

Uranium DRIVE IN

Chapter 1

MISSING

R ay Walker missed his daughter's wedding last night."

Billy Pederson spoke without inflection, as if to give away as little as possible, but then, the Montrose County sheriff's deputy always talked that way.

"Missed it?" Tom asked. "You mean he just didn't show up?"

To learn of a missing man from Deputy Pederson was a professional responsibility for Tom, who was the editor as well as the publisher of the West End Forum, but he was also a member of the small community of Naturita and neighboring Nucla, and was friendly with Ray Walker, so it hit him on a personal level at the same time.

"Sarah says they didn't have a fight or something like that to explain it," Billy said, referring to Walker's wife. "Says he was really looking forward to it. Plus, he still hasn't come home yet. Sarah says he got a service call on Wednesday afternoon, took off in his rig, and never come back."

"He missed Angie's wedding?"

"Yep," Billy said.

"And they went ahead without him?"

"Had to. It was all planned and paid for."

"That must have been a real fun wedding."

"Real fun."

"Why didn't Sarah report it quicker that he was missing?" Tom asked. "That doesn't make sense."

"There'll be time to ask her that, I reckon."

"Damn."

Tom leaned back in his chair. His mind was flooded with more questions, but he had an immediate concern: Would he have to rip up his front page and write a new lead story for the Forum? Press time was only an hour off.

"He probably run off the road somewhere," Billy said. "I need some help looking. If he run off the road and survived it, then he's hurt and we gotta find him fast."

"Well, if that's what happened, he's probably dead," Tom said. "He's already been out there four nights. It's been cold."

"Yep." The deputy was grim but matter-of-fact. "But maybe not. And even if he is dead, we've gotta look anyway."

"Got a picture?" Tom asked. "I'm sure I've got one somewhere, but…"

Billy was already sliding a snapshot across the desk. Tom picked it up. Ray Walker was in his early forties, his face weathered by a life lived mostly outdoors on the West End. He wore a full beard and a mesh cap emblazoned with the name of his business, Walker's Auto Repair. Ray worked on Tom's ancient Toyota, and half the other cars in the West End. He stared into the camera as if he were posing for a mug shot, no trace of friendliness or a smile in his expression. Ray was a good-natured guy, but there was no suggestion of that in the photograph. Sarah Walker, or whoever had given it to Billy, had not taken the time to look for the most flattering picture of the missing man, but had grabbed one that came immediately to hand. Tom shuddered at the thought that Ray could be lying off the side of a highway, trapped in his mangled truck, maybe unconscious, slowly dying, wondering if he would be found in time, if he was conscious at all.

"Paper's out tomorrow, right? We'd appreciate a story if you can get it in," Billy said. "Maybe somebody's seen him or his truck. But we've got to start searching now. Cross the street in an hour."

"Right," Tom said. "Let me write it up and get the paper out; then I'll help."

* * *

Tom studied the front page he had been about to send to the printer. President Bush was reelected the week before, and the lead story, under the headline "West End Is Bush Country," reported that the president had won 81 percent of local votes. Tom removed that story, thinking he'd move it below the fold, and also removed the story that he had placed there earlier. That was a story he'd downloaded from a wire service about how the meth epidemic had hurt military recruiting in precisely the areas, like the West End, where those efforts had always been most fruitful.

Tom liked how the two stories talked to each other: Bush was reelected at the same time potential soldiers were lost to drug addiction. He liked to think that by running the stories together on the front page, he was, in his own way, educating his readership; it was unlikely, but maybe a few readers outside the 19 percent who voted against Bush would see the connection.

Tom typed the headline "MISSING," in 36-point type, all caps, boldface, at the top of the page. But when he placed the mug shot of Ray beneath the headline and kept it at its proper dimensions it took up almost the entire page, leaving room only for a few words about Ray Walker's disappearance, and no room for Bush.

At first, Tom wasn't sure if that was the right way to go. But blown up large, the image of Ray had an iconic quality, even before it was reproduced several thousand times and widely distributed. In soft focus and slightly off-kilter, the snapshot created a strong if inadvertent impression that Ray was already fading away and difficult to visualize with clarity as someone you might see driving past in his tow truck on any given day, someone whose hand you would shake when you ran into him at the Merc, someone you'd see cheering on the sidelines of every sports event involving either one of his two kids. Besides, it was satisfying to push Bush off of page 1 by something of much more immediate interest to his readers. Tom went with it, placing the election story on page 3. That left no room for the story about the army's recruiting difficulties. But he knew he could afford to hold that one for another week, since neither meth use nor the need for military volunteers to fight the war in Iraq were going to abate in the next seven days.

Tom clicked "send" to upload the paper to the printer in Cortez and walked across the state highway that served as the town of Naturita's main street to the Maverick Café, where a group of Ray's friends had gathered. Tom grimaced to see that the flyers with Ray's mug, already posted in the window, carried the same headline he had just written. But perhaps "MISSING" was simply unavoidable. It was odd that no synonym worked. Ray wasn't "lost," "gone," or "absent." All of those words had entirely different connotations. Nor was Ray "misplaced," like a set of keys or a wallet, although he could be said to have "vanished." If you said he had vanished, though, that would imply something supernatural and would further suggest that neither the missing man, nor even a trace of him, would ever be found. That seemed, at the moment, unlikely, as Sally Morgan, who owned the Maverick, promptly observed from her station behind the coffee shop counter, just as Tom walked in.

"Hell of a thing," Sally said. "A person doesn't just vanish into thin air." She meant it as encouragement to the search parties that were beginning to form: Start looking and you'll find him.

This was a reasonable assumption because there were far likelier explanations for Ray's disappearance than a vanishing into thin air. Anyone who lived on the West End could imagine taking a curve too fast on one of the remote highways that traversed the canyon country, skidding off the road to where they'd be invisible to anyone driving past. It could happen while swerving to dodge a deer or a rock on the road, or from skidding across black ice on bald tires. And while a single-car accident was the likeliest reason that Ray Walker would miss his daughter's wedding, it was not the only thought that crossed the minds of the men and a few women gathered at the Maverick.

If Ray took a call from a stranded motorist, then who called, and where were they now? Did he crash after he repaired the traveler's vehicle and sent him on his way?

Perhaps the call had been to assist a four-wheel drive vehicle stranded in the backcountry. SUVs got stuck out there and had to be rescued all the time. If that were the case, then Ray could be far from a main road, far even from a secondary road. He could be virtually anywhere in a vast area of rugged canyons and mesas, scrubland and mountains, an area covering hundreds of square miles traversed by nameless and numberless dirt tracks and long-abandoned mining roads, not to mention sandy streambeds, salt flats and slickrock, where vehicles ventured freely.

Or was Ray called out under false pretenses by somebody with criminal intentions?

On one point, everyone was agreed, and it was Sally, typically, who voiced it: "Ray always doted on that little girl of his. He would not spoil her wedding, not if there was any way on God's green earth he could help it, that's for sure."

"Everyone find a partner," Billy said, "and I'll assign you a stretch of road. There's only a couple of hours of light left. You've got to drive real slow and look on both sides of the road."

"I'll ride with you, if you'd like," Dave Best said to Tom.

"Sure," Tom nodded. Dave owned the West End Merc.

"That was one helluva strange wedding," Dave said, as Tom steered west out of town, down the San Miguel River canyon.

"I bet."

"It was half wedding, half funeral, with Ray not showing up," Dave said. "Sarah did her best to keep it together, but everyone was just trying to think where he was at."

"Man, that's harsh."

"It was a real shame for Angie and Craig to start their married life like that."

"No doubt."

"And there was no drowning of sorrows neither," Dave added. "It was a dry wedding. Some of their friends just come out of rehab so they didn't want to put temptation in front of them. Craig's step-father's a part-time preacher from Paonia, and he performed the service. This guy sells insurance during the week, and he made all these cracks about how following Christ and buying State Farm is one and the same thing. 'It's all insurance,' he says. That's what he preaches."

"Guess I'll burn in hell," Tom said. "No religion. Or insurance."

Dave laughed, then continued with the story.

"I mean, he was trying to sell fucking insurance while performing the nuptials while everyone's mind is on Ray. I guess Ray didn't miss much. Or maybe he did. He'd have gotten a good laugh out of it, and then it would have been OK for me to laugh, too. We could have snuck out for a beer, maybe. But instead, I'm just listening to this guy try to sell insurance wondering where the hell Ray was. Or where he's at now."

They drove in silence for a moment.

"I've known Ray Walker my whole life," Dave said. "We played Little League together. He was a hell of a pitcher."

"Oh yeah?"

"You know the Springsteen song, 'Glory Days'? That was Ray and me and a bunch of us when we were 12 and won the Southwest League. We beat a Cortez team, the D'backs, who hadn't lost a game in a couple of years. Ray had the winning hit, right over the short-stop to center field. The parents of those Cortez boys were in shock, man, they were crying, their eyes all red. They'd worn their ace pitcher down in the tournament and that's why we won, because he was usually unhittable. After the game this kid says to me, 'I pitched bad,' and I say to him, 'Nah, you pitched good, Ray was just on, man,' I was just trying to make him feel better, and then the kid's dad grabs him by his *pitching* arm, which was probably about ready to drop off him as it was, and yanks him away like he shouldn't be talking to me because I'm the enemy…."

He shook his head.

"I wonder where the hell he is."

Tom turned onto the Paradox Valley road, toward the Utah state line, and slowed down.

"I'll look left, you look right," he said.

Despite their purpose, Tom found himself glancing up to admire the scenery. He couldn't help himself. People who had grown up on the West End were oblivious to the landscape. Tom had been there only five years and still drank in the long views of distant blue peaks and rocky red-hued canyons spiked with juniper and pinion that fell away to a vanishing point. There were many places in the region where abandoned cars sat rusting away on some ledge or precipice where they had landed after their driver had crashed them, not worth the effort for anyone to try to salvage them. Most such wrecks dated from the forties or fifties, though, when uranium prospectors ventured into what was then even more remote country than it was now.

If a driver were to lose control of his vehicle and shoot off the highway at a high speed, how far from the road would he land?

"He could be too far from the highway for us to see him," Tom said.

"Look for fresh skid marks," Dave said.

But there were many places where slickrock on the side of the road would not show any skid marks.

"I'm afraid Ray might have been mixed up in some bad business," Dave said.

"What kind of bad business?"

"Meth."

"I never would have guessed that," Tom said mildly. "Why do you think it?"

"Dunno. It just seems like everything that goes bad lately around here has meth at the bottom of it."

"He doesn't seem the type."

"Awww, I guess you're right. He's a straight arrow."

Tom wondered if Dave was trying to tell him something, but didn't ask any more questions. He would be "new" on the West End even if he stayed another forty years and died in old age at the West End Clinic. His obituary in the Forum at that point, whoever wrote it, even if he wrote it himself from his deathbed, would describe him as an Easterner. "Tom Austin of Boston, longtime owner and editor of the West End Forum, died Friday at the age of 79 at the West End Clinic...."

But if Tom could never be a true West Ender, he had been there long enough to know that aggressive questions would only push the answers away. He had run into a wall of resistance when he first arrived and tried to write an exposé of uranium's legacy of poisoned land and water and ruined health. How the Cold War had domestic victims. Even though he had abandoned his ambition of writing a big story, he was still considered a troublemaker by members of the old mining families he had tried to interview for it. He guessed that if Ray Walker's disappearance had anything to do with methamphetamines, he would learn the sad details soon enough.

* * *

"We've called for a helicopter," Billy told the searchers who had returned to the Maverick just after dark. "It'll be here tomorrow morning. So, we don't need any more search teams right now. Sheriff Martin will be here tomorrow to lead the investigation."

Martin was based in the county seat, a hundred miles to the east, making Billy the only law enforcement officer within a 50-mile radius.

The deputy shuffled his feet and added, "But so far as the law is concerned, we don't even have a missing person yet. He hasn't been gone all that long, and most times when an adult disappears, they've just gone off on some private business and they turn up in a day or two."

This was clearly wisdom Billy had just received from his boss, and it was obvious he didn't entirely believe it himself.

Sally called him on it. "You know that ain't true about Ray, now don't you, Billy Pederson?"

Billy tried to ignore her.

"Thanks for all your help," he said. He started to back away, toward the door, but nobody else moved.

"I know it's probably pointless," said Brandon Muller, who Tom guessed could have been another of the 1976 11- and 12-year-old West End Sox. "But I'm gonna keep looking, even if I have to do it by myself."

The others murmured their agreement and Billy couldn't object. Instead, he quickly took charge. If the search was going to continue, he would be damned if it would be without him.

"All right then," he said. "We'll put new teams on sections of road another team's already checked. New set of eyes might see something."

Ray Walker's dozen or so neighbors searched all night long, Tom among them, peering into the outback with flashlights that barely penetrated the vast darkness, their shouts swallowed up by the wind, finding no sign of the missing auto mechanic.

Chapter 2

A REAL STORY
TO CONTEND WITH

The helicopter didn't find anything either. Ray Walker, it seemed, had not run off the road, but had either left on his own accord or had met up with foul play. To those who knew him, foul play was the obvious answer, since the Ray Walker they knew would never abandon his family. But to Montrose County Sheriff Trace Martin, the alternative explanation was far likelier.

"Many people have secret lives," the sheriff told Tom in an interview at the Forum office, upon completing a day's search from the air. Martin, who was in his sixties, relished his role as a Western sheriff out of central casting, dressing the part in cowboy shirt, boots, Wranglers, a big hat, and a potbelly. He made no pretense at all to being modern and suffered no job insecurity, routinely winning reelection every four years without spending a nickel or a minute's time on a campaign.

"People in law enforcement find out pretty quick, when an adult disappears, ninety-nine times out of hundred, there's been no foul play," the sheriff said. "So, we have to investigate the other possibilities first. People disappear when they run themselves into debt, or if they have a fight with their spouse, or fall in love with somebody they're not supposed to, or when they get depressed."

He pronounced it "dee-pressed," as if it were a foreign word for a concept he'd heard about at a law enforcement seminar but had never actually seen, much less experienced. So, too, the four reasons persons typically disappear sounded textbook.

"Now, I'm not trying to say anything about Ray Walker," Martin hastened to add. "I don't know that boy personally, and I'm not trying to in-sin-u-ate anything about his character. But odds are he'll call home in a day or two or he'll turn up and he'll be terribly sorry for all the worry he's caused."

* * *

Tom could not discount the sheriff's wisdom. He knew firsthand about disappearing acts.

The very idea that Tom Austin was the publisher and editor of a small-town paper in the smallest town in the most remote and sparsely populated corner of the United States would have seemed impossible to Tom or to anyone who knew him just ten years before. Then, living within ten miles of where he was born in suburban Boston, Tom himself couldn't have imagined a place that was a seven- or eight-hour drive on mostly two-lane highways from any of the four closest cities of Denver, Salt Lake City, Phoenix, or Albuquerque, even if you drove the entire distance speeding at 80 miles per hour. The town of Naturita was even more isolated than that: well over an hour's drive from the nearest towns with a modern supermarket—Cortez, Colorado, and Moab, Utah.

By another name, not yet having changed it to the pseudonym

Tom Austin, he had been a young reporter for the Worcester Union-Leader, with no shortage of ideas or ambition. Right out of journalism school, he eagerly took any assignment handed to him, covering school board meetings without a murmur of complaint, anticipating a quick rise in the ranks, and soon, he imagined, job offers from bigger papers and then, a Pulitzer, followed by book contracts or an assignment as an overseas bureau chief for The New York Times — all by the time he was 40. Like the other junior reporters, he pitched ideas at story meetings and was shot down, and often had his best ideas stolen by senior reporters who utterly mangled them.

Then he got a break, the assignment of reporting the reaction within the town's tightly knit Hmong community after a Hmong grocer shot and killed a couple of hunters who challenged him after he trespassed on their private hunting reserve. The Hmong man was not crazy, Tom believed. He just felt threatened. The assignment was to do a sidebar to a hard news story about the incident, but Tom went big with it, working overtime to interview dozens of people and detailing the community's isolation from the society around them, explaining how the tragedy emerged from cultural assumptions on both sides. Against the odds, the paper's top editor saw the quality in the story and ran it on page one.

Then known by the name on his birth certificate as Ken Hanley, Tom was recruited by The Boston Mail. Not yet 30, he was recognized as a comer and was given good assignments and turned in stories that won him increasingly more latitude to range widely.

Ken led the good life that went along with the bright career: an apartment near Fenway and enough money to buy Red Sox tickets without a second thought, even from a scalper who marked them up two hundred percent. He had some drinking buddies with whom the conversation never got too heavy. He saw his mother, who still lived in his childhood home, every couple of weeks for dinner or Sunday brunch at her club, sometimes joined by his sister, who was just finishing law school, and her stockbroker husband. He operated on the assumption that his life would continue to progress according to plan, from one logical stage to the next, each with its own set of manageable challenges. Someday, but not too soon, he would meet the right woman and they would settle down; first, they would get a dog, and then they would have children.

Only later, after reinventing himself as Tom Austin, did Ken realize that he had been operating in a rare and fragile state of grace.

*   *   *

The first days after Ray Walker's disappearance had an unreality about them. Tom — then Ken — was reminded of his father's funeral, when he was 13: the long line of cars to the cemetery as he rode in a black limousine with his mother and sister at the head of the procession in the first car following the hearse. Out the window he saw a woman holding a little girl's hand as they waited to cross the street. He could clearly read the woman's expression as she wondered what dignitary had died who was so important to have a funeral so fully attended, with such a long procession of mourners.

It's just my dad, Ken mouthed, but she couldn't see him behind the darkly tinted window. Her life was interrupted for only as long as it took for the funeral caravan to pass. His life, and his mother's and sister's lives, were interrupted forever. His father's life was over, cut short by a heart attack. But life itself went on, without remorse, that very day of the burial in a series of mundane moments that had a striking crispness to them. Even at the cemetery, while his mother appeared steady and calm — an impressive display of dignity, it seemed to Ken — and his little sister wailed, equally heartbreaking, Ken found himself quietly cataloging these banal details: a plane flew overhead leaving a white contrail, wind rustled the leaves in a tree, the priest droned, a man waiting by a small bulldozer to fill his father's grave with dirt tapped his fingers restlessly against his knee. His father's best friend whispered something irrelevant to his wife. Were they making dinner plans? With each passing moment, and each observation Ken registered, his father was left further in the past.

But it was not at all clear that Ray Walker was being left behind as life continued in its usual way in Naturita. Indeed, it was quite possible that it was just the opposite, it was the community of Naturita that had been abandoned by Ray, and he was carrying on with his life in new surroundings, leaving the town behind to continue its slow decay into the landscape, as if it were an isotope of radioactive element, with a half-life of, perhaps, fifty or sixty years. And yet there was still the sense of heightened reality Tom associated with death, a sense of the abnormal in the familiar, in the sounds of a truck passing on the highway, a screen door slamming, or a telephone ring. Any of these, after all, could be the first indication that Ray had returned home with an explanation of where he had been, an explanation so simple that nobody had thought of it. Or that he had been found, dead or alive.

The Forum was rarely called upon to cover a breaking story. Instead, Howard Knapp, the publisher from whom Tom bought the paper, had told him that his first priority was supporting his advertisers, and he introduced him to Dave Best at the Merc.

"If you and Dave aren't great friends," Howard told him, "then you lose your business."

People pick up a community paper to see what's on sale at the grocery store, and to see pictures of their friends and children, and to see their own names in print, Howard had explained. Of course, it was essential to cover the Naturita Town Board, school sports, local business and church news, and the latest outrage perpetrated on the community by bureaucrats at the federal Bureau of Land Management or the Colorado Division of Wildlife, who were under the thumb of radical environmentalists over in Denver and up in Telluride, the closest upscale alpine resort and "a yellow jackets nest of damned liberal atheists," Howard said. More than anything, though, the Forum was a community bulletin board. The paper's most important feature might be the school lunch menu, faxed over to him every week by Sarah Walker, Ray Walker's wife, who worked as a secretary at the Naturita School.

"Are you sure you want to do this?" Howard had asked when Tom eyed him skeptically as Howard showed him how to process the lunch menu for publication.

But Howard misread him. This was journalism that made perfect sense to Tom, beautifully artless, and his expression did not speak of any misgivings; it spoke instead to the fact that he appreciated the simple honesty of it. There was something reassuringly specific about the school lunch menu. "Monday: franks and beans, lime Jell-O. Tuesday: hamburger pizza and green salad...." Tom was more than willing to treat the school lunch menu with respect, and the social calendar, too, and especially the obituaries.

The Forum had about a thousand out-of-town subscribers, virtually all of them old-timers who had moved away, many living in nursing homes in Grand Junction, Montrose, Cortez, Farmington, and Moab. As he hand-labeled the papers for mailing each week and the names of the subscribers became familiar—there were more than a few Redds, Pattersons, Bests, and Morgans—Tom started to feel as if he knew them personally. The subscribers shared news of one another's passing through the Forum's pages, Howard told Tom, and it would pay to make a few phone calls to gather some details about the deceased and write something more than what the mortuary sent over. Tom could not help noticing how many of the old-timers died of cancer, and particularly of leukemia, and lung and kidney cancer, all associated with long-term exposure to low levels of uranium, and he quietly kept tally of it.

* * *

When he first took over the Forum, Tom had toyed briefly with the idea that he would do some serious journalism. He was the publisher, editor, copy editor, production manager, and senior writer, not to mention advertising director, circulation director and janitor. He was free to assign himself any story he wanted to do, say, a feature about what commuting 160 miles round trip to a minimum wage job in Telluride could do to a worker's family. He was quickly enlightened when he made those few ill-fated inquiries into the legacy of uranium mining, sharply reminded that there are stories people don't want to tell and don't want to read, and to do them justice requires more devotion and insensitivity than he was prepared to give to it, especially now that he planned on living and working in Naturita for years to come. An ex-miner could be dying of leukemia and still believe that the tragedy of his life was when the mine company shut down and put him out of work. It didn't matter. Tom soon found that the routine work of publishing the paper and meeting his weekly press time was plenty to keep him occupied, and was comforting in its predictability, whereas his erstwhile ambition, when it asserted itself on increasingly rare occasions, was just a distraction.

Now, though, Tom had a real story to contend with. To ignore it was not an option.

On Monday, November 14, the fifth day after Billy Pederson walked into his office to tell him that Ray Walker had missed his daughter's wedding, and after Tom had given two days to helping with the search, he drove over to Walker's Auto Repair, a quarter mile down the highway from his own office, thinking that if nothing else he'd take a picture of the business for the upcoming Thursday's paper. The place was tightly locked up, the already ubiquitous poster depicting its missing owner taped to the door. Tom peered in through a window that had not seen a spray of Windex in a decade. In the dim light he could make out the front counter, and behind it, Ray's desk, papers strewn, a coffee mug sitting there as if Ray had just set it down.

Tom walked around to the back where several cars in various states of disassembly were littered in the yard, along with a small junkyard's worth of car parts. They were a couple of Ray's stock cars, which he rebuilt in his free time and raced on weekends. Tom looked through a back window into the garage, where another vehicle was under repair. He tested the rear door, but it, too, was sealed tight.

Tom had no real purpose in being there. He already knew the place, having had his car serviced by Ray, work that Ray was always willing to trade in exchange for some newspaper ads. It was extensive barter that made it possible to survive on the West End on a meager income.

Tom felt a little foolish snapping pictures of this unremarkable business, which looked as if its owner had locked the door and had stepped away, and would probably be back in a few hours. But he felt a growing sense of responsibility to the story of Ray Walker's disappearance, and to his readers, who would be looking to the Forum for a sense of what had happened, and what was being done about it.

Chapter 3

A CHEMICAL REACTION

Ray and Sarah Walker and their two children lived in an aging doublewide a mile outside of Nucla, on a gravel road lined by an irrigation ditch where wild asparagus grew abundantly in the spring. The trailer was shaded by a couple of towering cottonwoods. A half-dozen old cars, some on blocks, occupied much of the yard; further back there were fruit trees. The trailer and vehicles, a couple of sheds, and the orchard spread across about an acre of rocky land, surrounded by irrigated green pastures. The fields stretched for a few miles across the mesa, beyond which the land fell away to canyonlands, with the snowcapped San Miguel Mountains as a distant backdrop to the east and the La Sals, just over the Utah line, on the western horizon.

Just to the side of the driveway where Tom parked, there was a new slab of concrete and a basketball hoop mounted on a pole, where a boy, undoubtedly the Walkers' son, Ray Jr., was the only outward evidence that anyone was at home. He had been shooting hoops when Tom pulled up, and he rested the ball on his hip as Tom climbed out of his car.

As he approached, Tom put out his hands to receive a pass. Ray bounced the ball to him. Tom spun around and took the jumper. The ball bounced off the rim. Ray rebounded and dribbled to the back of the court to set up his turn on offense. Tom defended the basket as Ray drove past him for the easy lay-up.

"Nice," Tom said, bringing a faint smile to the boy's face.

Tom guessed that it was the first time Ray had smiled since his dad's disappearance. His easy warmth resembled his father's, as did the deep set of his eyes and the broad forehead; in a few years, if he chose to grow out his beard, the family resemblance would be striking.

"Tough time," Tom said.

"Yeah."

"I'm sorry."

Tom passed the ball, which he had rebounded, back to Ray.

"I lost my dad when I was about your age. How old are you?"

"Thirteen."

"Same age exactly, except my dad didn't disappear. He died of a heart attack. But I might have some idea what you're going through."

"Maybe. I dunno."

Ray's smile had been replaced by a scowl, and Tom knew that he had said too much, too soon. But he also remembered that it was everyone walking on tiptoes — and their hushed, solicitous tones and prolonged silences — that had most disturbed him when he was Ray's age and facing similar circumstances. It was better, he felt, to be direct.

"I'm Tom Austin," Tom said, extending a hand. He introduced himself as the owner of the Forum, an identification that made no discernable impression on the boy.

"Is your mom at home?" he asked.

Tom had not called ahead and did not know if Sarah Walker would be there, just one week after her husband's disappearance, or would be out searching, or was perhaps staying with friends.

"Yeah," Ray said. "She's in the shed."

He nodded in the direction of a small addition at the rear of the doublewide. Then he turned, dribbled once, and took a shot from beyond the free-throw line, nailing it.

* * *

Although she had sent him school lunch menus for five years, Tom had not met Sarah Walker. Their longest conversations on the phone followed a couple of occasions when the faxed menu didn't arrive as expected, and he called her to ask about it. He was surprised to discover, when she answered his knock on the door, that she was the woman who had caught his eye when they saw each other shopping at the Merc or elsewhere around town; he never would have pegged her as Ray Walker's wife, a school secretary, or a mother of two. She was too young, only in her mid-thirties, and too alternative for any of those roles. She looked like someone who had taken a disastrously wrong turn off the interstate at Grand Junction while driving through from one urban center to another, from Salt Lake to Denver perhaps, or even Los Angeles to New York. She wore her blonde hair short and fashionably spiked, with streaks of black, and a small diamond stud in her pierced left nostril. She dressed simply in tight jeans and loose embroidered shirts.

He had guessed that maybe she was an artist, a contemporary Georgia O'Keeffe, living alone and quietly making fabulous ceramics or paintings or jewelry in a remote studio and selling her high-priced work at some prestigious gallery in Santa Fe, Aspen or Telluride, where she made rare appearances. Or she was an urban refugee like he was, who had found herself in the West End by a path as unlikely as his own. She always met his glance and held it a beat longer than she should have—unless it was her intention to give him the wrong idea. He'd enjoyed the flirtation and the fantasy that they were destined to meet someday and have an affair, but instantly upon learning she was Ray Walker's wife he knew that she'd probably recognized him as the man to whom she faxed the weekly school lunch menu, and that was all she'd meant to convey by making direct eye contact and smiling at him.

"Sarah Walker," he said, upon instantly connecting his fantasy of her to the reality. "I never put the name and face together."

"I knew that."

"You knew?"

"You always looked like you were hoping I was single. I could tell you had no idea who I was."

"Why didn't you say something?"

She shrugged and Tom couldn't help feeling a little deflated. While Sarah had enjoyed his interest in her and had encouraged it, she'd never really been available. It was a married woman's harmless flirtation, and nothing more; worse, in the context of their first face-to-face meeting, it was trivial.

Tom could see in the workshop behind her that she was, just as he had imagined, involved in some kind of craft and true to her artsy demeanor, though it wasn't immediately obvious what she produced there.

"I hope I'm not interrupting anything," he said.

"I was just making a batch of soap. It doesn't require constant attention at this point."

"Making soap? How do you do that?"

She stepped back, a gesture that wordlessly invited him inside for a closer look.

"You basically mix warm oils and lye dissolved in water to create a chemical reaction called saponification."

"There's a word you don't hear every day."

"When you're stirring it, you can see the oils and lye water turn into soap before your eyes. It's called tracing when that happens. Then, when it reaches the right consistency you add color and texture and scent. This batch is lavender."

"Then what?"

"Then you pour it into molds and let it harden and cure, and you cut it into loaves and let it cure some more."

There was soap at all stages of the process she had described in the shed. Tom reached out to touch some that was sitting in a mold on a shelf, but she stopped him.

"It's not safe to touch yet," she said. "It has to cure for six weeks before all of the lye has been neutralized."

"Sorry."

"Did you know your skin is the body's largest organ? And that most commercial soaps aren't really soap at all. They're chemical detergents made from petroleum products and they draw moisture from your skin."

"I didn't know any of that."

"Real soap contains glycerin, which is a natural emollient, so it moisturizes your skin."

"Very interesting."

"The glycerin part?"

"No, the whole thing, making soap. I didn't know people made soap. I thought it was made in factories and people bought it at the Merc or Wal-Mart."

"Most people do buy it at the store, but I find it therapeutic to make it. Especially now, with everything that's happened. I like how the chemicals always react exactly the way they're supposed to. They're a lot more predictable than people are, that's for sure. As long as you have the temperatures and proportions right, and you use good ingredients, you get beautiful soap. I like how you take lye, something caustic and dangerous, and turn it into something soft and wholesome and clean…."

Sarah stopped herself, shot him an awkward glance, and laughed.

"Sounds like a bunch of bull, right?"

Having completed the tour of the soap studio, they had stepped back outside, into the sunlight.

"Not at all," Tom said. "Sounds a whole lot better than taking something beautiful and turning it into something nasty, which is what a lot of people spend their time doing."

"You got that right."

"What do you do with the finished product? You can't use it all yourself."

"I wrap it in nice paper and tie it with straw and sell it at a couple of shops up in Telluride, and at the farmers market there. The rich people up there like it and I make a little extra money. Heck, Dave Best even sells a few bars of it at the Merc. I'd like to get it into more shops, farther away, but I can't produce enough volume or find time to market it like I should. I can only really put time into it in the summer when there's no school. I keep thinking that someday, if I stick with it, it might grow into a real business."

"Maybe I could do a story about you and your business, for the paper."

"Missing man's wife makes soap," she said sardonically. "Why, that'd make a catchy headline, for sure. Might even sell a few papers."

"It might, but it's not what I was thinking."

"I know. I'm sorry. I know you mean to help. And I'd appreciate a story, I really would, maybe in a few months."

"Of course. Not now. I didn't mean now."

"No."

"I'm so sorry about Ray."

"Well, thank you for that. Everyone's sorry. Ray has sure made one heck of a mess."

She glanced out toward the horizon as if she might right then spot a plume of dust kicked up by the tires of Ray's truck, a herald of his belated homecoming.

"Where the heck is he, anyhow?"

A teenaged girl emerged from the back door of the doublewide and stepped up behind them. She was pale and slight, dressed in a worn Aerosmith t-shirt, torn jeans and flip-flops, and she held a new-born. She was blonde and resembled her mother, just as Ray Jr. had inherited his father's darker colors.

"This is my daughter, Angie," Sarah said. "And my grandson, Tyler."

"Hi, Angie," Tom said.

"He's fussy *again*." Angie said, addressing her mother as if Tom weren't there and making no effort to mask her exasperation. "But he *can't* be hungry. I just fed him."

"Well go back in the house and try and rock him, but do it *gently*, and I'll help out in a bit, after I'm finished talking with Mr. Austin."

Tom was surprised that nobody had thought to mention that Ray Walker's newlywed daughter was a new mother. But then, it was probably because everyone else knew. He was some newsman, he thought: always the last to hear the most salient local gossip.

He knew Angie slightly, having interviewed her his first week running the Forum when she and Ray stopped by the office to submit a photograph for publication. It was a picture of Angie, posed rifle in hand, with the carcass of a mountain lion she'd shot.

"I just got lucky," she said when he asked her to describe her kill, and didn't have a lot more to offer. Angie was just being shy, her father interjected. To take a lion requires nerves of steel, he explained proudly. If Ray was right, Tom remembered thinking, Angie's courage was well camouflaged by adolescent diffidence. But perhaps a proud parent can see depths in his offspring that are obscure to anyone else. Or maybe, and this was likelier, Ray, who had surely helped his daughter hunt the lion, was trying to endow her with some of his own courage.

To see Angie again now, still a child to Tom's eye but with a baby of her own — and one she was struggling to nurture — Tom wondered if her trophy lion might have been not only the bravest but also the luckiest moment in her life, not unlike her absent father's game-winning hit in a Little League championship a couple of decades before, and would remain her biggest accomplishment even if she were to live to an old age. It was no wonder that the bread-and-butter for a small-town paper like the Forum was coverage of kids' sports and snapshots of hunters and fishermen with their trophies.

"I'm sorry about your dad," Tom said to Angie.

"Uh-huh," she said, offering no hint that she recognized him.

"Who is it?" a male voice bellowed from inside.

"It's all right, Craig," Sarah shouted. "It's for me."

Sarah turned back to Tom as Angie retreated.

"My new son-in-law," she explained. "We couldn't cancel the wedding, even with Ray not being there, after it was all planned. We had the caterer booked with a big chocolate cake with white chocolate

frosting and a disc jockey and people coming from out of town...."
Her tone was apologetic.

"It must have been difficult."

"Well, it was still nice, I suppose, if you could put it out of your mind that Ray wasn't there. I kept thinking he'd walk in any minute and tell us why he was late and say he was sorry. Of course, if he had shown up like that with some lame excuse, I don't know if I would have hugged him or slugged him. Probably would have hugged him and then slugged him, and that would have spoiled the wedding more than him being gone. But what can I do for you?"

"I can come back another time if you need to help out with the baby. I was just hoping we could sit and talk a bit."

"Angie can't expect for me to jump every time Tyler whimpers," she said firmly. "She's got to learn to care for him by herself sooner or later, and now's as good a time as any."

"As good a time as any" sounded like Sarah's resignation to fate. He had observed before in his reporting career that a person in a state of shock following a trauma can sometimes open herself up in just this way, as if her defenses have been entirely breached, or because she has nothing left to defend.

"I'm here more or less to do my job," he said. "I want to make sure that what I write about Ray in the paper is right."

She gestured toward a worn redwood picnic table and the two of them sat.

"He's out there for hours at a time," Sarah said, looking toward the basketball court, where Ray Jr. was still at it, practicing free throws.

"It must be something he and his dad did together."

"They built the court together last summer."

She turned her attention back to Tom.

"I've got no idea what you can write about Ray that people don't already know," she said. "Everyone already knows he's gone missing. We made up hundreds of those posters and put 'em everywhere. And you put it in your paper, of course. And I've talked to everyone, too, to ask them if they know something."

"You must have some idea what happened to him."

"All I can think is an accident. But it seems like if that's what it was, they'd have found him by now. So, I guess I don't know."

"Ray lived his whole life here?"

"His whole life, except when he was in the army for a couple of years. Even then he didn't get all that far away. He was stationed over in Fort Carson, you know, next to Colorado Springs."

"And you too? Lived here your whole life?"

"Yep. Born and raised. Never been anywhere else. Well, except I've been to places around here like Telluride and Grand Junction. There's a nice store in Junction that sells my soap. And I was in Denver once. Ray and I kept thinking we'd travel someday, when the kids were all grown."

"Was he out on the road a lot, answering service calls?"

"A couple of times a week, more in the summer when there are tourists passing through on their way to Arches or Mesa Verde. The next closest tow truck is Junction if you head north and Moab if you head west, or Cortez to the south, so he got more than his share of the calls from Triple A. But he never was gone more than a few hours, not until now anyway."

"It's a real mystery, isn't it? How he could just be gone like this."

"I would certainly say so. I don't really know what I should be doing, you know? Should I be out looking for him? But where would I look that people haven't already looked? Do I need to stay here by the phone? Or should I just go to work like it was any other day? I can't afford not to work, or to lose my job. They're not going to let me stay home forever."

She hesitated, as if she wasn't sure whether she should say more. This can be the key moment in an interview, Tom knew, when the reporter's job is to remain silent.

"Ray was…." she stopped herself and started over. "Ray *is* the kindest, the best man I've ever known. I told the sheriff he would never have run off, not with Angie getting married in a few days and a new grandson to spoil. He wouldn't ruin her big day. Not on purpose. And it just burns me that he won't believe me and thinks I'm some kind of idiot that would lose her husband. I've got no idea what it is, but I know something real bad happened to Ray. I just know it."

Tom then asked the obvious but indelicate question: "How can you be so sure?"

She looked at him sharply, as if it was his impertinent question and not her tone of absolute certainty that had sounded off-key.

"Why, what on earth else could it be?"

To Sarah, it was just that self-evident. What else could it be? Her quick response — unvarnished, unrehearsed and unself-conscious — made for a convincing bit of testimony.

Sarah Walker had an edge, but Tom felt he could see past it to her underlying vulnerability. To him, she seemed authentic, but he wasn't surprised to learn that the sheriff was suspicious of her. He had seen how a crime victim's family can come to seem tainted in the course of an investigation; how, in their public display of grief, or their insufficient demonstration of grief — of either one or the other — observers can discern something unnatural, something that brought the tragedy to them. Thus, does humanity begin to separate the wounded and the weak from the herd. Even so, Tom wondered if the sheriff knew something that gave him good reason to harbor misgivings about Sarah Walker. As close as she professed to be to her husband, and as deeply as she seemed to love him, was it entirely plausible that she had no idea at all, truly none, what had happened to him?

To take Sarah at face value, the only possible explanation for Ray's disappearance was something random, an accident or a violent encounter with a stranger, just as she insisted. Though it was certainly possible that she was hiding something, any implication to that effect did not belong in The Forum, or at least not yet.

Chapter 4

SOUR MILK

**WALKER'S FAMILY AND FRIENDS
SAY FOUL PLAY IS ONLY POSSIBILITY**

No Sign of Missing Naturita Man

By Tom Austin

Devoted father. Loving husband. Stockcar racer. West End native. Loyal friend. Little League coach. Great mechanic.

These are the descriptions that are offered up when Ray Walker's friends are asked about him.

The Naturita man has been missing a full week and a half, since last Wednesday, just three days before he failed to attend his daughter Angela's wedding.

The people who know Ray Walker best say that it is completely out of character for him to miss the family occasion that he had been planning with his wife, Sarah. They are convinced that foul play or an accident are the only possible explanations for his disappearance.

Walker was last heard from on Wednesday afternoon, when he called Sarah to say that he had received a call from a stranded motorist and was going to provide service. Walker owns and operates Walker's Auto Repair business in Naturita. A major part of his business is towing stranded vehicles. Triple A has told the Montrose County Sheriff's Office that it did not refer the call to Walker.

Sheriff Trace Martin said on Thursday that he is pursuing a number of leads, but repeated what he said last week in an interview with the Forum, that missing adults almost always disappear for personal reasons and turn up on their own after they realize the ruckus they have caused. Martin added that he is ruling out a traffic accident in the West End as the cause of Walker's disappearance, having searched all of the roads by vehicle, including remote jeep roads, with the help of dozens of volunteers, and from the air by helicopter.

"If Ray Walker had run his rig off the road in my county, and most of the neighboring counties, for that matter, we would have spotted him," Martin said. "Heck, his truck is painted bright red."

That leaves foul play as the only possible explanation for Ray's disappearance, his wife said on Thursday, a week and a day since she last heard from him.

"Anyone who knows Ray knows how much he was looking forward to Angie's wedding," Sarah Walker said. "I know that he just would not have missed it unless something real bad happened." Walker said she did not report the disappearance for a few days simply because she kept expecting her husband to call or walk in the door at any minute.

As she put it, "You don't know when exactly someone has truly gone missing and when they're just running late. You wait another hour, and another hour and then suddenly a whole day has gone by, and then you wait another hour."

Sarah Walker made an appeal to the public to notify the sheriff's office at 970 355-3333 with any clue, no matter how insignificant it may seem.

"Did anyone see a car stranded out on a highway last Wednesday?" she asked. "If so, that could be the most important clue of all. I am afraid that whoever called Ray may have had criminal intent. What other explanation is there?"

Ray and Sarah Walker have been married for 20 years. They have two children, Angela, 19, and Ray, Jr., 13, and an infant grandson, Angela's son Tyler. Angela was married to Craig Pellison of Naturita last week, at the ceremony her father failed to attend for reasons yet unknown.

Sarah Walker works as a secretary at the Naturita School and does the books for Walker's Auto Repair. She also owns and operates the San Miguel Canyon Soap Company, selling petroleum-free, all-natural soaps that she makes herself by hand.

Ray Walker was born in Naturita in 1967 and has never

lived anywhere else, except for a two-year stint in the army. His mother, Elizabeth Walker, a longtime Naturita resident, now lives at the Manor Nursing Home in Cortez. His father is deceased.

Walker's friends, consisting of pretty much the entire population the West End, have gathered at the Maverick Café to talk about his disappearance all week, and to organize search parties.

* * *

Tom was at the Maverick rereading his own words, wondering if the plug for San Miguel Canyon Soap was too blatant, when Dave sat next to him. It was lunchtime.

"Nice story," Dave said, dropping his copy of the Forum on the table. "Course, like usual, you're missing the main point."

In the five years they had been friends, Dave had never before offered a single criticism of a story in the Forum.

"What did I miss? And what do you mean, 'Like usual'?"

Tom was offended. He'd already fielded compliments from readers who said they were glad he explained why Ray's disappearance was so disturbing: because it was so out of character and therefore inexplicable. He had anticipated the same from Dave, the familiar small-talk, even if the subject was bigger than usual.

"Aww, I guess it don't matter."

"Right," Tom said sarcastically. "It don't matter. You say I get my stories wrong, *usually*, but it don't matter. Oh, and by the way, Dave, I bought a quart of milk the other day at the Merc, and it was sour. In fact, and I've gotta be honest with you, your milk is *usually* sour."

They sat silently, chewing their burgers, each searching for the few words he might utter next.

"You know, you are still pretty new around here," Dave said.

"Always will be," Tom said, and then he pointedly shifted gears: "You picking the Broncos over the Giants on Sunday?"

"Probably not. Giants are looking too good."

"There's absolutely no evidence it has anything to do with meth," Tom said after another long pause. "Just because you said it might, if that's what you're thinking."

"I know. I don't even think that anymore. That was just trash talk because I was so worried."

Another five minutes of glum silence.

"I can only report what people tell me."

"I suppose."

"If you know something you're not telling me, you can't expect me to put it in the paper. His wife couldn't tell me much except that Ray is the kindest man she's ever known. Sheriff Martin and Billy Pederson aren't saying much. If they know anything, that is. What the hell do you want me to do? I'm not some goddamn detective or investigative reporter. I run a small-town community paper."

Dave was finished with his lunch and pushed his chair back.

"Maybe this don't matter neither," he said. "But maybe you'd like to know."

"Don't bother telling me something I can't use," Tom said, cutting him off. "I mean it. It's not like I'm gonna be the one who solves the mystery of what happened to Ray, and if it's gonna piss you off again if you tell me something I can't print, then just don't tell it to me in the first place and you can save us both the trouble."

"Yeah, well," Dave said. "It's all right. You don't need to print it.

It's just a fact you might find interesting. And I don't know why it bugs me so much that you got it wrong except that it was *not right*. Ray's father isn't dead, like you wrote.

"Ray is Dick Klein's bastard son."

Chapter 5

HY-PO-THETICALS

There was no reason to doubt Dave's revelation. On a moment's reflection it was not at all surprising that Dick Klein, the richest man in the entire Four Corners, had an illegitimate son. Why not? The Uranium King's legend was based on his having lived by his own rules, which was precisely what had enabled him to find a mother lode of uranium ore where others had failed. If the Uranium King had an illegitimate son, it could be Ray Walker as easily as anyone else. This would be another open secret, like Angie Walker's premarital motherhood, that Tom alone out of the entire population on the West End was not privy to. Tom could understand why the illegitimate son of a prominent man, and that son's wife, had cultivated the habit of saying his father was dead. They would have needed a polite explanation for the hole in Ray's biography. The world is full of this sort of useful fiction.

The relevance of this piece of intelligence to Ray Walker's disappearance was immediately obvious. Though uranium mining had long since ceased in the region, the Klein family still owned hundreds of thousands of acres around Naturita, and half of the property in town.

They were involved in developing high-end resort property in Telluride, and had recently opened the family estate on North Mountain as a high-end guest ranch. While Dick Klein, the old man, was in his 80s and rarely seen in public, his youngest son, Albert, as the principal overseer of the family's interests, was a familiar figure.

How was this degree of conspicuous wealth and prominence possible when Albert's half-brother, Ray Walker, lived in the same small community in virtual poverty? The possibilities for resentment and conflict were easy to imagine, far easier to imagine than it was to understand how they might be able to live side-by-side peaceably. No wonder Dave, who had already expressed a sense of solidarity with his childhood friend, was disgusted. As deep as the mystery of Ray's disappearance itself, there was a secondary mystery about why the investigation hadn't turned immediately to questions about Ray's relationship to his father. If the community of Naturita had a deeply ingrained habit of looking the other way when it came to anything untoward related to the Kleins, Dave was asking for more than that from Tom, who—as Dave himself had pointed out—was not really one of them.

The power of denial is strong, though, and Tom felt a pulse of resistance to being drawn into the swamp, a sixth sense warning him that he would regret it if he allowed himself to become overinvolved. Better to ignore Dave's tip, and Dave's expectations of what the newspaper ought to do, and nobody would ever know or care. If Ray Walker had lived his entire life on the West End without feeling any great need to identify himself as Dick Klein's son, why should Tom report it now? But he had another edition of the Forum to publish, the relentlessness of a deadline, so he picked up the phone and dialed Sheriff Martin.

Martin kept Tom on hold for only a few minutes.

"I'm trying to stay on top of this Ray Walker story, Sheriff," Tom said. "And I'm wondering if there are any developments in the case."

"Not a one, Tom," Martin growled. "But let's remember that Ray Walker is a competent adult and that no crime has been committed, not that we know of."

"Does that mean you're not investigating?"

"Now I didn't say that. We're following all the standard procedures we take in any missing person case. We've sent out a bulletin to all the law enforcement agencies in the region. And my deputies are keeping their eyes open."

"Could Ray Walker have been mixed up in anything that might have put him at some kind of risk? I assume you've interviewed his family and friends…."

"Yes, yes, of course we have." The sheriff sounded impatient, as if he were running late for lunch. "Can we talk off-the-record, for just a moment?"

"Sure."

"Let me just ask you a question, a hy-po-thetical question. Now I'm not saying that Ray Walker was having an affair, but let's just *say* he was having an affair with a married woman, and let's say her husband found out about it. Do you think it would be appropriate for me to tell you about that and for you to put it in your newspaper? I mean, so far as I know, it's not a crime for a married man to have an affair with a married woman, though I will admit it that some preachers wouldn't like it, and it is the kind of thing that might cause him to hightail it, especially after her husband found out."

"Are you telling me that Ray Walker was having an affair with a married woman, sheriff?"

"Oh, no, no, no, no, I didn't say that. That was a hy-po-thetical. But you hear what I'm trying to tell you? These are just some of the complexities of a missing person case that law enforcement has to think about. You've got people's privacy to consider, the privacy of the missing person, and of the people he's left behind. You start asking too many questions and you can end up with a big ole mess you never dreamed of."

"That's interesting, sheriff."

"Why, I'm sure you have similar concerns in your business, Tom. You don't always report every detail you know, now do you?"

Tom found it unlikely that Martin cared as much as he insisted he did about such niceties as personal privacy or the reputation of an innocent bystander, but it was fundamental to the ethos of the West that people should be left alone as long as they weren't hurting anyone else. Martin's strong libertarian streak was the basis of his popularity.

"I understand that Ray Walker is Dick Klein's son," Tom said.

Martin didn't skip a beat.

"Now that's just exactly the sort of thing I'm talking about, Tom! Another hy-po-thetical!" he exclaimed. "And it might be true, but if it is true, I don't see how that is of any concern at all to law enforcement. Where's the crime?

"Now I want to say something *on the record*," the sheriff said, "and you can write this down and put it right on page one in your newspaper with a picture of my pretty face and a big ole headline if you want to. I want to assure you and all of your readers and all of Ray Walker's friends and loved ones that this case is open and is being investigated aggressively. The Montrose County Sheriff's Office is doing everything possible to find Ray Walker."

* * *

So, Ray Walker might have run off with a married woman, though there was no report of a missing woman in the West End, making this a completely hypothetical possibility, as the sheriff said. Unless the sheriff was not, in fact, trying to tip Tom off, but was trying instead to mislead him. The sheriff had no reason to tip him off, unless he hoped that Tom would blow the case open and spare him the necessity of doing it himself. Martin just might prefer to let the newspaper tarnish Ray Walker's sterling reputation as a family man by reporting that he was having an affair, if that was where this thing was going.

Then again, if Walker was having an affair, a jealous husband might have done something about it, a hypothetical on top of a hypothetical. Or maybe Walker's own wife did something about her philandering husband, though that was highly unlikely, Tom thought, given the obvious grief his disappearance caused her. She was not entirely convincing when she insisted that she had no idea where Ray was, but she did not strike Tom as potentially violent. Still, they could have argued and he might have walked out, or she might have kicked him out, and that would better explain her delay in reporting that he was missing. If that's what happened, it would just add a layer of guilt to her grief, making her appear all the more aggrieved, and that wasn't implausible at all.

Then there was Dave Best's suggestion, albeit retracted, that Ray Walker could be involved with methamphetamines, not at all unlikely given the meth epidemic in the rural West. Meth was soul-destroying, and if Ray Walker was a meth addict, or was involved with meth addicts, foul play was not merely hypothetical, but given his disappearance was likely.

Though the list of possibilities was growing, it seemed clear that Sheriff Martin was not particularly interested in pursuing any of them. And for that, there was now a ready explanation: Ray Walker was Dick Klein's son, but not a legitimate heir to the discoverer of the Whispering Jim lode, founder of the Uranium King Mining Co., and still the region's most illustrious citizen, even in his dotage. To aggressively investigate Ray Walker's disappearance could risk disrupting the arrangement, whatever it was, that enabled the legitimate Klein family to enjoy their life of luxury at their estate on North Mountain just a dozen miles away from where their bastard relative labored as an auto mechanic. This could well be what Martin was concerned about when he spoke of "a big ole mess," a risk to the Kleins. Because one thing was certain: Trace Martin had not remained sheriff of Montrose County for 36 years by crossing the Uranium King.

Even if the sheriff had an ulterior motive, he had nonetheless posed a challenging question. Apart from the generalized and inchoate anxiety Ray Walker's disappearance had clearly caused in Naturita, absent a corpse, what did it matter? And if there was no crime, who was responsible for finding him?

People disappear all the time, Martin had declared, and this no doubt was true. To investigate could be an infringement on the missing man's privacy or, from a law- enforcement perspective, a waste of time. What if the missing man didn't want to be found? Was it his right to vanish?

Tom knew that a man might disappear for any number of reasons, for potentially as many reasons as there are men. He knew that there is nothing more personal than a man's disappearance.

Chapter 6

HOW PEOPLE BREAK

Tom's career in journalism — Ken Hanley's career, to be more precise — had come too easily. He enjoyed being a rising star, a form of celebrity measured by the time that his editors were willing to devote to his stories, his virtually unmonitored expense account, and the frequency with which his stories were given page one placement. He didn't mind the jealousy he inspired in other reporters, most of them older than he was.

He lacked only someone to share it with, and that problem was solved when he spotted Miranda Morcineau in Mallory's Tavern one day after work. He was captivated by her olive complexion, green eyes, and African-black curly hair: she was from Bahia in Brazil, a mixed-race beauty, all the more exotic because she was an executive with the Banco do Brasil. They were professional equals, each employed by a famous corporation, and they made a sexy and glamorous couple. He had given up his Fenway bachelor pad and had moved in to her chic Back Bay apartment within a few weeks after they met.

Unlike young romance as portrayed in the movies, no tiresome negotiation had been necessary. Miranda was not given to a lot of reflection or self-doubt, or at least none that she ever expressed to Ken. Shortly after they'd met and they had spent a series of nights together at her place, he mentioned that he needed to run home for some fresh clothes.

"I could just move in with you," he joked. "It would be easier."

"Why not?" she shrugged.

Could it really be that easy for a young man to find himself living with a beautiful woman? Was this how a soulmate identifies herself? With a shrug? Ken couldn't help but wonder if she was his only because he was the first man to come right out and ask if he could move in with her. If another guy had come along and had asked before he had, would she have answered him with "Why not?" She probably would have, as long as that other guy, like Ken, was willing to escort her to the clubs night after night.

He couldn't keep up with her. What came effortlessly to Miranda, working by day and spending every night on the town, was impossible for Ken. Was it something Latin in her, something cultural or genetic, that enabled her to drink and snort cocaine and dance with him all evening, and then wake up the next morning after just a few hours of sleep and put on her face and a business suit to join the executive class? Or was it something lacking in him that made it impossible for him to do the same thing? What made her so comfortable in her party animal skin while he felt increasingly like an impostor in his? The alarm clock would sound, his head would be pounding, and she would already be putting time in on her treadmill while watching the Today Show, having put a dark Brazilian roast up to brew.

Vanity, Tom later mused, when he tried to understand why he had wrecked his career, should have been one of the deadly sins. Of the classical seven — lust, gluttony, greed, sloth, wrath, envy, and pride—pride might be nearly synonymous with vanity, but in modern usage pride may be justified or virtuous, whereas vanity is pride charged with narcissism, for which there is no respectable alibi. So, it was his vanity—or just because he could—that led Ken to start cheating at work. Without his noticing how it happened or when it started, it was easier for him to invent a detail to give extra color to a story, especially when he was hung over. He had long since won the right to keep his own schedule and he started to abuse it, rarely showing up at the office before noon. To keep up with his outsized reputation, since he was often too wasted to do much legwork, he would sometimes have to make up an interview subject, and nobody would be the wiser. What really propelled him was that he was good at it. It seemed to be no accident that the more fabrication there was in a story, the more his editors seemed to like his work and the less they messed with him.

Of course, he took it too far and was busted. He strolled into the office at noon one day to hear from the receptionist, who was unfailingly chipper but now looked uncomfortably away, that he was wanted immediately in the managing editor's office. Was it just his imagination or were people in the newsroom stealing awkward glances at him as he strode through? Were some of the reporters he had snubbed over the years wearing a look of smug satisfaction? Later, when he remembered that walk enroute to his own execution, it all unfolded in slow motion, his injuries as gory as if they'd been sustained in a car wreck.

He had loved working in a big city newsroom; even before it slipped away he was starting to miss it.

"Close the door," his longtime champion Elaine Weiner said.

"What's up?"

She looked at him coldly.

"It's all a lie, isn't it Ken?"

"What's a lie?"

"Every last thing about you."

"Hey, slow down. I mean, that's awfully harsh, isn't it? Did I get something wrong?"

She tossed pages she was holding, evidently some of his copy, onto her desk.

"This kid you wrote about makes for a great story. Home schooled up in rural New Hampshire, groundbreaking work on the disappearance of frogs from local ponds. Being recruited by a dozen major universities that are offering him full scholarships. And you wrote it well. The only problem is, he doesn't exist. You invented him."

"I...."

"Don't bother."

"But, Elaine, you've got it wrong.... He's a composite...."

"A what?" She was incredulous.

"A composite."

She shook her head in disgust.

"I've got a team reviewing all of the stories you've written that we've published," she said. "So far, at least a dozen contain major fabrications."

"I can explain."

"No Ken, you can't explain. You've betrayed me. You've betrayed this newspaper and everyone who works here. You've betrayed your profession. And you've even betrayed yourself. At this point there's only one thing left that you can do."

He looked up at her hopefully, but her eyes were set hard.

"You can get the fuck out of here."

"Won't you give me a chance to...?"

"To do what? To explain? To make things right? What is there to explain? Do you have any concept of what you've done? You've not only ruined your own career. You've destroyed mine."

"Elaine, I'm sorry."

"I don't believe you and I don't care. You'll say anything. You're a sociopath. Just get out. Go."

Ken picked himself up and stepped back into the newsroom and now there was no question at all that everyone was staring at him. He tried to smile but could produce only a grimace. He knew instantly, right then, that in his arrogance he had failed to cultivate a single friend there. If there was nobody at The Mail sorry to see him get his overdue comeuppance, he was a sickening spectacle, nonetheless. When he reached his cubicle, thinking he would take refuge there and collect himself, that he would buy a little time to figure out what to do next — to attempt, at least, to recover a shred of dignity — he found instead a security guard, who handed him a carton containing his personal belongings.

"I'll escort you out," the guard said.

Ken nodded his acquiescence and once again had to walk the gauntlet, back through the newsroom, now serving as a garish example to all the other reporters and editors of just how low the mighty can fall. Passing the men's room he felt a wave of nausea. He handed the carton to the guard and ran inside and vomited.

Then, suddenly, he found himself on the street, holding the small box, which might have contained the ashes of his career, not moving, as if the only purpose he had left in life was to impede the orderly flow of pedestrians.

His cell phone rang. It was Miranda, calling to discuss where they would meet after work.

"I don't want to see you anymore," he heard himself blurt out. "I've moved out." He hung up before she could reply, with no idea what he might do next.

That's how people break, Tom thought, a half-dozen years later, when he wondered about Ray Walker's disappearance. It is so simple, really, and no mystery at all: They just fold under pressures that nobody suspects.

Chapter 7

PAPER'S FOR SALE

Ken Hanley's disappearance had been all-too-easily explained. Just three weeks after he abruptly walked off the job, The Mail ran a lengthy accounting of all the frauds he had perpetrated in his last two years at the paper, documenting a dozen of them in detail. Ken was on page 1 for the last time, albeit for the first time as the subject of a story, this one headlined, *Mail Reporter Fabricated Articles*, complete with an unflattering head shot. The story reported that new measures had been implemented to guarantee that no reporter in the future could do what Ken had done, tarnishing the reputation of a major American institution.

Tom read the story online from the Florida Keys, where he had fled after tossing a few clothes into a bag, riding the train to Logan Airport and boarding a plane to Miami, without so much as making a phone call to his mother or leaving a note for Miranda. He wasn't thinking clearly enough to foresee that he would never be back to the apartment he and Miranda had shared. His disappearance, to the two women who cared about him — three, counting his sister — would be every bit as hurtful as Ray Walker's. But this was something Tom was slow to comprehend, finally grasping it only when he witnessed the pain caused by Ray Walker's sudden absence. Caught up in his own personal drama, Tom assumed at the time that he was doing Miranda and his family a favor by vanishing, sparing them the humiliation of being associated with him and his scandal. It was a collateral benefit that he spared himself their pity. Their forgiveness, if they had extended it, would have been even more intolerable than that.

Moreover, Tom knew that by the time the story of his malfeasance broke, those he abandoned would know why he had left. By then, he had begun a new life as a bartender who introduced himself as Tom Austin—a name concocted by marrying one childhood friend's first name to another childhood friend's last name—in an aging Holiday Inn near Marathon, a motel that had been a fabulous resort in the 1960s and had comfortably settled into existence as a vacation alternative for the budget-minded. He grew out his hair and his beard to suit his new identity as a Keys eccentric, and imagined that sooner or later he would apply his facility for fabrication to a novel. He had always been an effortless writer, too effortless as it happened, but it was easier to drink than write and easier still to accept his apparent destiny as a beach bum. Wisecracks and small talk with strangers at the bar were a tolerable proxy for friendship. When he felt a little lonely, or had a yearning for body contact, with no effort at all he could bed one of the tourists for whom he poured an endless supply of rum drinks. A hotel guest could always be trusted to check out and be gone within a few days.

Tom was almost happy or felt that he could have achieved a variant on happiness, if not for a mind game he started playing. The mere thought of suicide was initially so frightening that he let it pass without trying to hold on to it. But then it would flit past again, and he would ask himself, clinically, Is this a suicidal thought? I'm not con-templating suicide, but am merely thinking *about* suicide, so does this constitute a suicidal thought?

If so, then: Am I suicidal? Are there degrees of suicidal inclina-tions? Can a person be a little bit suicidal, or is that like having a lit-tle bit of lung cancer?

From there: If I *were* suicidal, how would I kill myself? Would I have the courage to pull it off?

And then: Here are some easy ways I could kill myself. And he imagined swimming out to sea to the point where he was too far to return to shore, or crashing his car off a bridge, or shooting him-self in a display of machismo. All of this was abstract, as if he were considering suicide from a strictly theoretical vantage point. It was all conditional, each discrete thought taking the form of an if/then statement. And what was most unusual about the dialectic, which was taking place strictly as an interior monologue, even as he casu-ally popped the tops off longnecks and handed them to tourists, and talked sports and the weather, is that Tom wasn't depressed or even a little sad, just very matter of fact about the reality that he could and indeed might end his own life.

He wouldn't describe himself as unhappy, and yet the thoughts became increasingly insistent, pressing in on him, occupying more and more of his thinking capacity, driving out other thoughts, or per-haps filling the vacuum created by the absence of any other thoughts. If he tried to not think about suicide, then, in fact, he was thinking about it, and the more he tried to not think about suicide, the more he was thinking about it. He was in the habit of swimming almost every night after work, and he started going further and further from shore, and then one dark night he swam so far that he could barely see the beach. If he swam just a bit further and then swam in a circle, he would not know for certain which way to head to reach safety. He wavered, almost did it, and then started back. But his arms grew heavy, sooner than they should have. He faltered and gulped some seawater. He found himself coughing so violently that he had to struggle to keep his head above water.

Am I drowning? If I am, is it suicide?

The thought panicked him and then, unexpectedly, the panic produced a sense of resolve. He suddenly had a purpose: Making it back to shore alive. He kicked forcefully to lift himself up as high as he could out of the water and reorient himself to the beach. He could see the island, far, far off, or at least he thought it was land he saw, and he realized that he had actually been swimming in the wrong direction, parallel to the beach instead of toward it.

He remembered childhood tests of stamina: waiting at a bus stop in suburban Boston, the wind chill 35 below, thinking he would freeze to death, but then the entirely rational thought, *I'm not going to die here*, and sure enough the bus would come. Then he knew it was a self-dramatization, a mind game whose purpose was to chase away panic, but this time it was a mind game that had become unexpectedly real. He truly might die here. His arms were heavier with each stroke, the land so distant even after it came into view that it looked like a mirage. He had not known that his will to survive was so strong, and yet it seemed that all the will he could muster might not be enough. One ocean swell could sink him.

Somehow, he made it, painfully crawling on the beach not far from where he'd parked his car. He lay on the sand looking up at the dark night sky, the planets and the stars glowing brighter in the absence of a moon. The question was answered. He was not suicidal.

Once, when he was a child, Tom saw a snowflake precipitate out of the clear frigid air in front of his eyes. Just so, as he lay panting and gazing up at the sky, crystallized the awareness that there was no good answer to the mystery that had driven him to the brink of self-annihilation. He might answer that it had been simple hubris, but that only begged the question. What, then, were the origins of his deadly vanity? If it was a correspondingly outsized insecurity, then where did that originate?

If Tom did not know why he had sabotaged his career and had chosen to live on the margins of society, friendless and loveless, per-haps the reason was that there was no reason at all, or that there were too many reasons. He had been too lazy to do the work required, and clever enough to get away with cheating. He had been weak and he drank too much. He did not love Miranda enough. Or he loved her too much. His father had died too suddenly, when he was too young. He had never accepted religion or submitted to any other form of authority. In short, he'd had enough of a life that a shrink chosen randomly out of the yellow pages could uncover a dozen more rea-sons why he had been so self-destructive.

And so what? Mere carelessness is more than enough to shatter lives. There are mysteries of human nature, even of one's own nature, that can never be resolved by looking inward. That way, clearly, led only to despair. Answers were more likely to be found by looking out, precisely why he had become a reporter in the first place.

* * *

A week after he crawled out of the ocean, cleanly shaven, his hair neatly trimmed, looking fit and youthful thanks to his swimming regimen, Tom was on the West End. In the back of his mind, he had filed a story away, something he imagined he'd get to after he won the Pulitzer and had garnered enough prestige to write his own ticket: the underreported legacy of uranium mining in the West. Of course, now he had nobody to report it for. But it interested him, this apparent fact that in developing the bomb for the inarguable purpose of ending a world war America had poisoned some of her own, and moreover, that cleaning up the waste was to this day a story of corporate and government collusion. There was a health angle, an environmental angle, a political angle, and a human angle. Once, his goal in being a reporter was to be published. Now he found himself in the astonishingly naïve position of believing that reporting the story was its own reward. He had no idea where it would lead, probably nowhere, but he was still better off than he was just a few days before. He was moving forward.

Uranium country was more beautiful, and more desolate, than he had imagined it would be. Moab had become a tourist mecca, but the reason for it was the thousands of square miles of emptiness all around. The enormous landscape swallowed up the tourists, leaving more remote former mining towns entirely to themselves. In the hierarchy of the natural wonders of the Colorado Plateau, the San Miguel River Canyon was barely notable, but to Tom's eye it was spectacular. He saw a kind of decadent beauty even in the broken-down town of Naturita, which announced itself with a vast auto graveyard at its outskirts, the hundreds of vehicles slowly rusting into the rock and scrub. The town sat at the bottom of the canyon on either side of the river and consisted of a few businesses stretched out along the highway, the West End Merc, the Maverick, the Naturita School, the West End Clinic, the bank and an insurance company office, a couple of churches, a couple of gas stations, the Forum newspaper office, the Slickrock Motel, and a collection of maybe two hundred shacks and doublewides and a handful of fifties-era split-levels in bad need of paint, houses that would otherwise fit comfortably in an aging Denver suburb.

He drove through the town in a just a few minutes and started up toward the town of Nucla, just five miles away, or so a road sign indicated. When he reached the canyon rim and mesa stretching past it, he saw the marquee for the Uranium Drive-In. The sign was weathered and crumbling, its center — where the current attraction would have been posted — entirely broken out. The word *Uranium* was written in script and was painted in an electric aquamarine that when it was fresh had been meant to evoke glow-in-the-dark radioactivity. The sign's outline formed an arrow pointing up a rutted dirt track. Tom wrenched the wheel of his car in the direction the arrow pointed.

The road climbed over a small rise and then, behind a screen as decrepit as the marquee, the relatively flat expanse of the abandoned drive-in parking lot lay before him.

The operation had never been large. Like the marquee, the screen was undersized, and there were parking spaces for no more than thirty or forty cars. What had once been the concession stand and projection booth was a small two-story cinderblock building with its windows boarded up. A few of the posts that once held speakers at each parking space were still standing. Only a modest effort had been made to grade the area, which was strewn with rocks. The Uranium Drive-In had been scratched into the earth at the edge of a small mesa overlooking the San Miguel River and the town on its banks, and going to the movies in Naturita, even when it was at its peak of prosperity and miners earned good wages, would have felt more like roughing it than a night on the town. While mining companies built imposing mills and rail lines, their workers built towns of imperma-nence. Years after the ore was mined out or ceased to be profitable to mine, the works of the miners and mine companies rotted away at the same implacable rate, but there were people left behind, liv-ing in flimsy houses and trailers.

Tom got out of his car and walked to the rim of the mesa, where he could survey the town below.

Who lived here still? How did they survive? A few tourists trav-eled the highway from Telluride, eighty tortuous miles to the east in the San Miguel Mountains, to Moab, sixty even more tortuous miles to the west. Some stopped to fill their tank, buy a soda, or even to make a meal of a chili cheeseburger at the Maverick. There was some ranching. Off in the other direction, toward Nucla, Tom could see green fields, obviously irrigated. A few miles before he'd reached Naturita, he had seen a sign indicating the entrance to a power plant. He would soon learn that more and more inhabitants of the double-wides followed the route of the transmission line along the highway from the power plant all the way to Telluride. There they made hotel beds and served breakfast to wealthy tourists who came to the region from modern places like Boston, places so far away they could have been on another planet.

The air was dry and crisp, a bracing rejoinder to the humidity of the Keys.

An hour later, Tom had checked into the Slickrock Motel. He went for a stroll and found himself standing in front of the West End Forum newspaper office; it occupied a homely A-frame with a sheet-metal roof and a rectangular shed attached to the rear. When you are a national reporter covering a story far from home, you gen-erally start by making a friend at the local paper. Feeling like his old self, full of confidence and promise, Tom paused at the door to briefly consider—and quickly reject—the idea of introducing himself as Ken Hanley.

Taking a deep breath, he opened the door and walked inside.

"Tom Austin," he said, extending a hand to the slight man in his late sixties or early seventies who stood up from a desk behind a counter and approached him.

"Howard Knapp. What can I do for you?"

"I don't know. I'm a reporter. Working freelance. I was thinking I might do some journalism. I got the idea somehow that there might be a lot of good stories around here."

"Oh, we've got stories, all right. Plenty of stories. I've written hundreds of 'em myself. More like thousands."

Howard shook his head in wonderment, as if it had occurred to him for the first time what he had done with his life.

"I guess you saw my ad with the Colorado Press Association," he said.

Before Tom could answer, Howard continued: "Paper's for sale. Ad's been running for over a year. You're the first one to reply."

Tom laughed. "I trust you're a better newspaperman than you are a salesman," he said.

Two weeks later, after Howard personally guaranteed the loan from the West End Savings Bank, mortgaging his meager retirement savings against Tom's unproven ability to keep up with the payments, Tom owned the Forum. Better yet, it came with the real estate, which included, on the second floor of the A-frame, a small apartment equipped with a bed, bathroom and small kitchen: everything Tom needed.

Chapter 8

THE SAME OLD ARGUMENT

A dozen of the subscriptions to the Forum that Tom mailed out every week went to the Manor Nursing Home outside of Cortez. The home was filled largely with ex-miners and their wives, former uranium miners from Naturita and former silver and gold miners from Telluride. The two towns had traded their prosperity. First, starting in the late 1890s when the miners first unionized, through the late 1940s, Telluride was rich with well-compensated mine employees and their fabulously wealthy employers. Just when the cost of extracting precious minerals outpaced their value and Telluride started to decline into a ghost town, world war loomed and uranium became precious, even though at first its value was a highly classified government secret and widely misunderstood.

After Hiroshima and Nagasaki were destroyed by bombs that were fueled by uranium secretly mined on the West End and just across the Utah border, the nuclear arms race between the U.S. and the Soviet Union kept the region prosperous for another two decades. During that brief period, it was said that uranium was the most valuable substance on the planet. But then, abruptly, came the end of domestic uranium mining. America had more than enough bombs, the nuclear power industry was in steep decline after accidents at Three Mile Island in Pennsylvania and Chernobyl in Ukraine, and the uranium ore for which there was still a market was extracted in places like South Africa, where there were far fewer environmental and health regulations for mine companies to contend with. By the late seventies it was Naturita that was occupied largely by ghosts, while Telluride had found new prosperity as an elite mountain resort.

The former gold miners of Telluride and uranium miners of Naturita shared their senescence in nursing homes in nearby cities. They were all children of great mining companies, with sweet memories of life in a company town in its heyday, when their employer provided every service from running the grocery store and the bowling alley to providing free dental care—and now, retirement benefits. The only differences between them were that the uranium families experienced far greater incidences of certain cancers, and there were many more uranium miners' widows.

* * *

"I'm here to see Elizabeth Walker," Tom said to the orderly at the nursing home reception desk.

"Elizabeth Walker," the orderly replied tentatively, as if he had never heard the name before.

"She lives here, doesn't she?"

"Yeah, but you'll have to wait a minute," he said. "Have a seat."

The orderly picked up the telephone and muttered into it. A few moments later Tom was approached by a tall, thin woman in her fifties, her red hair turning a pink shade of gray.

"Are you here to see Elizabeth?" she asked, extending a hand. "I'm Beverly Tarbell, the director here. We've all been very concerned about Elizabeth's son. I don't suppose you have any news."

"No," Tom said, handing her his card. "I'm Tom Austin. I publish the West End Forum."

"I guess if anyone had news, it would be you. We all learned Ray had gone missing from reading your paper. It's been the talk of the home. We have many residents from the Naturita-Nucla area. But I don't believe Elizabeth can tell you anything. She hasn't seen Ray in at least a month."

"Did he visit her often?"

"Every couple of months. He was here in October, I believe."

"Does she know that he's missing?"

"There didn't seem to be much point in telling her until we learned something definite. I'm not sure what we would say at this point. He's all she's got, and she upsets easily. I'm quite sure that nobody has said anything for fear of that."

"Can I see her?"

"I don't know. As I explained, she becomes upset so easily. I'll have to ask her if she'd like a visit from a stranger. Frankly, I doubt it. Why do you want to see her?"

"I didn't know it would be a problem."

"We are a private residence home, Mr. Austin," Tarbell said firmly, looking at his card as a way of avoiding eye contact. "Our job is to protect our residents from disturbances. With Ray gone, we are all the more responsible for her."

"Of course," Tom said. "Is there anyone else who has visited her….?"

"Let me stop you right there," she said, cutting him off and looking him in the eye. "I can't tell you anything personal about one of our residents, even if you are a reporter. It's against policy and would violate her privacy, and I've probably said too much already. But I'll tell you what I will do. Give me a few days to talk to Elizabeth, and then I'll call to let you know what she says."

"Why I would really appreciate that," Tom said, confident that the officious nursing home director had no intention of doing any such thing.

Tom retreated to his car and drove to a vantage point uphill on a nearby street where he could discreetly observe the nursing home below. He could see the director through her office window as she passed back and forth. He could see the front and rear entrances of the building and all of the cars in the parking lot. As darkness fell, the building lit up, including the light in Beverly Tarbell's office window.

Sitting in his car waiting for the director to leave, Tom wondered why he had not simply been ushered in to visit Elizabeth Walker. The orderly had clearly been instructed to notify his boss if anyone asked about her, even though, to judge from his reaction, nobody ever had before; and the boss, Tarbell, tried to discourage him from meeting with her, stopping just short of simply saying that he couldn't. But why? Was it as simple as Tarbell's explanation that Elizabeth Walker was excitable and difficult to manage and she wanted to protect her from the trauma of learning her son had disappeared until there was more definitive news? That would be a plausible and sufficient explanation for the nursing home director's behavior. But given Tom's growing sense that there was a degree of opposition to his investigating Ray Walker's disappearance, there could be more, and that was enough to keep him engaged.

Shortly after dark, Tom saw the light flicker off in the director's office, and he watched the spindly Tarbell climb into her car in the parking lot and drive off. The orderly who Tom had first met had left earlier, leaving nobody at the nursing home who would recognize him.

The attendant at the front desk looked up when Tom walked in.

"I'm here to visit my great aunt Myrna Patterson," Tom said.

Patterson was one of his subscribers, and one he knew had a large family—there were a dozen Pattersons still living in Naturita and several dozen more between Cortez and Farmington to whom he mailed subscriptions—so Tom calculated that she was likely to receive frequent visitors and particularly at suppertime. She was also highly social, having called him more than once with detailed information about the recently departed.

The attendant nodded and Tom strolled past, down a corridor that opened up to the dining room where a number of residents were sitting down to supper, several of them joined by their adult children and other younger visitors. Nobody paid much attention to him, so he stopped one of the residents who pushed by with the aid of a walker to ask where he could find Elizabeth Walker.

"That old bird don't eat much," the old man said. "She'll be in the day room."

* * *

Elizabeth Walker sat in a rocking chair in the otherwise empty, glassed-in dayroom overlooking a garden, knitting. She appeared to be in her early eighties. The man who'd told Tom where to find her was not speaking metaphorically: she did evoke an old bird, possibly a buzzard. She was all skin and bones. Her hair was pinned in a bun on top of her head, exposing a long white neck; her shoulder blades resembled wings, her nose a sharp beak; her eyes were magnified by the thick lenses of her glasses.

"I'm Tom Austin, Mrs. Walker. I publish the West End Forum."

She was not one of his subscribers and Tom could not tell if the mention of the newspaper stirred any recognition in her.

"I'd like to talk to you. Can I sit down?"

She looked up at him and stopped her knitting for a moment, but didn't say a word. Since she didn't object, he sat in an armchair across from her.

"Did you call the gas company?" she asked sharply. "We need to get propane in soon, afore it gets any colder. I can't do everything all by myself. I'm old."

"How are you doing, Mrs. Walker? Are you OK?"

"How do you think I'm doing? I'm an old lady whose son never comes to visit, not even on my goddamn birthday." She choked back a theatrical sob. "Not one visit in ten years!"

"He was just here last month, wasn't he?" Tom said.

"I've got a good mind to tell your father how bad you treat me. He expects you to look after me. You know there ain't nobody else to do it."

"My father…?"

"Now don't you go bitchin' about him again! He done what he could for us. This house we live in ain't nothing. There's not a one of us on this Earth chooses our parents. I've done right by you, as right as I could."

"I know … mom," Tom said. "Tell me again about you and dad, how you met."

For the first time since he sat across from her, she set her knitting down in her lap. She pushed back in her rocker and closed her eyes.

"All the girls, they made eyes at him, but not me. I just served him up his bacon and eggs. Eggs over easy. But I'm the one he wanted. Mr. Klein, they called him the King, but I wasn't afraid of him, not one little bit, and that's why I was the one he liked. And there's a lesson in that, boy."

She looked Tom in the eye.

"You must never think you are not as good as some other person just because they got money and you ain't. Being rich, well, you just take one look at your father and you know it ain't everything. Money don't make a man happy, not if he's married to a bitch that won't let him go!"

"You met at the Maverick...."

"Not the Maverick, no, no," she said, annoyed. "The diner!"

"Right, the diner...."

"Then he invited me to the drive-in picture show, but I said no. I made him ask me again and again. He knew then that I'm not some kind of cheap tart. But there was a Lana Turner picture, and he had a nice big car for watching pictures, a Cadillac. I wanted to see that picture. He had a bar right there in the car, with ice and Scotch whiskey. We saw other pictures, too, with Betty Grable and Joan Crawford, and he said I was prettier than any one of them. He loved me.... He did love me. And then I got pregnant with you...." Her voice drifted. "Mr. Klein, he is a very important man, a very busy man, and of course he couldn't lose his entire company because of a nasty divorce. That woman would take him right down, I knew she would, and we couldn't let that happen, of course not, so when I got pregnant, well, he bought us this house and he never, never once, forgot your goddamn birthday."

She wiped away a tear and resumed her knitting.

"My, my we had fun," she said.

"But there were a lot of hard years," Tom ventured.

"Now don't you start in with your whining. There is hardship in life. Who in this world doesn't know that? People get sick. There's war and there's pestilence. Sometimes the river runs dry and there's heartbreak, too. You just remember that your daddy loves you, like your momma loves you. There are things that make it hard for him, he has important work, and you just need to understand… that he can't always do everything we…. Did you order the propane? It will be cold soon and we'll need propane."

Tom reached over to touch her hand.

She sighed. "I don't know why we have to have this same old, same old argument all the time," she said, shaking her head. "You are a stubborn boy, Ray Walker. A stubborn boy. Always have been. Since you was three-years-old."

· · ·

Tom drove back from Cortez, across the vast Disappointment Valley, under a full moon. High on North Mountain, looming ahead, he could see a cluster of lights: the Uranium King Ranch, lately converted into a luxury guest ranch operated by the family, overlooking the Klein empire consisting of hundreds of thousands of acres and the entire town of Naturita, of which Tom himself, like it or not, was now a subject.

Tom reordered the list of theories that could explain Ray Walker's disappearance. Perhaps Ray had gone to his father and had asked for something, for money, for a future. Or maybe he tried to blackmail Klein, threatening him with exposure. As a resentful child of a poor single mother, Ray would have been subject to her control, and it was obvious that she knew a thing or two about control. But she was senile now, powerless, and Ray had grown, and there would have been nothing to stop him from trying to take matters into his own hands, to make demands of his father, to claim some inheritance. Maybe he thought he was simply testing his mother's theory that his father, appearances notwithstanding, cared about him.

How would Dick Klein react to having his bastard son show up on his doorstep with some kind of demand? Probably not well. But at this point, with Klein himself in his eighties, a demand might have been directed to Albert Klein, the half-brother, and that might be met with even less forbearance. If either Klein turned Ray back, how would Ray have reacted? With anger? In a conflict between Ray Walker and the Kleins, who would prevail? There was little question about that. The Kleins were never known to be reticent about exercising their power and influence or protecting their interests.

Ten miles outside of Naturita, Tom stopped his car at the entrance to the ranch. He got out of his car to stretch his legs. The gate was imposing in a style typical of large Western ranches, constructed of rough-hewn logs, the name Uranium King and the brand, an entwined U and K, burned into the log that formed the overhead arch. The gravel road beyond curved into the woods before it began a series of switchbacks to the flat, forested mesa just below the summit, where the ranch buildings were located.

In his younger days, Klein hosted legendary events there; he invited the whole town to meet a candidate for governor or to celebrate the Fourth of July. Since its conversion by Albert Klein into a resort, Tom had been there several times, when it had been first opened up to the public and for several promotional events since. He was torn between an impulse to drive up the road and talk to Dick Klein or Albert Klein, to investigate further and find the truth, and a sharply competing impulse to drive by and forget the entire thing. He couldn't see the percentage, at that moment, in questioning the Uranium King about his illegitimate son or Prince Albert about his interloper half-brother. On the other hand, he was drawn by the pull of the mystery and a growing conviction that if he didn't solve it, nobody would.

It was no contest, really. Tom got back in his car and drove home.

Chapter 9

WHISPERING JIM

When Tom acquired the Forum, he took possession of its entire archives, several dozen dusty black volumes containing every issue of the Forum and its predecessor paper, the Center Times, dating back to 1873.

Center was what Nucla was called before changing its name in 1949 in honor of the National Uranium Corporation of America, which operated the major mines and mills in the area. The region had proved a tough setting for the "Utopianists" who had founded the town half a century earlier. These were the region's earliest non-indigenous inhabitants: a group of Mormon pioneers who went far astray enroute to Salt Lake City, and settled their own desolate region, subsequently diverging into their own short-lived fundamentalist Mormon sect. Such schisms were not uncommon in early Mormonism, since the religion's very premise was that God could offer revelations to latter-day prophets like Joseph Smith, the church's founder.

Though Center's prophetic founders dreamed they would originate a new world order—hence the town's name—Center never prospered like Salt Lake did, and not for lack of religious zeal. When

Smith's successor Brigham Young decreed that the Salt Lake Valley was "the right place," he had the good sense to pick a location where plentiful fresh water flowed down from the high elevations of the Wasatch Mountains that formed the valley's eastern wall. In Center, it was the other way around: the essential fresh water flowed in a river canyon below the mesa that was suitable for cultivation. This required Center's founders to devote their first decade to the construction of a ditch, before they could plant a single turnip. They started out working collectively to bring water to the mesa, but as soon as the ditch reached a plot of land that someone had claimed for a homestead, that fortunate landowner stopped digging and started farming, resulting in a constantly shrinking workforce as the ditch grew longer, slowing the mesa's cultivation all the more.

Starting at such a sharp disadvantage in building their utopia, Center's pioneers failed to expand their religious franchise. Instead of a community of the faithful, they devolved into a group of isolated ranchers, struggling to supply themselves and the miners in Telluride with beef, mutton, milk, eggs, and vegetables.

"You will be the guardian of all this history," Howard Knapp had stated, as he prepared to turn over the keys to the Forum offices to his successor, grandly gesturing to the wall where the volumes of bound newspapers filled the top two shelves in a floor-to-ceiling bookcase.

Had Knapp kept the lower, easier-to-reach shelves empty in consideration of the future?

"In the century and a half that the Center Times and the West End Forum have published you will be only the ninth publisher," Knapp continued, as if he easily read Tom's mind and was happy to answer the question.

Knapp evidently expected Tom to devote his next forty years to creating volumes that would start to fill the third shelf, Tom realized; and when he was ready to retire, he would hand the keys to the tenth publisher, just as Knapp was handing the keys to him. In a mere three hundred years, the bookshelf might be full.

The years of labor that went into publishing what was in most years a slim newspaper by generations of lonely publishers represented an impressive commitment to some kind of legacy and, to Tom, a touching faith in the very idea that recording events has inherent and lasting value. Someday, the shelf of volumes seemed to propose, the stories contained herein, this carefully documented past, would matter to someone. From the Utopianists to mining the ore that went into the manufacture of the world's first atomic bomb, the history of the West End could be, should be, of more than local interest. Yet during Tom's tenure at the Forum, only he and Molly Buford, who wrote a weekly history column for the paper, cracked open the volumes of newspapers that Howard Knapp and his seven predecessors—and now Tom—compiled and guarded.

Arriving home from his visit with Elizabeth Walker, Tom sank into an armchair and found himself gazing at the wall of old newspaper volumes. He wondered if Elizabeth herself ever made the news. Had there been an announcement of her son's birth? Or was a rich man's bastard son unmentionable in the 1960s? He wondered when Dick Klein himself might have first been mentioned.

Tom pulled down a volume of newspapers covering the early 1940s and started flipping through it. The nation was on the verge of war.

On December 11, 1941, after Pearl Harbor, an uncredited writer, presumably the paper's editor or publisher, sought to convey his and his community's resolve:

THE UNITED STATES IS AT WAR

This peace-loving nation, which has ever shunned imperialism, has been attacked without warning by a mongrel yellow race that has dreams of dominating and controlling more than half the face of the globe.

Our nation apparently already has suffered heavy losses. Our people are face to face with the knowledge that we must wage a long, burdensome struggle to maintain our free American way of life and the right to conduct friendly commerce with all parts of the world.

This nation will meet the challenge. No matter what sacrifices are involved, the United States of America will win this battle of the Pacific, just as it will help to rid both hemispheres of the curse of dictatorship.

Our people are now united in a common resolve to make Japan rue the day it attempted to match forces with this great republic. No matter what the cost, no matter how long it will take, this nation will emerge victorious.

We of the West End will put forth every effort to help our country in this grim struggle. Through the purchase of government bonds, through aid to the Red Cross and other welfare organizations, this section of the country will not be found lacking. Scores of our young men are already in the armed forces—others will enlist from time to time as their services are needed. The West End is "all out" to win this war—just as all other parts of the nation are.

In succeeding editions, the Forum voiced pride that the local mining industries had geared up to defend America. Vanadium was a strategic mineral of great importance, used to manufacture the bullets and airplanes and rifles that American soldiers would need to defeat the enemy.

"The metal mining industry is a vital part of the war program," the paper preached. "Without metals, the tanks, guns, ships, and airplanes needed cannot be produced in sufficient quantity to meet the needs of the soldiers at the fronts. In this emergency every ounce of metal is a sacred trust. Every worker in the metal industry is a vital soldier in a war against evil. Not only is every ounce of metal a sacred trust but everyone connected with the mining industry has a sacred duty to perform."

The region boomed and Naturita sprouted on the banks of the San Miguel as large corporations operated mines and mills throughout the region, purchasing carnotite ore from independent miners. In 1943, the paper was indignant that Secretary of the Interior Harold Ickes declared millions of acres of public land off-limits to prospecting, stating it was being reserved due to the likelihood it contained minerals of strategic importance: vanadium, magnesium, and potash.

In a futile attempt to deduce why the land was withdrawn, the long-gone Forum editor supposed there was "a nigger in the woodpile," since the withdrawal did not advance but actually seemed to slow the production of strategic metals. Of course, Tom realized with historic hindsight, it was uranium that was being safeguarded, and it was uranium, not vanadium, that was being extracted at the region's "vanadium" mills, as part of the then top-secret Manhattan Project. Like the miners themselves, who were being kept in the dark as to the real value of their ore, the Forum demonstrated no awareness at all that the region's contribution to the war effort was so essential to the ultimate war strategy. Before the detonation of the first atom bomb, perhaps nobody—not the politicians who authorized its development, nor the physicists who split the atom—could truly comprehend what uranium meant. Before Hiroshima and Nagasaki, it was an abstraction. But after the war, the government made itself the only legal buyer of uranium.

In early 1952 the Forum reported that the year 1951 had seen over $300 million in uranium mining and milling activity in the region. The U.S. Atomic Energy Commission had not only set the price of uranium high enough to encourage prospecting but paid generous bonuses to new claims that produced a minimum volume of ore, setting off the uranium rush. Congress authorized the AEC and U.S. Geologic Service to build roads to access mining districts and connect them to mills. The population of Naturita spiked tenfold in 1951, from about a thousand to ten thousand, with most of the new inhabitants living in tents, shacks, or trailers, scrambling to stake claims or, failing that, working to support the booming new industry in mines, mills, and ancillary businesses. Among the population, Tom surmised, was the young Dick Klein and his family.

Tom scanned the pages of the Forum for any mention of Klein, and found it unexpectedly, in a brief story dated November 14, 1952.

GEOLOGIST REPORTS MISSING MAN

Geologist Dick Klein told authorities on Monday that his partner, Jim Stewart, is missing in the vicinity of the Iberia Canyon mining district. Klein said that he and Stewart were prospecting in the Iberia Canyon, 40 miles southwest of Naturita, when they became separated.

Klein said he searched for Stewart but found no sign of him. After searching for a full day, Klein returned to Naturita for help looking for the missing man. A search party had no luck.

The Iberia district is rugged country, with numerous side canyons. It would be easy for a man to become disoriented there, or to lose his footing and fall a great distance, searchers said after they returned to Naturita.

Klein said that Stewart is known as Whispering Jim because of his soft-spoken manner of speaking. He said that Stewart is single and has no family in the area.

That was all. But this was clearly how Klein's famous uranium strike, the Whispering Jim Mine, got its name.

If the disappearance of Whispering Jim did not command more ink, perhaps it was because the paper published so much misfortune. The Forum was full of stories of men and women "called by death" or "summoned home." Sometimes death "beckoned" or it "found" the unlucky deceased. There were constant stories of miners struck by falling rocks and wives taken by sudden illness. There were frequent mine cave-ins, and ranching accidents involving horses or bales of hay, and a couple of fatal car accidents every week, it seemed, drivers taking curves at too high a speed and running off the road. Constant though these mishaps were, the Forum duly noted that the death "was a keen shock" to the surviving family or a "sharp blow." Friends almost always extended "heartfelt sympathy to the bereaved."

Tom found himself engrossed in this litany of lives cut short, flipping the pages of the old newspapers past numerous stories with the name Klein, or the Uranium King, in the headline, thinking he would come back soon to read them all.

It was pure luck that he opened a volume to a story that seemed to resolve the mystery of what had happened to Whispering Jim. It was from the summer of 1971.

HUMAN REMAINS BELIEVED TO BE WHISPERING JIM FOUND IN IBERIA CANYON

Montrose County Sheriff Trace Martin said Tuesday that the human bones found last week in Iberia Canyon are probably those of Whispering Jim Stewart, the miner who went missing almost twenty years ago, and who Dick Klein's Whispering Jim Mine is named after. Stewart was Klein's partner before Klein made his famous uranium discovery.

If the remains are those of Whispering Jim, a mystery is solved. The only bones that were found are those of a man's arm below the elbow. The bones were found wedged behind a boulder in a slot canyon. There was a rusty knife nearby. Sheriff Martin says it appears that the boulder fell on the man's arm, trapping him.

There is no way to know for certain if the bones are those of Whispering Jim Stewart, but Klein told the Forum he is convinced they are.

"It looks like a boulder fell on Jim and trapped him down there in that canyon where he was prospecting and that's why we could never find him," Klein said. "We looked all over that area. He must have been dead or unconscious, so he couldn't even shout out for help when we were looking for him. Poor Jim. I only hope he died quickly."

The bones have been sent to a medical examiner in Denver for analysis.

A few months later, the Forum published a follow-up story.

WHISPERING JIM MAY HAVE CUT OFF HIS OWN ARM

The state medical examiner has determined that the arm bones believed to be those of Whispering Jim Stewart show signs of knife marks at the elbow joint.

"It sure looks like Whispering Jim cut off his own arm," Montrose County Sheriff Trace Martin said. "He got trapped down in that slot canyon by a boulder that must have come loose on him, and he must have used the pocketknife we found to free himself by amputating his own arm. Then he wandered off and died, probably of shock and exposure and maybe blood loss."

Whispering Jim Stewart went missing in 1952, while prospecting in the Iberia Canyon vicinity with his partner Dick Klein. A search for the missing man did not find him. Klein later found the mine he named after Whispering Jim.

"This just shows what kind of man Whispering Jim was that he had the strength to cut off his own arm," Klein said after learning of the medical examiner's conclusion.

It is not surprising that no other human remains have been found, Sheriff Martin said. The bones trapped by the boulder were protected from predators and the elements, but if Jim severed his own arm and walked off before perishing, predators and the elements would have dispersed any remains in just a few years' time....

Just as Tom had surmised, the long-serving sheriff of Montrose County, Martin, and the county's most prominent citizen, Klein, went back decades together. Martin would have been newly installed as sheriff when Whispering Jim's remains were found.

To all appearances, the mystery of Whispering Jim had a logical resolution. If there had been any further developments, the Forum did not report them. But Whispering Jim's demise had been suspiciously convenient for Dick Klein, and Trace Martin's investigation into the circumstances surrounding it could have been every bit as cursory as his current investigation into the disappearance of Ray Walker.

Was it improbable or even unlikely that behind the Klein fortune there might have been a crime?

Chapter 10

INHALE, EXHALE, HOLD YOUR BREATH, AND SQUEEZE

The West End Historical Society occupied an old ranch house in the Naturita Town Park, next to the rocky baseball fields where the town's entire population gathered to watch their kids play in the spring and summer. The building's yard was littered with rusty old ranching and mining equipment. It was far more evocative of a junkyard than an aspiring museum exhibit.

Tom found Molly, his history columnist, behind the wooden desk just inside the door, patiently awaiting any tourists driving between Telluride and Moab who might have enough of an interest in local history — or enough time to kill — to stop in. Occasionally, she once told Tom, somebody actually did. In her eighties, Molly was the descendent of Utopianists, but she had not lived her entire life on the West End. She worked for a major book publisher in New York for most of her adult life. She had never married. When she retired, she returned home and devoted herself to the history of the West

End, not only writing for the Forum and operating the Historical Society, but also seeking out old timers and recording their stories.

"Ray Walker is not the first missing man around here," Tom said, after they got through their greetings.

"Oh, my goodness, no!" Molly said. "In the forties and fifties, with men prospecting far and wide, many were reported lost. More may have disappeared without anyone noticing. So many were bachelors."

"I was looking back through old newspapers," Tom explained. "People died and took sick and even disappeared all the time in those years."

"Life here has always been hard. Ranching and mining are the two most dangerous occupations a man can have, according to the government, and that's all we've got here; it's all we've ever had, mostly, except for a little tourism nowadays, and people living here who commute to jobs in Telluride. And there are jobs at power plant, of course. But as hard as it is now, it's better than it used to be and that's why something like Ray's disappearance hits so hard. I suppose people took it more in stride when it was more common."

"I was reading about Whispering Jim Stewart."

"He is one who disappeared, that's right."

"The paper reported it, but as a story, it seemed to go away fast," Tom said. "It's not like this story now with Ray…."

"He was a bachelor, and as I recall, he was called Whispering Jim because he didn't talk much."

"Did people think it was, I don't know, kind of convenient for Dick Klein that Jim disappeared when he did?" Tom ventured. "I mean, after he struck it so big not long after, was there talk or malicious gossip?"

"I suppose there was that sort of talk. You know how people are. But nothing came of it, and I don't suppose there'd be any way to prove what you might be thinking. What got you started down this path?

"I was just reading old newspapers. That's all."

"Klein had a certain ruthlessness, I suppose, and was single-minded. But he became so revered here that nobody would ever accuse him of killing his partner. He built the mill and provided good jobs. He built the clinic, gave money to the schools, and set off fireworks every Fourth of July. He flew sick people on his private plane to the hospital in Denver."

"I've heard the stories."

"It didn't last more than twenty years, but for as long as it did he was so good to the people here that you'd just never think of him as greedy."

"When they found Jim's remains…."

"There wasn't much left of him. Just a few bones, as I recall."

"And a knife…"

"Oh, yes. His own knife, probably."

"The newspaper story said he was trapped by a falling boulder and then cut off his own arm."

"Can you imagine?"

"I really can't. It's not possible. Nobody could cut off his own arm."

"Well, in fact, a man can do just that," Molly said. "Why, some years back there was a hiker out in the canyonlands over near Moab who got himself trapped, just his arm, like Whispering Jim," Molly said. "This boy's arm was crushed under a boulder. He was stuck there for a few days, and he realized that nobody was going to find him. If he didn't do something dramatic, he was going to die there. So, he tied a tourniquet around his arm, cut his arm off at the elbow to set himself free, and walked right out."

"I couldn't do that. I'd just die waiting to be rescued."

"People can do amazing things; things they don't realize they are capable of doing."

"Do you know Ray Walker's mother? Elizabeth Walker?"

"When I came back from New York on my vacations, I'd take my father to the diner for dinner, and she always waited on us. She was there for decades. She was such a fixture that when she retired, the diner had to shut down."

"She's at the Manor Nursing Home in Cortez."

"She must be almost as old as I am."

"She's got some kind of dementia."

"Oh, the poor thing."

"Do you know that she was Dick Klein's mistress?"

"She never made much of a secret of it. It was the biggest thing in her life." Molly paused, but only for a moment. "So, if Dick Klein was capable of killing his partner back in the fifties, maybe he has something to do with his bastard son's disappearance now?"

"Something like that."

"Now that's so far-fetched that it's funny," she said with a laugh, drawing a half-apologetic grin from Tom.

"What do you think might have happened to Ray Walker?" he asked.

"Maybe he got himself trapped in a slot canyon by a falling boulder," she shrugged. "I mean, without more to go on, one theory is as good as another. I can see why you find it interesting that he's Dick Klein's son. But it's not as if that was ever all that much of a secret, and it sure doesn't mean Klein had anything to do with his disappearance. Before you can develop a hypothesis like that, it strikes me that you need some evidence for it, or a motive at least."

• • • •

Tom was stopped at a guardhouse a few miles up the access road to the Uranium King Ranch.

"I have an appointment to see Albert Klein," he told the armed guard. "Name's Tom Austin."

The guard glanced at a clipboard and nodded.

"He's expecting you. He's at the shooting range. Do you need directions?"

"I've been there."

The guard waved Tom on, and he drove the remaining few miles up the winding road deeper into the woods to the cluster of buildings on the relatively flat mesa near the summit. He parked next to Albert Klein's polished black Hummer, which occupied a place of honor in the lot adjacent to the main lodge building.

There was plenty of parking available. Despite efforts to promote the latest Klein family enterprise, the UK Ranch was never very busy. Tom's first visit there had been at Klein's invitation to join a reporter from Telluride, who was doing a story about the region's exclusive new resort. The intention, clearly, was to capitalize on Telluride's growing reputation as a chic destination, even though it was eighty miles away, along with any mystique associated with the ranch's history. The first autumn the resort was open, Tom had been a guest at a sad, sparsely attended Oktoberfest, the staff bravely outfitted in dirndls and lederhosen, a yodeler providing the entertainment, and brats, kraut and beer on the menu; a year later he had attended an open house at the resort's most unusual amenity, the Olympus Shooting Club, featuring demonstrations of every way it is possible to engage with a firearm. The initiation fee was $10,000, leaving Tom well out of the running as a prospective club-member.

Getting out of his car, Tom was struck as he had been on previous visits by the eccentricity of the place. The historic, sprawling ranch house and a few traditional ranch outbuildings, still the personal residence of the Klein family and off-limits to resort guests, sat at the compound's edge. Sometimes the stooped figure of the elder Klein, the Uranium King himself, could be spotted from a distance, passing time on the expansive front porch. He occasionally waved to visitors. By comparison, the new resort buildings seemed out of scale and ill-placed on the hilly, densely forested landscape. There was an oversized main lodge building housing the elegant dining facility, a bar, a spa, and hotel rooms, awkwardly sited overlooking an artificial pond. Nearby there were guest cabins in the woods, a wedding chapel in a clearing, and the shooting club facilities, adjacent to Tom's destination, the shooting range. As Tom headed up a paved walkway in that direction, he encountered another of the armed guards.

"Good afternoon Mr. Austin," the guard said, having been alerted by his colleague at the gatehouse that Mr. Klein's guest was on his way up. He had, undoubtedly, been sent to ensure that Tom was not straying from the path to his appointment.

Was the guard's attentiveness offered as a taste of the resort's discreet five-star personal service to the visitor, intended to ensure that he was finding his way and in no need of assistance? Or was it something more? The ambiguity seemed intentional.

Indeed, the pervasive obsessions with weaponry, self-defense and security at the UK Ranch Resort bestowed a degree of paranoia that may well have been intentional. Albert Klein's marketing concept when he converted the family homestead into a hotel was that as the world's only five-star resort that incorporated a shooting club as its premier amenity, North Mountain would attract titans of corporate America and the ultra-wealthy from across the globe, powerful individuals with realistic concerns about their personal safety. In addition to marksmanship, the club offered courses and ongoing training in the martial arts and self-defense, some expressly for women. Klein was especially proud of the state-of-the-art "scenario house," which he personally designed with help from Hollywood special effects experts, where hostage incidents and break-ins could be staged and defended against using live ammo, because the bad guy targets were holograms. As a community service, Klein had opened up the shooting club at no cost to law enforcement agencies from the entire Four Corners region, for their officers to practice and perfect their marksmanship and other SWAT-team skills.

The day was cold and overcast, threatening snow, and Klein was the only shooter on the field, which would have been a sea of ankle-deep mud if the ground hadn't been frozen solid.

Klein glanced at Tom, and then greeted him by shouting, "Pull!"

An unseen assistant catapulted a clay pigeon into the air. Klein took aim, fired, and shattered it.

"Ever shoot a gun?" Klein asked, turning to Tom.

"Never have."

Klein handed Tom his shotgun. "Let me see you take aim," he said, pointing to a stationary target a hundred feet away.

Klein corrected Tom's form and posture, as Tom took aim.

"You are holding a fine precision instrument whose fundamental purpose is to kill," Klein said. "How does it feel?"

"Reminds me of the first time I took a seat at a blackjack table at a casino, when I was 22. My heart kind of jumped."

"In a minute, you'll squeeze the trigger and then it will feel like the first time you touched a girl's naked breast, when you were … how old?"

"I don't know. Fifteen, maybe sixteen."

"Late bloomer, I guess."

"Ha!"

"Marksmanship is about discipline and self-control," Klein said. "You need to be loose enough to adjust to the target, and quickly, if it's a moving target, and steady enough so that the recoil doesn't throw you back; you've got to be relaxed and steady at the same time."

"I see."

"It's not as easy as it sounds."

"I don't doubt it."

"Make sure you are balanced and comfortable," Klein coached. "Here's what you're going to do. Without trying to anticipate when the round will fire, because that will totally screw you up, you're going focus on the bullseye through the scope, inhale, exhale, hold your breath and squeeze."

"Sounds like yoga," Tom muttered.

"I wouldn't know. You ready?"

"Yep."

"OK then, inhale, exhale, hold, and squeeze."

Focusing on his breathing, Tom fired, missing the target, though by how much there was no way to know.

"How was that?"

"Good, I guess," Tom said, lowering the gun.

"That's all?" Klein sounded disappointed. "Just good?"

Tom laughed: "There's something better than good?"

"Most people get it right away," Klein shrugged, as if Tom had just confirmed that he belonged to a lesser category of human being. He had just confessed to yoga, after all.

"You're still welcome to come and use the club anytime you'd like, as my guest," Klein added, as if to display a hotelier's graciousness.

"Thank you. I appreciate that."

Klein took the rifle back and cradled it lovingly. He was tall, muscular, and bald, and had dark brown eyes. He wore a sheepskin coat. Abruptly he shouted "pull," and another clay pigeon flew into the sky. Klein smoothly turned to it, put the rifle on his shoulder, fired, and shattered it.

"If you're firing at a living thing, it's even harder because then your emotions may be engaged, even if it's just a pheasant whose life you're taking. A pheasant is a beautiful bird. That's why they had to invent machine guns. It's a rare soldier who can be expected to control his emotions in combat, but any idiot can suppress a wide area with an automatic weapon by spraying bullets all over the place. Marksmanship has evolved into a highly specialized skill. Its only real applications are for target shooting, which has become a sport but is really just practice for hunting and … can you think of the other application?"

Tom shook his head.

"Designated marksman. Sharpshooter. Pick off a high value target from a safe distance, whether it's a sniper like Lee Harvey Oswald carrying out an assassination or a SWAT team officer trying to prevent one. In combat, the DM is usually assigned to take out the enemy's commanding officers."

Klein reveled in his expertise.

"Interesting," Tom said.

"Pull!" Klein shouted, and he fired, but this time he missed the pigeon. He turned abruptly to Tom and asked: "You need a loan?"

"A loan?" Tom said. "Why would I ask you for a loan?"

"I don't know why you wouldn't," Klein barked. "Every damn business in Naturita asks the Kleins for money sooner or later. Even the damn bank. I've wondered why you haven't. The old man put thousands into the paper before you bought it. Town needed a paper, he figured. If he'd ever done any proper accounting, we'd own you, but he didn't bother. I thought it was just a matter of time before you came around with your hand out."

"Actually, I came to ask you about Ray Walker."

"What about him?"

"You must have some theory about how or why your brother disappeared."

Klein scowled, an expression that might have reflected nothing more than lifelong irritation at the mention of his half-brother's name.

"Pull!" he shouted, and he fired, knocking off another clay pigeon.

"I've got no idea," he growled. "Is that all? Because if it is, you've wasted your time, which is fine, but I won't let you waste any more of mine."

The interview, such as it was, was over.

· · ·

Klein's flat denial that he had any interest in or concern about his illegitimate stepbrother's disappearance brought Tom to a dead end. There was really no other lead to follow, nobody else to interview. He had already gone much further than he'd intended in pursuit of the mystery, brazenly and pointlessly confronting Albert Klein for reasons that very likely had more to do with himself than with Ray Walker. He had been driven by his basic curiosity, but also something deeper, something to do with his understanding of his profession and his betrayal of it, and his sense of himself and how and why he had ended up in Naturita. But those were all subjects he preferred not to think about very deeply.

In any case, having been thwarted, Tom thought about how Ray Walker's disappearance had already receded far enough into the past after only a little more than a week that it now felt virtually preordained. Something unlikely or unthinkable suddenly happens and is shocking, but then it is simply a fact. To take a huge example of the same phenomenon, three years earlier the World Trade Center towers in New York disappeared from the city skyline. Who other than the perpetrators who planned and executed the attack could have imagined such a gigantic effect? But the essential appeal of violence is that it changes something, whether it's the entire world, a small community like Naturita, or an individual's private world. Even if a shattering event was predictable, nobody can know exactly how it will unfold. Once it takes place, both the reality of it and the sharp details of how it occurred make it seem as if it were predetermined. Isn't this why human beings often imagine they can foresee the future? Because the instant the future becomes the present, and just as instantaneously slips into the past and later is remembered, it all seems so obvious in retrospect?

The phrase that ran through Tom's mind was, *that's what happened.* Tom's father died without warning when he was 13. The World Trade Center towers were destroyed in 2001. Ray Walker disappeared in 2004. In the 1940s, physicists working just a few hundred miles away, at Los Alamos, New Mexico, learned how to refine uranium mined on the West End and manufacture nuclear weapons from it, and soon after that Hiroshima and Nagasaki were bombed into oblivion. All of those things happened, and the world was not the same afterward. They, and countless other occurrences, significant and trivial, complex and simple, affecting individuals and all of mankind, cumulatively bring the world to its present moment. History itself might be written as nothing more than a series of simple declarations of what happened and when, but not necessarily why they happened when they did. For another example, as Albert Klein casually noted, in 1963 a sniper's bullet killed President Kennedy. Everything may change, but the world keeps turning.

Chapter 11

GETTING PERSONAL FAST

A week before Ray Walker disappeared, the Naturita Town Board had taken an action that created a ruckus. The board unanimously followed the recommendation of the superintendent of the West End School District and made Fourth Street one-way between Main and Herron where it passes by the school.

Now, barely a week and a half after Ray Walker's disappearance, the town meeting hall was full of citizens up in arms that such a momentous action had been taken without more public discussion.

Tom sat in his usual place at the back, taking notes.

"When there is a controversial matter before this board," Anne Carson, a former board member said, "then you need to ask your constituents. You need to put something in the newspaper, so we know what you are up to."

Oh, but I did, Tom thought to himself as the crowd murmured agreement, a reminder that his journalistic efforts were an exercise in futility.

"This was not controversial at all," Mayor Harry Denny said. "At least none of us thought it was at the time."

"Well, as one board member, I apologize," Greg Holstrom said. "I am sorry I made the motion."

"I submitted this request to turn the road into a one-way in sound mind," Superintendent Larry Tice said. "My daddy always taught me to make decisions that I could sleep with. After I asked this board to make the street one-way, and you did it, I slept like a baby. I don't think anyone on this board should apologize for anything."

"If the idea was to protect school kids, there was a better way to do it," Tom's friend Dave Best said. "Did you stop to think that the one-way would make it so trucks can't get down the alley behind my store? Now, how are we going to unload merchandise? Did you stop to think that speed bumps or a flashing light might work better?"

"What about teaching the kids not to walk in the middle of the street?" Lulu Lack asked.

"We've obviously got a problem," Mayor Denny said. "I guess we didn't necessarily make the right decision. But we voted unanimously and so now we have a law on the books that makes Fourth one-way, so what do we do about that? Seems to me this is a health-safety issue and if we go back on our decision we've got a real liability problem."

"That's right," Tice said. "I urge you not to go back to the way it was unless there is some other safety measure in place first. I wouldn't want to be a member of this board if you did that and then some child was hit by a car and killed."

Checkmate. You can win any argument, Tom mused, by threatening the life of a child.

"If I may," town manager Luanne Pillsbury proposed, breaking the silence. "The board could leave matters as they are, and before our next meeting in three weeks we could work with the neighbors who are concerned about the one-way and bring you some options."

. . .

It is far better that life goes on, Tom thought, as he walked back to his office, for what was the alternative? That everything should stop just because a man was missing? He himself was relieved. This was precisely the sort of story he preferred to spend his days reporting. Should Fourth Street be one-way or not? Despite the school superintendent's dire warning, this was not life or death.

Tom immersed himself in his daily routine. The school lunch menu sat on his fax, and he wondered if Sarah Walker had sent it. Had she gone back to work? He had some ads to build, one for Scenic Realty featuring single trailers and doublewides and tract homes, not one of them listed at more than $75,000. Dave delivered his Merc ad, along with a snide comment about the idiocy of the town board. Tom typed up the lunch menu. He wrote up the one-way street story. And then he wondered what, if anything, he should print about Ray Walker. Was it news that he had learned Ray's parentage? Clearly not. Would there be any purpose served in calling Sheriff Martin for another update? Doubtful. If this was a case when no news was news, then how long would that be true?

He decided to run the one-way street story as his lead, and to run the familiar picture of Ray below the fold, with a caption stating the basic facts, that he was still missing, and had been missing for 15 days, and that there were no new leads in the case. Walker had led the news after all, for two consecutive weeks. Pushing the story to lower prominence would be part of the healing process. It was time to let Ray go.

The phone rang.

"I just called to make sure you got the lunch menu," Sarah Walker said.

"You're back at work."

"I couldn't sit at home anymore, making soap and waiting for Ray to walk in the door."

"I understand," Tom said. "I'm sorry, Sarah."

She said nothing but did not hang up, either. He sensed that she was working to control her emotions.

"Are you OK?"

"Yes." But her voice was weak.

"Would you like to go for a walk after work?" he asked, absolutely unsure if it was his reporter's instincts kicking in, or something else. Either way, he was sure she had some as-yet unspoken reason for having called him.

She didn't answer quickly.

"Can you meet me at the drive-in?" she asked.

* * *

Desolate but on a hill, the drive-in offered both privacy and safety. A person could sit in her car at the drive-in and watch the single entrance to see who was coming well before they arrived. At the same time, it was possible to remain inconspicuous, parking off to the side or among the boulders at the edge of the mesa, behind the crumbling screen.

That's how Tom found Sarah, waiting for him, in the safety of her car, watching him approach.

When he pulled up, she got out of her car and joined him in his.

"You can't imagine how hard this is," she said.

"No."

"I feel awful for saying it, but it would have been easier if he'd been killed. Then, at least I'd know."

"I've thought about that. How a disappearance is worse in a way than a death. You must feel like you can't go on. How will you know when it's OK to keep living your life?"

"Every day I wake up and I'm living my life. It goes on, it just goes on. Why did you want to meet me?"

"I thought maybe you needed someone to talk to."

"I thought you might have questions you want to ask."

"I might."

"Do you think I have secrets? That I know more than I'm saying?"

"Do you?"

"Doesn't everyone?"

Though he'd been looking forward to seeing her, he hadn't anticipated they would be sparring, each seeking some kind of tactical advantage, even if their underlying purposes were unclear. He had imagined something gentler, but she looked at him hard, an expression that could be read either as a challenge to try harder to uncover her secrets or a warning to back off, or maybe she was toying with him for the hell of it. Regardless, her aggression presented a bigger question: Why had she called him in the first place? Surely it was not, as she professed, to make sure that he'd received the school lunch menu. That was far too easy an alibi. Her suggestion that he had initiated their meeting was not exactly accurate, either, or had he only imagined when he heard her voice on the other end of the phone, purportedly to ask about the school lunch menu, that she was inviting a further interaction? She had sounded hesitant, to which he had responded, but it is easy to misread the silence in a pause. If this was a seduction, it was not clear which of them was more interested in pursuing it. Each had, after all, revealed an attraction to the other before Ray disappeared, before he knew she was married to Ray, when they had innocently flirted with each other.

In any case, just when Tom had convinced himself that the story of Ray's disappearance was nearing its conclusion, however unsatisfactorily, she was drawing him back in. But why? The calculus involved so many variables, emotional and mercenary, and so many unknowns, that Tom could not be confident he'd accounted for all of the possibilities. The simplest and least compromising was that she was lonely in her husband's absence and needed someone to talk to.

"Do you think I'm mysterious?" she asked. "That I know what happened to Ray?"

"Maybe you do," he said, a tacit acknowledgment that she made a plausible femme fatale. "You haven't been at the top of my list of suspects. At least not until now."

"Go ahead and ask me something. Maybe I'll give you a clue I don't even know I have, and you'll be the one to figure out what happened to him."

Her gamesmanship demanded an worthy response, so Tom delivered one.

"Did you know that your husband, that Ray, was conceived here?"

"That's getting awful personal awful fast!" she exclaimed, her armor dented, but for no more than a second. "But it's a safe guess. I'd say half the people born on the West End were conceived here. And that's why the place is dying. The drive-in movie theater is shut down so there's no place for people to make babies so that they have to get married and stuck here for the rest of their damn lives."

He frowned and nodded, as if to process what she said.

"Of course," she added, "Angie figured it out somehow, even without the drive-in. Or maybe they did get pregnant right here."

"Is that what happened to you? You got pregnant and stuck?"

"Not exactly."

She didn't volunteer more, so they sat silently for a moment.

"I suppose I'm impressed," she said. "Mostly people from away never understand the first thing about this place. But you've got it all figured out."

"You know Ray was Dick Klein's son…."

"I've been married to the man for 20 years."

"But you told me his father is dead."

"What else would you expect me to say for you to put it in the paper?"

Her tone had shifted, signaling that she was finished teasing him and was deploying a different element of her game. She was a complicated woman, subtler and more in command of how she presented herself than he had expected.

"Listen," she said, "I called because I wanted to tell you something."

"Yes?"

"I don't want you to investigate my husband's disappearance."

"I'm not," he said, surprising himself with his own hurried denial. "I'm not an investigative reporter, and even if I were The Forum is too small, I'm too small. I don't have the resources it takes to investigate anything."

"Why did you go meet Elizabeth?"

How did she know? Had the nursing home director found out about his visit and reported it back to the family?

"Why wouldn't I?" he asked. "I'm reporting a story of a man's disappearance, so I met with his mother. The same way I interviewed you. It would be odd if I didn't. But it's not an investigation. I guess you keep up with her."

She turned to face him and look him in the eye to impress upon him that she was serious.

"You wrote up your interview with me and put what I said in the paper," she said, sounding like a prosecutor grilling an unfriendly witness. "It was *mostly* true...."

Was she referencing her husband's not-so-secret parentage? Or something more?

"I read the Forum sometimes," she continued. "Especially lately. I haven't seen a story about your interview with Elizabeth."

"I discovered she was senile. Has dementia. She didn't give me anything I could publish. It was a wasted trip."

"You don't know what you're getting into," she said, enunciating every word for emphasis. "It could be more dangerous, much more dangerous, than you think."

Did she also know he'd met with Albert Klein?

"Dangerous how?"

She didn't answer.

"Was Ray having an affair?"

"No!"

"Was he using meth? Or cooking it?"

"No! Why would you ask those things?"

"What other danger is there? There's sex if he was having an affair, or drugs if he was messed up with meth, or possibly money if the Kleins are involved. Doesn't that cover everything dangerous? Sex, drugs, and money?"

"There's always a boring old car wreck," she said without conviction.

"Everybody is telling me something different," Tom said. "And I have to wonder why."

He told her about Dave Best's suggestion that Ray might be involved in some "bad shit," meth, and that Dave wanted him to know that Ray was Dick Klein's son. He described Sheriff Martin's warning that an investigation can lead to "a big ole mess" after Tom asked if he knew that it was Dick Klein's son who was missing. He told her the sheriff hinted that Ray was having an affair.

"Those are all the clues I've got," he said, omitting what he learned from Elizabeth Walker, and failing to reveal he had also interviewed Albert Klein. "And now you're telling me that he wasn't having an affair or doing meth and that it's no big deal who his father is, and you also don't think he was in an accident, but you don't want me to investigate because of some vague danger. Whatever happened to Ray can't be that complicated. It's got to be simpler."

Sarah seemed to choose one of the complications to tell him about, whether to appease or misdirect him he wasn't sure, or even, just possibly, because it was relevant.

"There was a woman who lived here, a beautiful Russian woman, she lived in town for a year and then she left, about six months ago, and I don't think she touched but one or two lives…. Ray's life, and mine, I suppose," Sarah said. "She worked at the auto shop."

"Oh?"

"Ray taught her how to install windshields, and repair cracks in them. He could have done it himself and saved what he paid her, but he just felt so terrible for her. She needed the work, and she needed to get out of the house, and Ray, he was so kind to her, to Anya, she was so cultured, not just another West End hick like the rest of us, you know, she was … *educated*, and she had this *spirit*. She was blonde and so skinny, and she had these high cheekbones and bright eyes, and she laughed a lot, even though she was sad. She was from St. Petersburg, over in Russia, and she came here as a mail-order bride.

"I'm sure you never heard of Mark Brubaker, either. He is a trucker, lives out on the mesa, doesn't know anyone and nobody knows him.

He's one of these guys who has his own rig, and he only works when he has to and he lives as cheaply as he can between jobs, and that's why he lives here, outside of Naturita, because it hardly costs him a cent. He can live three or four months off of what he earns on one long haul and then he can sit around in his underwear and drink beer and fart all day long. He paid for Anya to come over here, with her son, Nick, but he lied to her. Her life in Naturita was nothing at all like what he told her. She hated it, probably thought she'd ended up in Siberia or someplace god-awful, and she hated him, too. She is so beautiful, and he must have sent her a fake picture, or she would have chosen someone else, because he's a toad. I mean, a complete loser. You can't imagine how anyone could have sex with him.

"Anyway, Anya decided to leave him, there was nothing else to do, and Ray helped her. Brubaker took off on a long road trip, and Ray helped Anya and Nick pack up their things into a truck he rented for them. They were great friends. I caught them once horsing around, playing like a couple of kids, he was pushing her around in a wheelbarrow, and they were both laughing. The plan was that her husband would come back home from a long haul, and she'd just be gone. He wouldn't know where to find her. She would disappear, kind of like what happened to Ray, how Ray disappeared from my life. And that's exactly what happened to Brubaker, and it would make me feel sorry for him if he wasn't such a creep. I mean, we have this horrible thing in common, except he knows that she left because she couldn't stand him, and I have no idea at all what happened to Ray. But I really don't believe they were lovers, Ray and Anya. I don't know if I could have blamed Ray if they were lovers, because she would be hard for any man to resist."

"You shouldn't... You're beautiful, too, you know."

She brushed past his awkward attempt to console her or to get more personal, if that's what it was.

"If they were lovers, Ray would have tried to keep it all a secret," she continued. "Because he is not cruel, and he would not have wanted to hurt me or his children. But he didn't do that. He was perfectly honest that they were friends. She was different from anyone else Ray could ever meet, so foreign, and you can't blame him for being fascinated by her."

"Her husband might not believe they were just friends, and might have been jealous even if they were," Tom said. "And if he knew that Ray helped her leave him, he could have wanted revenge."

"Sheriff Martin is convinced that Ray and Anya were having an affair. He can't believe two adults of the opposite sex could be just friends. He figures that if they *were* lovers, well, then, obviously Ray ran off with her, and that's that. Case closed. That's why he's not investigating."

"I'm sure they questioned this trucker about Ray's disappearance."

"Probably. But maybe not. Who knows?"

"And Anya? It seems like somebody should find her and ask if she's heard from him...."

She interrupted to complete his sentence: "...to see if Ray ran off with her and they're living happily ever after. But that's not what happened. I know it isn't."

"How do you know?"

"I just know."

"Why would Ray become so involved with Anya and her son if he didn't care about her? Maybe he cared more than you want to believe. If he didn't care, why would he take the risk?"

"He couldn't bear the idea of her getting stuck here, like the rest of us. He wanted to help her get away. It's that simple. If you knew Mark Brubaker, you'd understand. And if you knew Ray better, you'd understand. That's the kind of guy Ray was … *is*, the kind of guy he *is*."

That's unlikely, Tom thought, confident that the mystery was all but solved, and that it really was that simple, although not simple in the way Sarah imagined. No wonder the sheriff was disinclined to investigate. It seemed obvious that Ray Walker had fallen in love with another man's beautiful and exotic Russian mail-order bride and had run off with her. What hurt most was Sarah's unavoidable recognition that even she couldn't blame him if he did.

The Sheriff was right. There was no crime, and there wasn't even any news. There was only the terrible vulnerability of the woman left behind. As much as he admired her gallantry, Sarah was in a state of denial so deep that she preferred not to know the truth. That's why she wanted Tom to leave the story alone, not because it was dangerous to investigate, but because the truth hurt too much. The danger was to her fragile psyche. Whether Ray was or was not with Anya was irrelevant to Sarah, which was precisely the point she intended to convey by telling Tom about their "friendship." Either way, as far as she was concerned, the case of Ray's disappearance was, or ought to be, considered closed.

Tom was touched. He reached over and put his hand on hers.

Chapter 12

ANYA

Tom carried a crowbar and was prepared to break into the Walker Auto Repair shop, having already observed a week earlier that it was tightly secured. But it wasn't necessary. Somebody had already broken the pane of glass in the rear door and the door itself was loose on its hinges. He entered the garage through the broken door all the more cautiously, wondering who had beaten him there.

It was dark and his flashlight provided minimal illumination. The air was acrid, and he was drawn to the strong smell of ammonia in a corner, near the restroom. In the shadows he could make out a couple of overflowing trashcans filled with empty antifreeze containers and other detritus. That might be expected in a garage, but there were also hundreds of empty cold tablet packages and empty plastic bottles of rubbing alcohol and broken glass beakers. There were used coffee filters, stained red, and a hot plate, and other waste that looked suspicious, but wasn't readily identifiable by Tom.

Tom reached for the hot plate and touched it to assure himself that it was cold. He kicked at some of the trash on the floor and a mouse skittered out. Startled, he jumped back, upsetting one of the trashcans and spilling its contents on the floor. The noise of the aluminum can hitting the concrete floor echoed loudly across the garage, making any effort at stealth Tom might have entertained irrelevant.

"Speedy mouse," he muttered out loud, as if to confirm his presence, or his clumsy lack of guile, to anyone who might be lurking in the shadows. He swung the beam of the flashlight to one dark corner of the garage and then another. There was nobody there. He stood perfectly still and tried to slow his breathing so that he could listen intently. The only sounds were the ambient hum of the space, a truck passing by out on the highway, and possibly the ticking of a clock coming from the direction of the front office.

The garage was unmistakably being used for a meth lab. Surely the sheriff had discovered it in the aftermath of Ray's disappearance but had looked the other way. Why? Not only did it present a strong lead, but someone eventually would have to clean up the hazardous waste site. Or maybe not.

Maybe a longtime sheriff of Montrose County was habitually blind to an environmental hazard, just as he had a finely honed sense of when to look away from shady activity that occurred off the highway or behind closed doors. So much on the West End took place at the periphery of what was legitimate. Nobody wanted to think very hard about the enduring waste from uranium mining, which had enriched Dick Klein and his heirs and a few others who held the claims; had enabled the United States to build a nuclear arsenal and ultimately establish itself as the world's only superpower; and had allowed the mine workers to live in a fools' paradise of company largesse, as if to distract them from the price they paid in ruined health, at least while it lasted. Meth presented the same kind of devil's bargain to the

West End, only without the rationale of defending freedom and the homeland. Like uranium, meth was a toxic substance so addictive that people couldn't resist it, despite overwhelming evidence that to use it was not sustainable. Like uranium, meth promised easy riches to whoever produced it, and a seductive illusion of power to anyone who used it, but at the same time it threatened to ruin anyone who touched it. Both uranium and meth were explosive. Meth labs were prone to bursting into flames. Like uranium, meth left vile residue where it was produced.

Dave Best was right. How could Sarah not know her husband was cooking up meth in his garage? She had said that the garage, the business, was his, not hers. Though Ray Walker was evidently a master of compartmentalization, meth addicts were notoriously out of control. Maybe that is why he had to flee: the walls between his various selves were collapsing under the pressure of his addiction.

While it was still likely that Ray had run off with Anya, meth changed things. If they were not just cooking meth but were also using it—which was certainly likely—it might have made Ray and Anya overconfident of their ability to manage the jealous husband, who remained a potential suspect. Or maybe they were producing the drug to raise money for their escape. The meth dealer necessarily interacted with desperate characters in secret, out-of-the-way locations, and handled large quantities of cash. That reopened the possibility that Ray had been a victim of foul play out on a lonely highway, where he could have gone to complete a transaction. A meth addict might easily decide to shoot his dealer and steal the goods.

Tom flicked off the flashlight to ensure that he wouldn't draw attention from anyone out on the street as he made his way to the front office. There was enough light filtering in through the grimy front window for him to make his way. He found what he was looking for in the single filing cabinet next to the desk: folders containing bills, paid and unpaid. He found a U-Haul bill for a truck rental, to be picked up in Grand Junction on June 4th and dropped off in Albuquerque a few days later. And he found a copy of a lease for an apartment in Albuquerque, rented to Anya Nemerov, guaranteed by Ray Walker.

. . .

It was a seven-hour drive from Naturita to Albuquerque, across the high desert of northwestern New Mexico. Tom arrived after ten p.m., too late to drop in on Anya, so he checked into a Motel 6 on the edge of the urban sprawl, next to a truck stop so brightly lit that the air itself seemed juiced. There was a Waffle House across the parking lot. Truck traffic thrummed past on the interstate.

The talking heads on late night cable were analyzing Bush's comments that he "had earned political capital" in the election and "planned to use it."

Tom used to care, but he now clicked the TV off and lay awake in his bed, feeling exposed under a thin sheet. The motel room curtain did not block all the light and the room was cast in a yellow hue. Shortly after he fell asleep, a shrill fire alarm went off, jolting him awake.

He pulled on some shorts, opened the door, and stepped outside onto the balcony. There were no flames, no smoke, no sirens, and no move from anyone to evacuate.

"You see anything?" he asked a paunchy guy who had emerged from a nearby room wearing only a towel.

"Nah."

The guy retreated back inside. Tom followed his lead and turned the air conditioner up high to drown out the noise. After a few minutes, the alarm went silent.

He woke up shivering before dawn and went down to the Waffle House. For a moment he thought that the waitress was Angela Walker: thin, stringy hair, blotchy complexion, sunken eyes rimmed in dark eyeliner, only this girl's teeth looked like they'd been filed to sharp points.

"Rough night?" he asked.

"Hell yeah," she said. "I got called in when the girl on the night shift walked off, and after I worked all day yesterday. A customer pulled a gun on her 'cause he thought she was ignoring him. A fucking tweaker."

"Damn."

"She'd have been all right, probably. We're used to whackos on the night shift, but this one fired a shot. Bullet hole is right up there."

She pointed to the ceiling.

"I was at the Motel 6 and didn't hear a thing," Tom said.

"There were sirens and all kinds of commotion."

"Who knew slinging waffles is a high-risk occupation?"

"How about that?" she replied. "In Bush's America."

* * *

Tom parked in front of the rundown apartment building, not far from downtown, where Ray had rented the apartment for Anya.

He knocked, drawing the sound of anxious voices speaking in Russian, likely discussing who it might be at the door, and debating whether it would be safe to unlock it.

"Hello," Tom said. "I'm a newspaper reporter from Naturita. I'm here to ask you about Ray Walker. He's gone missing."

With that, quick footsteps, fumbling with a lock, and the door opened a crack.

"What do you mean missing?" Anya said.

"Unless he is here, with you."

"I had a bad feeling," she gasped. "He has not called me in two weeks, and nobody answers at the shop."

Anya opened the door wider to size Tom up.

"You must tell me."

Anya extended her hand. She was just as Sarah had described: poised, outgoing, and forthright, angular; blonde and blue-eyed. Tom had seen her shopping at the West End Merc, always with her son by her side. He had wondered about them.

"Please, come in."

She spoke with a thick Slavic accent. The boy sat at the kitchen table eating a bowl of cold cereal. He was in his early teens and was dark where his mother was light, his close-cropped hair and eyes a deep shade of brown, evidently inherited from his absent father.

"This is Nicolai. Nick," Anya said. Nick nodded as if he recognized Tom, and then listened intently as the adults talked.

"What do you mean when you say Ray is missing?" she asked.

"Nobody has seen him or heard from him in two weeks," Tom said. "He went on a towing call and didn't return."

"And you thought that maybe he was here, living with me."

"Yes."

"I am sorry," she said, her blue eyes filling with tears. "He is not here, and we are not lovers, but it is my fault. I am sure that the man who thinks he owns me, Mark Brubaker, has done something." She spit out the name with contempt, repeating his full name in the next sentence as if she enjoyed lacerating it with her tongue. "Mark

Brubaker is a very cruel man, a primitive man. I told Ray that he should not help Nick and me because this *animal* would do something for revenge. But Ray only laughed at this danger. He did not think Mark Brubaker could hurt him."

"Did he think that you and Ray were lovers?" Tom asked, uncomfortable to be talking so frankly in front of the boy. But Anya apparently shared everything with her son.

"An educated person cannot know how a primitive animal thinks," she said. "He knew Ray Walker was my boss. But Mark Brubaker is not right…."—she tapped her forehead as she searched for the right word—"he is *paranoia* and he is cruel and he wanted me to stay in Naturita for all of my life as his slave. He thought he owned me because he paid for us to come from Russia. He did not understand that I am mother, and I must help Nicolai to study maths and physics. I was trained as engineer in Russia, as chemical engineer. That is why we are here, in this city, for the school, for my son, so he can have future. For me, it does not matter. I will fix windshields for all of my life, since Ray taught me how and I cannot get job in America as chemical engineer. Can I get you coffee?"

They sat with Nick as she poured coffee and sliced coffee cake and put it on plates. She stopped abruptly; her careful composure suddenly broken. She sobbed, and Nick quickly went to her side and put his arm around her.

"Maybe you should go now," Nick said to Tom.

"It is OK, Nicolai," Anya said. "I am glad Mr. Austin has come here with news, even if it is bad news. I am just so sorry for Ray. I accept his kindness and now look what happens! I had the needs of mother, and so I let Ray help, but I meant him no harm. Now his kindness led only to murder.

"But Nick now must go to school. You must go Nicolai, or you will be late. I will be safe with Mr. Austin. He is good man. Like Ray."

Nick eyed Tom suspiciously as he packed his books, dawdling until Anya spoke to him in Russian. They talked for a few minutes, and only after they apparently reached some kind of understanding did Nick reluctantly back out the door, leaving his mother alone with the stranger.

"He worries about you," Tom said, after Nick had left.

"He is very good boy," she agreed.

"He must be upset to learn that Ray is missing."

"Yes. He is upset. But I told him there is nothing he can do, and I will tell him everything when he comes from school. First of importance, he must not let anything to interrupt his studies."

"You are a good mother."

"I am trying," she said, and she sank down onto a tattered sofa and buried her face in her hands. "But…"

It was awkward to stand over her, so Tom sat next to her on the sofa.

"But what?" he asked.

"You can see that I am all alone, with no man," she whispered hoarsely, "and this is what makes it very much more difficult."

"Where is Nick's father?"

"He was in the army in Chechnya. He was lost there. Now, I do not know…. I think he must be dead."

"So, you decided to take Nick to America?"

"There was no future in Russia for him. I sign with agency, and they send me to Mark Brubaker. Only it was not Mark Brubaker in the photograph. And this agency was not for romance, but to sell women for slavery. But I learned of this treachery only when I came to Naturita."

She was not nearly that naïve. Surely, she had known what would be expected of her when she accepted the tickets and visa, certainly forged, to go to America to live with a strange man who had paid her way. And yet Tom was impressed by her determination to escape dreary circumstances and find a better life, if not for her, for her son, even if she had to sell herself to do it. And she had done it at least twice, first by escaping Russia and then by escaping Naturita. Now she was calculating whether Tom would be her next provider.

"You have not had an easy life."

She answered with a sob and pressed herself into his arms. He could so easily take advantage of her neediness, and it was almost tempting. She was an attractive woman. But the price of getting involved with her would be high, in the form of endless complications, as Ray had apparently found out. She must have offered herself to him in just this way.

"Ray must have found you attractive," he said, "and difficult to resist."

"Do you find me attractive?"

"Yes, of course."

He could feel her breath against his chest and her fingers fluttered suggestively on his shoulders. But he didn't make the next move and after a few beats she pulled away from him and quickly recomposed herself.

"But Ray is married, and nothing came of this attraction," she said. "You are also married?"

Tom decided not to answer. Her disappointment seemed directed more at him than at Ray, but it was nothing to take too seriously. To find another man to rescue her was her most finely honed survival skill. As if to distract herself from that very thought, as if she felt just a twinge of shame, she quickly reverted back to the safer subject of Ray's disappearance, taking more responsibility for it, perhaps, than was justified.

"Yes," she said dramatically. "Nothing came of our friendship except for Ray's death."

"What makes you so sure that Brubaker killed him?"

"What else can it be? There were many times I feared for my life, and for Nick's life, from this animal, Mark Brubaker, when he would be crazy man and violent."

But Tom knew there was another strong possibility, related to the fact that Ray Walker was running a meth lab out of his garage. Ray was always willing to help others, Sarah said. He would give a stranger the shirt off his back. Ray treated Nick like a son, Anya said. He was the father Nick never had. Could this sainted man—who resisted the unquestioned temptation of Anya to stay faithful to Sarah, and at the same time may have risked his life to help Anya and Nick—possibly also be a crankhead?

Why not?

"You must arrest Mark Brubaker!" Anya exclaimed. "You must make him say where is Ray."

"I can't arrest anyone. I'm not a policeman. I'm a journalist."

"I will call and tell the sheriff that Mark Brubaker killed Ray Walker!"

"What about the meth lab, for Christ's sake?" Tom said.

"What lab?" Anya asked.

Tom told her about his discovery in the corner of Ray's garage.

"This is new," she said. "There was no meth. I know about meth. Mark Brubaker, he is addict."

• • •

The long drive home allowed Tom plenty of time to turn the evidence over in his mind. It could be a coincidence that someone used the abandoned auto repair shop for a meth lab after Ray's disappearance. The fact that it had been abandoned by its owner was, after all, widely publicized, by none-other-than Tom himself. He had run a photo of the deserted business on the Forum's front page. Any meth addict could have deduced that the shop would be a safe place to cook up a batch or two, and that would explain why the door was broken.

If meth dropped as a likely factor behind Ray's disappearance, the theory that he had been done in by Mark Brubaker now rose in probability. It was not surprising to hear that Brubaker used meth. Long-distance truckers were a high-risk group for the drug, using it to keep themselves awake on long hauls. Brubaker was clearly unstable. Sarah had identified him as someone who chose to live in the remote West End because he wanted to be left alone, and he had bought himself a mail-order bride, so he was perfectly comfortable operating outside social norms. What was most persuasive was that the woman who knew him best described him as violent, and did not doubt that he was capable of murder. She had her own reasons for hating Brubaker, though, and assumed a burden of guilt over Ray's disappearance, and might therefore be quick to point the finger at what, for her, was an obvious explanation. Still, Tom concluded, he could hardly ignore the likelihood that Ray had been dispatched by a jealous husband with a meth habit and possibly psychotic tendencies.

But perhaps Dave Best was right, and Sarah and Anya were wrong, and Ray was involved with meth. Depending on how far gone he was, Ray could have become psychotic himself, disappearing on his own into the chaos of a growing addiction, more or less as Tom himself had once fled his life. He might have simply driven his truck out of town to spare his wife and children his agony. He was, by all accounts, a kind man at bottom. The true horror of addiction, Tom knew, is that the addict is fully aware of his own destructiveness, to himself and anyone who cares about him. He just can't help it. So maybe in a rational moment, Ray Walker decided to dispatch himself. Maybe Ray simply swam further from the shore than Tom had.

If Ray was manufacturing meth, too, he was dealing with shady characters, reintroducing that possibility to account for the mystery. And then there was Ray Walker's troubled relationship with his father, Dick Klein. It wasn't long ago, Tom recalled, that he had developed a theory that the Uranium King might have had something, or everything, to do with his illegitimate son's disappearance. That seemed less likely now, following Albert Klein's lack of interest in the matter, but could not be entirely discounted.

What about Sarah Walker's effort to discourage Tom from investigating the story? He was not necessarily wrong that she was terrified he would discover that Ray was living with Anya, and that she simply preferred not to know the ugly truth. But she had insisted that Tom would not find Ray with Anya. It turned out she was right. Could there be something else she wanted kept secret or was afraid of? She was not without guile, and it would be a mistake to underestimate her.

Finally, there was the relatively benign theory that Ray had suffered a one-car accident and had run his truck off the road, and that despite the search by his friends and neighbors, the wreck simply had not been found yet. It was entirely possible in the canyonlands. Whispering Jim had not been found when he was trapped in a slot canyon, even when the area was intensively searched. The car-wreck theory was not only benign, but simple, and therefore probable for that reason alone. Sure, there were plenty of suspicious circumstances surrounding the life and disappearance of Ray Walker, but that did not mean that the most innocent explanation for the mystery was wrong.

In any case, Tom was no closer to understanding what had happened to Ray Walker than he was the day Deputy Billy Pederson first told him the auto mechanic was missing.

"I will probably never know," Tom muttered to himself.

Mysteries have tidy solutions in movies, but not in real life, he thought. But Ray Walker was a deepening enigma. The more Tom learned about him, the less he understood him.

He was driving past the turnoff to the ruins at Chaco Canyon, where people had lived for a thousand years before they disappeared. Nobody knows why they left Chaco, although there are theories: maybe a prolonged drought, maybe decades of warfare. A recent theory held that they had been terrorized by cannibalism on the part of tribes from the south, and had dispersed, their culture destroyed. People lived at Chaco Canyon almost four times longer than the United States is old. Then they vanished from the earth, and nobody will ever know for certain why.

Chapter 13

THE TWEAKER

Tom could easily picture Anya's dread at the thought of being stranded in Naturita. Miranda had responded the same way at the remotest possibility of it.

About a year after he bought the Forum, and after the humiliation of his ruined former life had receded far enough into the past for him to come out of hiding, Tom had called the three people he had left behind who he thought might still wonder what had happened to him: his mother, his sister and Miranda. His mother and sister were quick to forgive him for the heartless way he had walked out of their lives, thankful he was alive and well. He was relieved to discover that they weren't ashamed of him but were concerned about his well-being. They made it easy for him to resume the uncomplicated relationship they'd had before, checking in with each other on birthdays, at major holidays, and at other odd times. For Tom, their easy acceptance and the connection to his past had inherent value, anchoring him in time just as his new ownership of the Forum rooted him in the specific place of Naturita. After the shame of his meltdown at the Mail, for him to acknowledge having come from somewhere and to be in contact with his family represented a necessary step toward normalcy, however modest and however tenuous.

Miranda was another story. Upon picking up the telephone and hearing his voice, she cursed at him in unintelligible Portuguese and then started sobbing. When she was done with that, she stunned him by making immediate plans to come see him in Naturita. He picked her up at the airport in Grand Junction. When she walked off the concourse, past the security barrier to where he was waiting for her, she stepped right up to him, handed him her carry-on bag, and instead of the peck on the cheek he anticipated, she slapped him, hard. She had clearly worked out the choreography of her arrival for maximum dramatic impact.

She was only mildly horrified by the banality of Grand Junction, as they drove through it. The empty spaces between the edge of the city and Naturita were of no apparent interest. Naturita, though, might as well have been an outpost on Mars. When they reached Tom's place she showered immediately and then drew him into bed. It was the first time he had been with a woman since leaving Marathon and he welcomed the human contact.

"I really did love you, you know," she said.

"No," he replied. "I didn't know."

"Maybe it's because you can't love."

"Yes. I'm sure that's it."

Tom's response sounded glib, even to his own ear, but that didn't make it false. If he hadn't been capable of loving Miranda when they lived together, it was also true that he hadn't yet healed and was no more capable of loving her now. He wanted to say more, to explain that it really wasn't her fault — that it was his failure and his alone, and that he was working on it — but that would have sounded even more selfish. After all that had happened, and from the vantage point of his new life, which he could not abandon and she could not share, there didn't seem to be any point. It was easier to accept blame, and it was more honest and kinder, too, just to let Miranda go.

The two of them had never talked that much; their affair was based on other points of contact, the sexy impression they created as a couple on the dance floor, the buzz of cocaine and blur of alcohol, their glamorous careers, but in Naturita there were no nightclubs, Miranda had no routine to follow, and the dust, the empty spaces and the silence broken only by the wind, the traffic on the highway and the occasional bark of a dog all conspired to drive her to a state of complete apathy. Tom felt badly for her and one night during her stay they drove to a cowboy bar in the town of Norwood, on the road to Telluride. He realized only later that he should have driven the rest of the distance to Telluride, where she would have felt much more at home.

Following the glum experience of trying to dance to country music while ignoring the ranch hands leering at her, Miranda rebooked her return flight home to leave a few days earlier than she'd planned.

Midway on the long drive to the airport, Tom broke the silence: "I'm sorry."

There was nothing more he could say. More words, he felt, would only undermine the sincerity behind those two words.

"I know," she said. "It's OK. I think it's better this way."

She was looking away from him, gazing out the passenger door window at the sheer, impossibly colorful canyon wall that rose hundreds of feet on the other side of the river, possibly contemplating the meanings of its green, yellow, black, and ochre bands of rock. The cliff was nothing more or less than a geologic accounting of the millennia, of long-gone oceans and extinct forms of life, volcanic eruptions, earthquakes, tectonic uplift, and erosion, against which human emotions were infinitesimal and inconsequential.

"Yes," she added a few miles on. "It's better for both of us. But I will remember you."

"I will remember you, too," he said.

$$\cdot \ \cdot \ \cdot$$

Mark Brubaker's house wasn't much different from Ray and Sarah Walker's, but with no evidence of a woman's touch, not a single grace note; not a wilted flower in a cracked pot or a tree cultivated by a human hand, not even a scrap of a faded curtain behind one of the filthy windows. It was just another crumbling shack built by a long-gone uranium prospector, surrounded by rusting junk on a dusty acre of land a dozen miles from Nucla, down a labyrinth of rutted roads where nobody would ever venture unless they were either lost or knew exactly where they were going.

Brubaker was evidently home: his rig, conspicuously shiny on the sere landscape, sat off to the side of the shack. Tom pulled up to the house and sounded his horn so that Brubaker wouldn't be startled, expecting him to emerge from the house, allowing Tom to introduce himself from a safe distance and ask if they might talk. But nothing stirred. He parked, opened the door of his car, stepped out, and pressed on the car horn again. Still nothing. He considered climbing back behind the wheel of his car, to start the engine and pull away. That would be the smart move. He had been warned more than once that Brubaker was dangerous and potentially violent. Instead, he told himself that Brubaker likely was away, slammed his car door shut, and walked toward the house. He knocked on the door and shouted, "Hello? Anyone home?" No response. He tested the door. It was locked.

Yes, he thought. Nobody home.

Tom walked around to the rear of the house. There was a small mountain of partially crushed beer cans just outside the back door, and thousands more cans sliding downhill into a small dry ravine that ran behind the shack. Tom stepped up to peer in a window when the adjacent door creaked open.

"Just what the *fuck* do you think you're doing?" a man's voice snarled.

Tom jumped back.

"I'm sorry," he said. "I'm looking for Mark Brubaker."

"You are fucking trespassing, dude. That's way dangerous."

Brubaker was about forty and not the least bit self-conscious about the fact that he was completely nude. Perhaps he didn't feel naked: He was covered from the top of his ankles to his neck and wrists with bawdy tattoos. Tobacco juice drooled out of the corner of his mouth. Brubaker's genitals were completely obscured by the overhang of his belly. The bright light of the outdoors clearly hurt the fat man's eyes, since he shaded them with his meaty left hand.

"I'm Tom Austin. Publisher of the Forum."

"What's that?"

"Local paper."

"Never heard of it."

"I was hoping we could talk."

"What about?"

Good question, Tom thought to himself. He was deeply regretting that he had come and was wracking his brain for a way to retreat.

"Nice place you got out here."

"It's a shithole."

"Yeah."

"But it's private."

"Sure is. Hard to find."

"You know, you are really starting to piss me off."

"That's probably not a good idea, is it?"

"Nope. Not a good idea at all."

Brubaker shifted his position in the doorway and Tom saw that he held a pistol in his right hand.

"Hey, I'm really sorry that I trespassed onto your property, man," Tom said. "I should have called first. I'll just leave the way I came."

"Don't got a phone," Brubaker said, squinting as he raised the gun and pointed it at Tom.

Tom made a slow move back the way he'd come.

"Not yet," Brubaker said, waving the gun. "Now you got me curious. Why the fuck are you here?"

"It was a mistake. I just got lost. Gotta go," Tom said, taking another step backwards, and Brubaker fired at his feet.

The noise was startling, far louder than Tom thought a gunshot could sound, louder than Albert Klein's rifle, which he'd recently fired on North Mountain, probably, it occurred to him in an instant, because this time he was the target. If he'd been shot in the head, that bang, that explosion, would have been the last experience of his life, the sound of his death. Or would he have heard it at all? They say you don't hear the shot that kills you, though of course it's only a guess: there's really no way to know if that's true. In any case, Tom's ears rang and his heart pounded, painful proof he was still alive.

"I could shoot you right now," Brubaker said off-handedly. "Your dead body would fall right down there, and I wouldn't have to do nothing to get rid of it. Coyotes would eat you in a day or two. They even eat the bones. Nobody would ever find you."

Tom raised his hands in a gesture of submission.

"Yeah," he said, wondering how many others had met just that fate in the ravine, and more specifically if Ray Walker was one of them. "Of course, you'd have to get rid of my car, too. Coyotes wouldn't eat that."

"Get your skinny ass over here."

The inside of the shack was as cluttered as the yard, and it stank of rotting food, stale body odor and, not faintly, of sewage.

"Take off your clothes," Brubaker said.

"You're not gonna rape me…?" Tom asked.

"Do I look like a fag to you?"

Tom shrugged as if to say, Got nothing against it if you are.

"Maybe you noticed I'm not wearing nothing," Brubaker said. "You want to talk to me, it's gotta be even. And I don't feel like getting dressed." He waved the gun.

"Are you sure about this? You don't want me to just go? Forget about this whole thing? Like I was never here?"

Brubaker answered with another shot at Tom's feet.

"Shit man!" Tom shouted as he started to quickly unbutton his shirt. "You gotta stop that. You're gonna give me a fuckin' heart attack."

Through the front window, past Brubaker's hulking form, Tom could see his car. It looked far away.

Tom soon found himself sitting unclothed on a filthy couch across from Brubaker, who occupied a chair he had moved to a critical position, cornering his hostage and blocking any escape. The image of Anya in this house, with this man, was more than Tom could summon up. Brubaker might not rape Tom, but he had surely raped his Russian bride, and probably her son, too. She had called him a cruel animal and a barbarian, but her words had failed to convey his complete debauchery. Of course they had fled. Of course, Ray Walker had helped.

"You think maybe you can put the gun away now?" Tom asked. "It's making me way nervous."

"No problem," Brubaker said, and tossed it on a stuffed armchair a few feet away. "You're not going nowhere, are you?" He laughed. "What can I do for you?"

He asked it as casually as if there'd been no threats or gunfire, as if the two men were not sitting naked across from each other, as if he were a plumber on a service call or a salesman in a hardware store.

There seemed to be absolutely no point in dissembling. Maybe Brubaker had been shrewd in stripping Tom of his clothes.

"I'm looking into the disappearance of Ray Walker," Tom said. "I heard you knew him."

"Fuck you!"

"Look, I'm sorry…"

"No, I mean it," Brubaker said, his eyes narrowing. "You are fucking gonna tell me who sent you."

"Nobody."

Brubaker shook his head slightly, sadly, as if deciding how to respond to an outrageous impertinence, a bald-faced lie, and then with lightning speed and astonishing agility he sprang at Tom and pinned him down on the sofa.

"You're an asshole and a liar!" he shouted.

Brubaker had planted himself on Tom's chest and was crushing the air out of him, pinning Tom's arms between his thick legs. Tom struggled but it was hopeless. Brubaker not only outweighed him by a hundred pounds, but was obviously tweaking, propelled by adrenaline, his strength superhuman, his focus intent on something only he could see.

Tom anticipated that Brubaker was going to try to rape him, and resolved to fight to the death, but that's not what Brubaker had in mind, at least not immediately. He heard the fat man's labored breathing as he worked a belt around Tom's torso, pinning his arms to his side, and buckling it tight.

"What do you want from me, man?" Tom asked, resorting to words to try to slow down the assault.

"That's not the right question," Brubaker said. "Who sent you here? Why are you here?"

"Nobody."

Thwack. Brubaker slapped him hard with the back of his hand.

"Fuckin' liar! I know it's Klein. But what did he send you for?"

Were the Kleins at the center of everything?

Tom had abandoned his theory that being the Uranium King's son had led to Ray Walker's undoing and was following an entirely different thread, one that tied Ray Walker's disappearance logically to a psychotic meth-addict who had enslaved his mail-order bride. There was no need for the Kleins or for any reference at all to Walker's lineage to construct a scenario ending in Walker's demise at Brubaker's hands. The trucker was more than sinister enough to account for any conceivable depravity all by himself. But now, even as he was under assault, Tom was cycling back and trying to construct a more complex narrative linking not only Ray Walker, Anya and the demonic Brubaker, but somehow involving the Kleins, too.

He couldn't connect the dots.

"No way, man," Tom protested.

"I'm not fuckin' stoo-pid!"

Brubaker was shouting and at the same time was tightly wrapping a bungie cord around Tom's ankles, and another around his knees. Tom's face stung and he could feel blood dripping from his nose.

Checking his work and satisfied that Tom was immobilized, Brubaker lurched to his feet. Tom watched him bend over a table and pick up a small, blue-tinted zip-lock baggie and dump some of its contents into a plate. Then he heard a "chop, chop, chop" sound, like cocaine being crushed with a credit card. But it wasn't coke. Tom knew it had to be crystal meth.

"What are you doing?" Tom asked. But Brubaker ignored him, concentrating on the task at hand, mixing the crushed crystals with water, boiling it in a spoon, filling a syringe with some of the resulting liquid and then he was leaning over Tom with the needle.

"Hey man," Tom said. "I don't shoot...."

"Just a little truth serum."

"I'm telling you the truth...." But it was too late. Tom felt a sharp needle prick on the inside of his thigh, followed by a cold sensation as the meth flooded the vein that Brubaker had expertly penetrated. Within seconds the cold flush rushed to his chest and then to his head and a drug-induced euphoria was battling the panic he felt at being tied up.

"Man, this totally sucks," he said. "You gotta untie me."

"Relax and enjoy it. All you gotta do now is tell me who sent you. If you do, maybe I'll let you out of here alive."

"I told you, man, nobody sent me. I'm just trying to find out what happened to Ray Walker, and I thought you could help."

Brubaker was calmer now, apparently satisfied that the truth serum was working, allowing him to relax.

"What would I know about it?"

"Didn't your wife work for him?"

"Yep."

"It must have pissed you off when she disappeared."

"Nope. She was a lousy fuck, like fucking a dead fish. Couldn't cook or clean worth shit, either."

"Did you ever talk to Ray Walker about it?"

Brubaker ignored the question, his interest in the subject spent, and concentrated instead on the baggie of meth, the plate he emptied it onto, the card to chop it with, and the water to dissolve it in, and he muttered to himself as he injected a syringe full into his own inner thigh.

"Salt Lake tomorrow," he muttered, "then Seattle and LA and Phoenix…."

"A lot of driving," Tom said.

"Yeah."

"You gonna untie me now?"

"Nah."

Beneath the flap of Brubaker's stomach, Tom could see that his dick had become hard, no doubt from the speed coursing through his veins. He wondered if the drug had had the same effect on him and glanced down to see that it had. To be supercharged with speed and trussed up like a chicken at the same time was an almost unbearable torture. There was nothing he could do to end it, but he could feel some give in the belt and bungie cords and wriggled them as loose as he could without being conspicuous about it, gaining an inch of slack.

"Meth makes me horny enough to fuck a dog," Brubaker said. "When it first hits, that first rush…." He had fallen back into an armchair and was playing with himself.

"You're not gonna try and fuck me, are you?"

"I told you I ain't a fag, didn't I?"

"Man, why'd you do this to me?"

"I didn't tell you to come out here."

"Am I gonna get AIDS or hepatitis from that needle you poked me with?

"Prolly."

Tom gazed up at the ceiling of the shack, covered in spider webs and ropes of dust that seemed to vibrate with life. More dust motes skipped about in the air. Across the room, he could hear that Brubaker was wanking with more energy now, grunting. Tom was at the center of a web, as tightly bound as a spider's prey. Brubaker was completely crazed, a tweaker over the edge, so paranoid that a stranger trespassing on his property had to have been sent with malign intent by Klein. Though it was Brubaker who had tied him up, Tom figured that the Uranium King or more likely his son, Albert, must be the alpha spider.

How much time passed? He couldn't tell. It seemed like an eternity but might have been just a minute or two. Brubaker was standing over him, still wanking. And then Tom felt himself being lifted up and flipped over onto his stomach. Brubaker was going to rape him after all. The fat man's weight pressed against him.

Tom struggled against the belt and found just enough slack to work his right arm free. Brubaker had him pinned, but Tom was able to grab an object, an iron fire poker. With a surge of energy, and as Brubaker had raised himself up to angle for position to penetrate his victim, Tom pushed him off and swung around, thwacking him with all his force on the side of his head.

Brubaker groaned and fell backward. He had already suffered his fatal injury, but Tom didn't back off. He was charged with his own meth-fueled adrenaline intensity and pressed his advantage, whacking his assailant again, landing a blow at the base of his neck, and another blow, crushing his upper right arm, by this point a completely gratuitous injury to the broken corpse of a man who was dead or dying fast. Blood was spurting from Brubaker's neck and flowing from his mouth.

Tom roared, a naked gladiator drenched in another man's blood, and breathing heavily he stared at the horror he had wrought: Brubaker's mangled and tattooed corpulence, his blood slowly spreading across the filthy floor; the dank odor of his death mingling with the preexisting stench in the house.

"It was self-defense," Tom muttered to himself, as if he were pleading with the sheriff or a judge or jury, or even to a higher authority than that, presenting his justification before the reality of the brutal killing he had just committed fully sank in, even before Brubaker's body had stopped twitching.

Tom freed himself from the remaining bonds as quickly as he could and backed away from the scene. Finding Brubaker's mildewed shower, he stood under a stream of hot water, watching with a kind of abstract fascination as Brubaker's blood flowed off of his body and ran down the drain. His mind was playing tricks. The bloody water flickered in strobe-light fashion from technicolor to even more disturbing black-and-white—right out of Hitchcock's *Psycho*—and back to color. He was far too stoned from the mainline injection of meth to rationally process what he had just done.

His mind was racing.

"This is what a tweaker feels," Tom said out loud. "What did I do?"

He got out of the shower and quickly got dressed, studiously avoiding the bloody mess he had made. He was unable to distinguish whether he was energized by the violence he had perpetrated or the drug he'd been injected with or by a combination of both, but he was charged with a strong sense of purpose.

If Tom wasn't categorically a tweaker, having never used meth before, the drug still had a beneficent effect on him, making him indifferent to everything that was wrong and focusing his thoughts exclusively on his own mission: to understand what had happened to Ray Walker. At that moment, nothing was more important. The solution to the mystery seemed more crucial than ever, critically important, an urgent necessity. It was the key to … Tom had no idea what, precisely … which was to say it was the key to absolutely everything, to eternal enlightenment and the very meaning of his sorry existence.

Brubaker had assaulted him and had died for it, but he had also provided him with good information, shifting the focus of the investigation back to the abiding enigma of the Kleins.

The sun was just setting to the west.

Chapter 14

THE URANIUM KING

Tom turned away from the sunset, east toward Denver.

But in his meth-fueled haste, his trip was nearly cut short. Only a mile from Brubaker's place, and well before he reached a paved road, he nearly crashed into an oncoming pickup, whose driver was speeding as fast as he was. Tom and the driver of the pickup saw each other and slammed on their brakes and wrenched their wheels simultaneously, both of their vehicles fishtailing on the gravel so that they skidded parallel to each other only a few inches apart. The driver was a young longhair, his gaunt face was a mask of rage as his car slid past Tom's in cinematic slow motion. Tom could see him shouting, "Fuck you, asshole!" and giving him the finger.

Another surge of adrenaline at this point was too much for Tom, and he thought he was having a heart attack. His car having screeched to a stop, Tom relaxed his painful grip on the steering wheel and worked to slow his breathing. How banal it would have been for the story to end like this, Tom thought, and just when he was making progress in putting the pieces together. Of course, it might have been something just this random, a car wreck involving Ray Walker, that had set off the unlikely series of events that had brought him to this precise moment, racing from the scene of a bloody death in a manner that would only seem to confirm his guilt as the cause of that death—if there had been anyone to witness it. Amid these meth-suffused musings, Tom vowed to drive more carefully.

He resumed his journey. The miles of empty canyon country rolled by until the road reached a broad plateau just south Grand Junction, the Grand Mesa rising to his right and the Dominguez and Escalante canyons falling to his left. There the horizon fell, and the world was suddenly dominated by a vast darkening sky. Overhead, Tom could see the contrails of a half dozen planes, brightly illuminated by light from a sun that had already slipped below the western horizon, carrying busy people to exotic destinations, from San Diego to Chicago, perhaps, or Phoenix to Billings, Omaha to Salt Lake. He wondered who they were, the people in the planes, and why they were in such a hurry. Was their reason for rushing as compelling as his? He wondered when he might fly in a plane again, something he once did routinely but had no plans to do again soon. Someday, he was sure, a plane would take him somewhere, but he couldn't guess where it might be. He had always wanted to see Vancouver and sometimes imagined himself trekking in Nepal, visiting the Buddhist temples at Angkor Wat, or on a safari in the Serengeti. He thought of all of the people at airports at that precise moment—children, wives, and husbands; boyfriends and girlfriends—waiting for a loved one to arrive. Every once in a great while, a plane crashed, carrying loved ones with it into oblivion.

As Tom reached the interstate at Grand Junction and joined the stream of traffic, he contemplated his initiation into a separate class of human being. He was a killer now, but a righteous one, a victim who turned the tables on his depraved assailant and killed in self-defense. He felt no guilt at all, at least not while he was still under the influence of the meth, and what made it even sweeter was his calculation that he stood a good chance of getting away with it.

He cataloged all the reasons he was safe and need never report what had happened to anyone. There were no witnesses and Brubaker's corpse might not be found for years or decades. Hadn't Brubaker himself observed that a body tossed in the ravine behind his shack would never be found? There were undoubtedly skeletons slowly disintegrating into dust in plenty of the abandoned homesteads, shacks and doublewides around Naturita, the remains of hermits like Brubaker who died alone. By the time Brubaker's murder was discovered, if it was discovered, his corpse would have been eaten by scavengers or rotted away and the trail Tom had followed from Sarah to Anya to Brubaker would be so cold that nobody would pick it up. Beyond that, any investigator would assume the death was related to the meth whose detritus would be fully evident at the scene. That would be true up to a point, and Tom was not a habitual tweaker and therefore not a likely suspect.

But perhaps what was most reassuring was Tom's confidence that Brubaker's life had been worthless, maybe even to himself. Surely, no one would miss him or seek justice on his behalf. He might not even have had a mother, but more likely crawled out from under a rock. Anyone who had so much as crossed his path would be glad he was dead. Very possibly, if and when Brubaker's corpse was discovered, the coroner, or whoever investigated, would not bother to look deeply enough into the circumstances to label the death suspicious in the first place, the bloody murder weapon, which Tom had left behind, notwithstanding. In the astonishing clutter of Brubaker's shack, the fire poker would hardly jump out. Or the death would be chalked up as just another bit of unremarkable meth-related violence in a world that had plenty of it. Who would have the time or inclination to look deeper?

On the other hand, Tom had been observed in the vicinity by the driver of the pickup. And he realized after he'd driven a hundred miles, he should have removed the fire poker, which was certainly covered with his fingerprints as well as Brubaker's blood, rendering it into a piece of physical evidence that could incriminate him well beyond a shadow of a doubt if it fell into an investigator's hands. Tom banished these harsh thoughts, at least for now, if only because there was nothing he could do about them. The driver of the truck could have been headed anywhere and would not tie Tom to the scene of the death unless Brubaker was discovered immediately, and what were the odds of that? In a week or so, the time of death would be impossible to pinpoint, making Tom's presence nearby less relevant. As for the fire poker, Tom resolved to return to Brubaker's place and retrieve and dispose of it later. Sure, that made perfect sense; it was a reasonable plan; he would go back to cover his tracks. Tom was able to observe his own sloppy thinking under the influence of the meth with clinical dispassion. But even knowing it was reckless, he didn't care. Raging on meth, to go for broke, fully confident that the needle could be threaded, felt not just sensible but mandatory.

Tom did not stop driving except to fill the tank of his car and empty his bladder, until he reached Denver, six hours later, arriving there before dawn. To Tom, the time seemed short, as if he had covered the nearly 400-mile distance from Naturita in just half an hour, as if his Corolla were his own personal Learjet.

He parked by the Colorado State Historical Museum. He found a coffee shop nearby where he picked at a plate of bacon and eggs that he ordered even though he had no appetite. He managed to down only a single gulp of black coffee and was waiting by the entrance when the museum library opened.

Within half an hour, he had found several magazine articles and chapters in books about Dick Klein.

From The Denver Post Empire magazine, dated July 23, 1953:

IN THE URANIUM BELT, A KING OPENS THE GATES TO HIS 'CASTLE'

By Kandee DeGraw

On the Fourth of July, you won't see a solitary soul on the streets of tiny Naturita, in the far southwestern corner of Colorado, just a few miles from the Utah border. Every last one of the townsfolk is up on North Mountain, a dozen miles outside of town, where the Uranium King is hosting them at his lavish estate. The festivities begin with a traditional barbecue, followed by an afternoon of baseball and other traditional games, all capped off with a spectacular fireworks display that would be worthy of any big city like Denver.

The Uranium King is Dick Klein, the prospector who put this town on the map when he struck a mother lode of uranium, the famous Whispering Jim Mine, which has already produced millions of dollars of uranium ore. The colorful Klein often says that he owes his good fortune to all the citizens of Naturita, the miners and mill workers and the town's shopkeepers alike. Last year, this year and as far as he can see into the future, Klein plans to host them all on Independence Day as a small measure of his gratitude.

Klein fashions himself to be a latter-day Horace A.W. Tabor, Colorado's legendary Silver King, who was for several decades before the silver crash of 1893 the richest man in the state. Klein owns almost every business in this town, including the Uranium Drive-In Theater, which he plans to replace with an indoor movie theater to match the famous opera houses Tabor built in Leadville and Denver. Also, like Tabor, who was a lieutenant governor of Colorado and a United States Senator, Klein promises that he will soon throw his hat into the political ring.

"I'm just waiting for the right opportunity," he told this reporter with a wink.

Up on North Mountain this past July 4th, the Uranium King himself was flipping burgers and turning hot dogs on the grill on the spacious patio behind his ranch-style home overlooking the San Miguel River canyon and the town of Naturita far below. He seemed to know every child by name.

Klein's gracious wife Betty handed out slices of ice-cold watermelon to one and all, assisted by her three young sons, Frank, Richard, and Albert.

After lunch, there were a three-legged race, a watermelon seed spitting contest, a greased pig catch, a tug-of-war, and other games.

When darkness fell, Klein said a few words.

"This old-fashioned celebration may mean just a little bit more to us here in Naturita than it might to folks in other places," he told the crowd, "because we mined the uranium ore that made the atom bomb that defeated the Japs and ended the war. We have helped make the United States of America the greatest military power the world has ever known. That doesn't make us better than other Americans, but it does mean that we are the guardians of the freedom we celebrate today. God bless America."

Then the Uranium King's guests sang the Star-Spangled Banner and fireworks filled the sky.

* * *

The story was illustrated with a half-dozen carefully composed photographs. There was one of the King at the barbecue, wearing an apron, wielding an enormous set of tongs, and grinning at the camera. He was surrounded by children with their plates held out like so many Oliver Twists. Another pictured Betty, described in the caption as "the most fabulous hostess between Denver and San Francisco," noting that she had hosted Mamie Eisenhower on North Mountain. Betty was as trim as a fifties' sitcom star, Donna Reed, not a hair out of place despite being surrounded by her three young boys. Another photograph depicted the spacious living room at the North Mountain estate, Betty and Dick perched on a couch. The house was furnished "in an eclectic mix of Western furniture, hunting trophies, and carefully chosen European Old Masters," the caption read.

The story of how Klein had discovered the Whispering Jim was legendary and repeated with a few variations in many stories. Graduating from the University of Colorado in 1942 with a degree in geology, he was ineligible for the army due to poor eyesight, so he worked for a couple of years for several copper companies in South America. He returned home after the war and took a job with Standard Oil, but was fired for insubordination for doggedly, some would say obnoxiously, pursuing a theory of underground geological formations that he had developed in South America, which his superiors found dubious. He was informally blackballed in the oil industry.

Out of work just when the Atomic Energy Commission established guaranteed high prices for uranium, with Betty pregnant with their third child, Klein borrowed a $1,000 stake from his mother-in-law to join the uranium rush. Among the thousands of hopeful prospectors on the Colorado Plateau, he was again the odd man out. Most prospectors guessed that uranium-bearing carnotite would be found in surface deposits, since that was where it had always been found. They searched for claims by traipsing across promising terrain bearing a Geiger counter. But most of the deposits they found were small and quickly mined out, and thus of little interest to Klein, who dreamed much bigger dreams.

Klein believed that the small surface deposits found by others meant there must be far larger deposits underground, where they were not subject to the forces of erosion. He prided himself on "sensing" what lay beneath the surface of the earth, knowledge to be gleaned from a study of surface features, informed by the experience of seeing what could be seen in existing mines and oil well core samples and comparing that to what lay above. He theorized that carnotite would collect in long-buried watercourses where minerals dissolved in water, like uranium, were the fossilizing agents of organic matter.

In searching for uranium, he adopted the prospecting tool of the oil business: drilling core samples in promising locations.

He found an acolyte, Jim Stewart, who was known as Whispering Jim, and the two formed a partnership to drill in places that Klein identified as likely to hold uranium deposits. For two years, the Kleins lived in a tarpaper shack outside Naturita, subsisting on the venison Dick hunted, dried beans, and oats. Klein and Stewart devoted hours to traversing terrain that was of little interest to other prospectors. Klein was looking for younger surface geology at higher elevations than the more eroded formations where surface deposits of carnotite were found. There was a strong element of faith in Whispering Jim's participation with Klein, as he could discern nothing different in the settings Klein found interesting than any other dry gulch or outcropping of rock. Was Klein a scientist or a diviner? When Klein finally staked a claim and drilled, Whispering Jim and Betty Klein and her children all had to develop a thick skin to fend off taunts about "Klein's Folly," especially when it turned up no uranium ore.

Jim didn't live to see his faith in Klein vindicated when their third and what probably would have been their final attempt to drill for uranium hit a mother lode. But Klein named the strike for his lost partner.

Klein leveraged his newfound wealth by establishing his own uranium mill outside the town of Naturita, a mill supplied not only by the Whispering Jim and ore from other companies' mines, but by Klein's own additional claims. The skeptics had no choice but to concede that maybe he did know — or sense — what the geologic structures beneath the earth's surface looked like. Luck simply could not account for his success. By the late 1950s, Klein's Uranium King Mining Co. was the biggest enterprise in the Four Corners, employing hundreds of men and diversifying into the other traditional West End enterprise of cattle ranching.

By the early 1960s, uranium mining on the Colorado Plateau was no longer profitable, the boom was over, and Klein's businesses shrank. If his gift was that he sensed what lay beneath the surface of the land in the Four Corners region, it did him little good when the minerals to be found there were no longer marketable. Other business endeavors—a marble quarry, a vineyard, resort development in Telluride—were marginally successful at best. He and Betty spent most of their time in a Denver mansion, near their sons, their daughters-in-law and their grandchildren. Betty died of Alzheimer's disease in the early 1990s and shortly after that, according to the business pages of the Denver papers, Dick became estranged from two of his three sons, the family split into two warring camps in a bitter legal battle for control of UK Mining, or whatever was left of it.

A particular flash point was the vast sum being spent to convert the family ranch into a resort. On one side was Dick and his youngest son, Albert, who was developing the resort. On the other side, the two older sons, Frank and Richard. Frank and Richard accused Dick and Albert of squandering the fortune on dubious investments, and none more dubious than the resort. Dick and Albert rejoined that Frank and Richard had forfeited their inheritance by virtue of years of disloyalty to the family.

There was not a word in any of this family history, of course, about an illegitimate son named Ray Walker.

Chapter 15

THE DISINHERITED

I got interested in the story when we started getting these weird press releases and promotional materials about the über-spiffy new resort at the Uranium King Ranch. The stuff they sent out made the place sound like a resort designed to entertain James Bond. I mean, how about a 'climate-controlled' cigar room? I had to check it out for myself."

Tom had called the reporter from The Denver Post and invited him to lunch. He'd explained he was working on a story about the most prominent family in his backyard and was looking for some additional background. The journalistic tradition that the big city reporter can always find a friend at a small paper is reciprocated without risk of being scooped. The Post and the Forum were obviously not competitors. And Tom knew that almost any reporter is a sucker for somebody else picking up the lunch tab.

"What did you do to your nose?" the reporter, Dan Bryant, asked.

"Oh," Tom said, self-consciously reaching for his face, which he hadn't realized had been so obviously bruised by Brubaker. "I walked into a door last night, in my motel room. In the dark… I was half asleep…."

Bryant nodded and continued with his story.

"I went down to Naturita and, sure enough, the UK Ranch Resort was one of the strangest places I've ever been," he said. "Have you been there?"

"Yeah."

"It's totally bizarre, right? Did you check out that scenario house? That alone must have cost millions, with all the high-tech gadgets in there. I started poking around and learned that there was this war inside the family. Basically, the two older brothers are totally pissed off about all the money spent on the resort. They had their lives all figured out. They were going to live quietly off their inheritance as soon as the old man died. It wasn't a huge fortune like it used to be, but it was enough, and the family still owns a lot of land that could be developed or sold off. But their whacko younger brother had other ideas. Somehow Albert got control of the parents and they let him do this resort.

"The big blow came in Betty Klein's will, leaving all her assets to Albert and naming him her executor and leaving just $1 to each of the other boys, Frank and Richard, because—and I remember this language exactly—'of their role in the deliberate obstruction of the UK Ranch Resort plan and the years of financial hardships and mental anguish that they caused their parents by their selfish ingratitude and dishonesty.'

"Frank and Richard responded by filing a suit contesting the will on the grounds that Albert dictated it to Betty, who by then was well in the depths of Alzheimer's."

"What happened?"

"It's still going on. There've been a couple more suits and counter-suits filed since that one. If you've got the time to spare, you could meet with Frank and Richard. You might find it interesting. They'll give you more material than you can ever use for a story. They're both listed in the phone book. And believe me, they've got nothing better to do than talk about their troubles."

*   *   *

Frank Klein answered the phone on the second ring, needing very little in the way of an introduction from Tom before inviting the publisher of the West End Forum to his place for an interview. He seemed disappointed that Tom couldn't arrive sooner than within the hour. He agreed to call his brother, Richard, to invite him to join them.

The two brothers were waiting on the front porch of Frank's modest Aurora bungalow when Tom pulled up.

The introductions were cursory. Nor were any questions from the journalist necessary.

"It's really a damn tragedy that mom and dad didn't succeed in spending it all," Frank said even before the three of them had settled into their seats around the dining room table. He was in his mid-fifties and bore a strong family resemblance to Albert.

Richard, who was a few years younger, nodded agreement. He sat behind several portable files bulging with documents, ready to present evidence if it was called for. Richard looked like he might have come from a different family; he was short, round, and had a full head of hair.

"When we were kids, we went from beans and oats to Swiss cocoa and filet mignon," Richard said.

"That was the easy transition," Frank interjected. "Going back the other way was the hard part. Back to beans and oats."

"Dad used to take us up in his plane to watch television because the signal didn't reach Naturita."

"The point is that he and mom thought they'd struck it so rich that the money would last forever."

"That's right. Fur coats and diamonds. Champagne and caviar."

"He bought the plane in the first place so that he and mom could fly to Denver for weekly rumba lessons. Then he had to build a landing strip for it."

"Dad thought he was literally a king. King Dick Klein."

"And mom thought she was his queen. Queen Betty."

"Wouldn't that make us princes?"

"In 1970, the estate was worth $120 million."

"And that was when a million dollars was worth something."

"You really have to work hard to spend that much money."

"Oh, they worked at it, all right!"

"Of course, nobody knew then that one of their children was a psycho."

"We only learned that later."

"After it was too late."

The two brothers jumped on each other's lines, pathetically eager to get the story out, and leave no sordid detail untold.

"Albert was always off," Richard said.

"We thought he was just slow. Especially after he fell off his bike and hit his head."

"He's plenty smart. From the time he was five, he was plotting against us."

"That's a bit much, don't you think?" Frank asked. "From the age of five?"

"You know, Frank, I really don't. We always underestimated him."

"How did he gain control?" Tom interjected.

"Through deceit."

"And fraud."

"He's a sociopath."

"He told Mom and Dad whatever they wanted to hear."

"So, you've sued him."

"Only five times!" Richard said. "I've got all the legal documents right here if you want to see them." He started rummaging through the files.

"Maybe later, if there's a story here for me."

"Oh, there's a story all right," Frank said.

"Yeah, *Bleak House*," Richard said. "You ever read it? Dickens novel about the lawsuit that goes on for decades and ruins everyone it touches. That's the story of the Kleins."

"Why not walk away?"

"It wouldn't be right," Frank said.

Richard nodded his agreement, his expression sober and sad. "It's a matter of simple justice," he said.

"Before Mom died, Albert got her will rewritten, and the two of us were completely disinherited," Frank said. "Of course, she had Alzheimer's, so it won't stand up when we get before a judge."

"Albert dictated it to mom. Now he's got the same control over Dad."

"Have you been to the ranch?" Frank asked Tom. "We hear it's absolutely grotesque."

"We can't visit," Richard explained. "Can't even visit our own family home, the place where we grew up. It belongs to us as much as it does to Albert. But he's got armed guards to keep us away. He doesn't want us to get within ten miles of Dad."

"I often think it's a pity Albert hasn't wiped us out completely. So that we couldn't keep fighting."

"Maybe he has by now."

"It might have been better if dad had never discovered the Whispering Jim in the first place," Frank said, closing the argument with the same sentiment he had started it with on Tom's arrival: Money is a curse.

The two brothers were done, and they sat there looking at Tom expectantly, as if now that they'd presented their case to him, a case that consisted of deeply bruised feelings and several cartons of legal documents, he would assume the role of a judge and set things right.

"It's quite a story," Tom said.

The Klein brothers nodded: quite a story, indeed, a story of hopeful lives undone by greed and malice.

"I'm actually looking into the disappearance of your half-brother, Ray Walker."

"Ray Walker?" Frank asked blankly, as if the name rang only a far distant bell.

"I haven't seen him in years," Richard said with a shrug of disinterest.

Frank nodded. "He was a lot younger than us," he said.

"I'm pretty sure Dad settled with him ages ago," Richard added. "Set him up in a business and made pretty damned generous arrangements for Elizabeth, too."

"She probably came out better than we have," Frank said bitterly.

"Did you know Ray's gone missing?"

"No."

"Hadn't heard anything."

"Not a word."

Walker's disappearance was of far less interest to the Klein boys than the epic tale of the disappearance of their inheritance.

"I don't think we can help you there," Frank concluded. The deflation in his voice was sad.

Maybe uranium is toxic in more ways than one, Tom thought, as he drove away, watching the forlorn figures of the Klein brothers recede in his rearview mirror as they stood on Frank's front porch. It had certainly destroyed them.

Chapter 16

BRRRRING. BRRRRING.

Tom was crashing. He'd hit a wall. The meth was wearing off. The symptoms were entirely familiar from his past alcohol and cocaine addictions, but greatly exaggerated by the overwhelming realities that confronted him: He had killed a man, *he had killed a man*, and could not understand why time itself didn't stop to force him to reckon with the enormity of that fact. A sacrament was required, but none presented itself. He was probably infected with a deadly disease by a dirty needle, another grave reality he couldn't ignore.

Worse, there was no compensation in the form of deeper knowledge about what had happened to Ray Walker. He had nowhere to go, no friend to seek out for solace or advice, no more meth to keep himself amped, and he cursed his own hunger for it. He knew that more of the drug now would only mean a worse withdrawal later, but he craved it anyway. As bad as he felt, the moment was hypercharged with the intensity of the present. He was like the protagonist in a sci-fi short story in which every puzzle piece imagined by the author was perfectly wrought to fit tightly together and form a coherent pattern, but the author's diabolical purpose was to keep him, the story's hapless hero, suspended in a state of complete and utter confusion.

He drove out East Colfax Ave., Denver's strip of cheap motels and all the unsavory trade they attract. He got a room and planned to sleep it off. But he couldn't sleep. He couldn't shake the image of the blood spurting from Brubaker's neck. He thrashed about on the sheets, experiencing a profound withdrawal even though he'd used meth just once. He hadn't *used* meth, exactly, but had been assaulted by it. It didn't matter. Damn, this shit was addictive, just as it was reputed to be, far more addictive than the drugs he'd abused in his past. If he could score just a little meth, just enough to get himself back home to Naturita, he thought, he'd break the incipient habit then.

Don't do it, he told himself: tough it out. And he thrashed about some more, sweating, his thirst so profound that he couldn't drink enough water to quench it, moving ceaselessly from the bed to the tap for more water to the toilet to pee; acutely aware of the noise of traffic out on the street, to the life underway on the other side of the thin motel walls, to the sounds of people having sex, laughing and talking. Toilets flushing. Televisions left on. He heard a man shout and a woman cry.

Crashing from any high brings paranoia, Tom knew, but he wasn't merely paranoid, he argued with himself. He had every reason to despair, even though only a few hours earlier he'd been exhilarated, and his sense of purpose then felt every bit as real as his current dread. Still, this acute isolation, this teeth-grinding, joint-rattling fear, this unquenchable thirst, this copious sweat, it was all as real as the ugly stains on the four walls that enclosed him.

He thrashed about and sweated some more. He saw faces, scornful, angry faces, in the pattern of the cottage cheese texture on the dingy ceiling. Nobody in the world knew where he was or cared. A shiver moved from his tailbone to the base of his neck at the thought of his loneliness. Was there ever anyone more alone than he was at that moment? Then he indulged a worse thought: what if there were people who knew exactly where he was, and who were closing in on him? Who would they be? How would they know and why would they care? Someone could burst in the door, and it might be a cop on the trail of Mark Brubaker's killer. Or Brubaker himself, not dead after all, but merely wounded and enraged and seeking revenge. Or it could be Dick Klein. Or Albert Klein. The shiver reversed direction and moved from the base of his neck down to his tailbone and then to his toes. He remembered how it felt to be suicidal.

He gazed at himself in the mottled mirror in the motel room bathroom, harshly lit by the green tint of a fluorescent light. Sometimes in a mirror, Tom saw a face he might describe as handsome, or at least inoffensive: sandy hair, symmetrical features, a ready smile, dark brown eyes. Expensive orthodontics as a teenager had given him perfectly aligned teeth. Now the corners of his mouth were twitchy, his nose swollen from the wound Brubaker had inflicted; his expression was drawn, his eyes blank but bloodshot from lack of sleep. He looked dangerous, even to himself. He dressed and stepped out onto Colfax and started walking, just to walk, to move.

It was past midnight and there were hookers working the sidewalk and johns cruising past, and all other manner of insomniacs and tweakers, muggers, gangbangers, and aimless youth. He passed a beat-up car parked in the shadows just down a side street in which a family, both parents and two small children, were trying to sleep, all of their belongings piled up around them. They looked familiar and

Tom thought for a moment that they might have come to this place, like he had, from Naturita. But they could as easily have come from Wyoming or Kansas. No doubt a cop would find them soon, shine a flashlight though the windows to wake them up, and make them move on. If the cop were kind, he would direct them to a homeless shelter.

Tom didn't walk five minutes before he was hit up.

"I know what you need, baby."

He eyed the tranny, all skanky 110 pounds of her, and shook his head. But she didn't take no for an answer, and instead reached into her bag to show him a familiar looking blue plastic zip-lock baggie.

"How much?"

"$100."

He followed her to the dark edge of an empty parking lot, where someone had thoughtfully broken the bulb in a security light fixture, and he emptied his wallet to complete the transaction. The tranny pressed herself up against him, her knee brushing his crotch.

"C'mon honey," she said, "Blow job's included, no extra charge."

He could have agreed, and he momentarily considered it—why not, after everything else he'd experienced in the last 24 hours?—but he felt a wave of nausea and pushed her away.

Though meth was something new, Tom was a connoisseur of addiction. Back in his motel room, he started out slow to test just how much of the drug he needed to snort to ease himself out of the darkest corner of the dark place he'd sunk to, and how much more it would take to fuel his drive back home to Naturita.

It wasn't so bad, really. He paced himself perfectly. By the time he got home the next morning, he'd been awake more than 48 hours. Then his body shut down, as if an internal timer had run out, and he fell asleep the second his head hit the pillow.

*   *   *

But this was a restless sleep. Tom's dreams were filled with ringing, incessant, endless ringing, and shouting, cries of anguish, whimpers, and groans that sounded precisely like the last noise that emanated from Mark Brubaker. He was deep in the canyonlands, prospecting for uranium, or maybe searching for a missing man, he wasn't sure. Whatever it was, the search was fruitless. He was lost in a labyrinth of canyons, sheer cliffs rising up high above him, hemming him in. There was no moon. "Helloo… helloo," he called. But nobody answered.

What is that damned ringing? *Brrrring. Brrrring. Brrrring.* It's *inside* him, the ringing, and he shakes his head violently side to side to knock it out, to dislodge it from his cranium.

He tries to climb out of the slot canyon he's been wandering for days, up a seam in the rock to where he can make out a ledge, but his foot slips and he grabs on to a rock overhead to steady himself. But the rock breaks loose and falls on him and carries him back to the canyon floor and comes to rest on his arm below the elbow. The pain is excruciating, his arm crushed beneath a boulder that must weigh two tons, he's pinned firmly to the ground. The word "excruciating," he remembers, comes from crucifix, and it is apt: he is indeed pinned like Jesus on the cross. He screams but is answered only by an echo, "Hellooo," and that damned ringing. *Brrring. Brrrring.*

"Helloo," someone is shouting, or is it just his own voice coming back at him for a second or third time, echoing off the towering canyon walls? Then, not a quarter mile away, on a ridge, he sees his partner, his friend. Tom recognizes the young Dick Klein in a dusty hat, a World War II-vintage canteen slung across his back, in dungarees, suspenders over a plaid shirt, and brown leather combat boots, peering at him through a pair of binoculars. Tom struggles to wave his free arm, he shouts, "Helloooooo," but Dick just stands there looking right at him and making no move toward him.

Tom grinds his teeth against the pain. His teeth feel loose and his jaw aches as much as his arm. The vision of Dick Klein watching him die must be a hallucination, because the figure on the ridge vanishes, dissolves into a rock outcropping, and then from the same rock the human figure reemerges. It is merely Tom's, or Jim's, fevered and vain hope for a rescue, for a miracle. He is weakening fast, delirious, his canteen empty; he is thirsty, so thirsty, his mouth tastes of grit. The boulder is absolutely fixed, it won't budge, and there is only one way Tom can see to save himself. He rips his shirt off and forms a tourniquet that he ties just above where he will make the cut. His crushed arm is so numb, so broken, that he probably won't even feel it when he hacks it off with his pocketknife....

But he's wrong about that. The pain is white hot, the worst pain a man can endure, and even worse than that because it is self-inflicted, and he screams with all his might — there is nobody to hear him, after all — as he forces the knife tip into the inside of his elbow in order to gain leverage against his own sinew and tendons and bones, working as quickly as possible to saw through his elbow joint and free himself. The makeshift tourniquet is no barrier to the blood that spurts from his torn arteries, he is clinically aware that his own heart is pumping his blood out of his body in steady but quickly diminishing spurts. In his agony there is a moment of release, literal release from the grip of the rock as the knife completes its work, and he stumbles to his feet, almost experiencing joy, having escaped his broken body, but he's lost too much blood and he falls on the ground and rolls over to look heavenward and there, looming over him, is Dick Klein, who coldly watches him die.

"I'm sorry, Jim," Dick says. "There was nothing I could do."

"Water…." Tom says. More than the betrayal, more than the physical pain, he is most acutely aware of his dry, parched mouth and wants nothing more than a little moisture to ease his passage into the afterlife.

• • •

Brrring. Brrring.

Tom bolted awoke to the sound of the telephone ringing downstairs in the Forum office. He was instantly aware it had been ringing for hours, but how many hours? It was four o'clock according to the clock by his bed, and it was not dark out, so it was late afternoon, but what day was it? His stomach was a knot of hunger and his arm ached—it had been pinned under his body while he slept, cutting off the flow of blood and numbing it—but he was even thirstier than that. He lurched into the bathroom, cupped his hand under the faucet, and drank deeply. He tried to shake his arm awake.

The phone started to ring again, and there were familiar voices and the sound of pounding on the door. They were forcing their way in.

"Tom? Tom?"

It was Dave Best calling.

"I'm here," Tom shouted.

"We're worried about you," Dave called. "What happened to the paper?"

"Can we come in, Tom?"

Tom recognized the voice: It was Deputy Peterson on what the police blotter would term "a welfare check," in response to a report that somebody might be in need of assistance.

"It's Friday, man," Dave said. "What happened to the paper?"

"Oh, shit," Tom said, and thinking quickly he ran what little meth he had left down the drain. "I'll be right down."

"What the hell happened to you?" Dave said when Tom straggled down the stairs. "You look like shit."

Dave and Billy were looking at him with expressions that mixed concern and, perhaps, disgust. Or was Tom just imagining that they now saw in him yet another formerly upstanding citizen of the West End undone by meth?

"I don't know what happened," Tom said. "I got sick and had a fever and passed out. I didn't realize how long I was asleep. I lost track of the time."

He knew how unconvincing it sounded. It had to be obvious to his friends that he'd had some kind of breakdown, almost certainly related to drugs or alcohol. But he was safe in trusting that they couldn't call him on it. This was, after all, the West End.

"I guess I'd better get the paper out."

"I'm just glad you're alive," Dave said.

Chapter 17

WARM PEACH PIE

Somehow Tom produced a newspaper, cobbling it together out of wire stories, press releases, and a couple of soft features he had prepared in advance that were held in the can to fill last-minute holes, and got it out and on the racks only a day late. And then the depression hit, as he might have expected it to, coming off meth and after having joined the fraternity of killers. Was it a product of guilt or just fear that Mark Brubaker's body would be discovered, and he'd be called upon to report in the pages of his newspaper the details of a death he himself had caused? He was in possession of knowledge he could not share with anyone, but even if there were someone to tell, what would they make of his fantastic story, starting with his rash motive in trespassing on Brubaker's property to begin with? Would anyone believe he had killed the tweaker in self-defense? With the clarity of hindsight, if Tom seriously thought he might be confronting Ray Walker's murderer, then what did he expect?

Is that why had Brubaker attacked him? Because he was Ray's killer and thought Tom was onto him? Not likely, Tom thought, because Brubaker's reaction to him seemed entirely impulsive. As the saying went, even paranoids have enemies, and while Brubaker had seemed uninterested in Ray Walker and even in the whereabouts of Anya, he clearly had something to fear from Albert Klein.

Or maybe not. Brubaker could have conjured the entire grievance out of thin air, just as Tom, in his own meth stupor, envisioned himself as Whispering Jim, amputating his own arm. That hallucination had an immediacy and degree of detail Tom had never experienced in a mere dream. If he weren't so fundamentally rational, he'd interpret it as a paranormal communication from the beyond, a desperate plea for justice from the restless spirit of Jim himself. But since he was rational, he gave it a different interpretation: it was his subconscious mind egging him on in his pursuit of the truth, now an urgent personal necessity following his encounter with Mark Brubaker. It didn't take a Freudian to see the amputation as a symbol for castration, or, more precisely, the very emasculation at the hands of Mark Brubaker that Tom had only narrowly escaped, the lingering emasculation of his failed career in big-time journalism, and the ongoing emasculation of being systematically thwarted in his pursuit of the story, for although he was reduced to publishing a small-town paper, he still had the instincts of a reporter.

Tom thought about reporting the Brubaker incident to the authorities, but the skeptical interrogation he'd receive from Sheriff Martin was all-too easy to imagine.

"You say he made you get nekkid?" Tom would be asked. "Now, why do you suppose he would do a thing like that? You saying he was a fag?"

The sheriff was privy to all sorts of distastefulness, but nothing more disgusting than this: obviously, a kinky homosexual tryst fueled by meth and ending in murder, an unsavory queer lovers' spat. While

Brubaker was dead and therefore inarguably on the receiving end of a violent act, Tom would be able to provide no evidence that he'd been attacked first, other than his own testimony.

"Say again?" the sheriff would probe, tirelessly and uncomprehendingly: "What exactly is it that were you doing at Brubaker's shack in the first place?"

The likelihood of a just outcome was so remote that Tom understood why rape victims so rarely bother to report the crime. From his perspective as a victim, albeit one who successfully defended himself, he could see that an investigation by the Montrose County sheriff would serve no good purpose. Reports of rape never turned up in the Forum police blotter, but did that mean that there weren't sexual assaults on the West End? That was impossible considering how rough life was by every other measure. Therefore, perhaps wisely, such unpleasantries were swept under the rug.

Yet at the same time, Tom now felt driven, where before he was only curious, to keep searching for the truth. Sarah Walker had been right in warning Tom that to investigate her husband's disappearance could be dangerous. But dangerous how? She couldn't possibly have anticipated that Tom would be attacked by Mark Brubaker. That was far too random an event to have been predicted, unless she only meant to express the ethos of the place and caution him against prying into any dark corners of the West End. He doubted that was what she intended, but it would have been a reasonable warning. Shine a light in a place that had been purposefully left dark and you might startle a rattlesnake, stumble on a toxic meth lab, or discover a moldering corpse.

What was Sarah alluding to? What other hidden dangers lurked?

* * *

Whatever she meant by it, Sarah owed him an explanation. Tom was exhausted and jittery, and felt as though a week's uninterrupted sleep wouldn't be enough for his recovery from the events of the previous few days. But he couldn't sleep. It was early evening, and he knew Sarah would be home from work, so he jumped in his car and drove to her house.

Ray Jr. was outside shooting hoops in the fading light when Tom pulled up and got out of his car.

Thump. Thump. Thump. Pling.

Tom grabbed the ball as it caromed off the rim.

"Hi Ray," he said. "Is your mom here?"

Ray nodded and Tom tossed the ball back. For Ray, it was easy to mask his disappointment that Tom wasn't interested in playing with him, even to take just a few shots: *Thump. Thump. Swoosh.*

"What happened to you?" Sarah asked, when she opened the door. She was wearing an apron dusted with flower.

"A lot," he said.

Though they had been together just a few days earlier at The Uranium Drive-In, so much had happened to Tom since then that it felt to him as if it had been months or years since he'd last seen her. He realized that she couldn't have the same perspective. She hadn't aged in the previous 36 hours like he had, and his unannounced appearance on her doorstep might strike her as aggressive. He was suddenly and acutely aware that, more than information, he needed her sympathy, or maybe just the warmth of her kitchen, but that he had no right to either. They scarcely knew each other. She was a married woman whose husband was missing but not necessarily dead. But he had been on an emotional journey that she was at the center of. She was the catalyst that sent him down the fateful path that took him first to Albuquerque and Anya and then to his devastating encounter with Brubaker. Given that, maybe he was entitled after all.

"Do I look that bad?" he asked.

"I was just making pies," she said. "Would you like a slice? It's still warm. It's peach."

He nodded. She did not seem either surprised or unhappy to see him, but somehow resigned, as if his visit was inevitable, sooner or later, or something to be routinely expected. He was either that persistent or had become a fixture in her life. She poured him a cup of coffee.

"Ray isn't with Anya," Tom said.

"I knew that."

"You seem to know a lot. More than you tell."

"How's the pie?"

"So good…" he smiled.

"I guess you found her."

"Anya's in Albuquerque. I went there to talk to her. She's convinced that Mark Brubaker killed Ray."

"I don't know," Sarah said tentatively. "It's possible, I guess."

"Is that why you told me it was dangerous to ask questions? Because of Brubaker? Were you concerned about me?"

"Let me ask you something," she countered. "Why do you care so much about what happened to Ray? An auto mechanic disappears and the only people it hurts are his wife and kids and nobody else. You didn't even know him all that well. Everybody else just wants to forget as quickly as they can. Why can't you leave it alone?"

"I don't know. I've become involved, I guess."

"Involved how?"

It was a good question with an obvious answer, but he couldn't say it. The killing of Brubaker had made him an integral part of the story, robbing him of any claim to detachment, journalistic or any other kind. He wanted to confess and tell her about his horrifying encounter with the fat, tattooed tweaker. He wanted to be absolved by her, as if that were possible, but her reaction might not be that simple and he couldn't afford to take the risk.

Thump. Thump. Swoosh.

"How are your kids doing?"

"All right. Angie's still working up in Telluride. Ray Jr., well, you saw him. He acts like a normal 13-year-old, doesn't he?"

"I didn't know there was a normal 13-year-old."

She smiled ruefully. "I could have been normal."

He ignored the chance to follow-up and get more personal, which in other circumstances would have been of interest but was, at this moment, a distraction from more pressing matters.

"I need to know why you said it could be dangerous for me to ask questions about Ray."

"I don't know," she said. "I can't say."

"You don't know, or you can't say?"

"I don't know. I don't know."

"How can I help you if you won't tell me the truth?"

"I never asked for your help," she replied a little sharply. "I don't need your help and I don't want your help. Especially if you're going to keep acting like I'm a liar."

"I'm sorry," he said. "I just wish you'd tell me what's dangerous."

"It's just time to stop," she said without conviction. "Nothing good can come of it, no matter what happened to Ray. That's how people survive here. It's what we do and we're good at it. We accept whatever happens and then we move on."

"Does it involve the Kleins?"

"Everything on the West End involves the Kleins," she sighed. "Nobody likes having somebody snooping around, asking questions about them, especially the Kleins. They probably know you went to see Elizabeth in Cortez. You ask a lot of questions, you know. Too many, probably."

"If nobody asks questions, you'll never know what happened to Ray."

"Maybe that's just as well," she said. "That's why I decided today that when I got home from work, I'd make pies instead of worrying. I've done enough worrying and it hasn't helped one bit."

"I can understand that," he said. "At least you can eat the pies and they taste good."

At an impasse, they didn't talk much more, but he made no move to leave, and she allowed him to feel at home. He lay down on her sofa while she cleaned up the kitchen.

Chapter 18

THE SCENE OF THE INCIDENT

His eyes fluttered open several hours later to the sounds of Sarah preparing for bed. He lay under a quilt that she had apparently thrown over him. Without turning his head, he could see her pass across his field of vision, dressed in a lightweight nightgown, her figure silhouetted against light spilling out from her bedroom. From the other side of the room, a television flickered, though the sound was turned off. Tom lay still and kept his breathing regular, deliberately allowing her to believe he was sleeping, even when she moved close enough that he could feel the air fanned by her efficient movement.

"How late are you going to be up?"

Her voice was low to guard Tom's sleep.

"It's Friday," Ray Jr. replied. "No school tomorrow."

"Well, you still need your sleep."

Tom felt an impulse to stir and draw her attention and test her response. He imagined how he might be able to push the intimacy of the moment by sighing loudly and then tossing on the couch so that the quilt fell to the floor, inviting her to replace it. If she did, he might press up against her, and she might welcome his touch. He wanted to lie there in the warmth of Sarah's living room until morning, and maybe longer, but there was another thought lurking on the edge of his consciousness. He had left something undone, something important, something he'd meant to do and could no longer avoid: the incriminating fire poker still lay where he'd tossed it aside after killing Brubaker with it, just waiting to be discovered if he didn't return to the scene of....

Tom interrupted his own train of thought, resisting the obvious descriptive ... *the scene of the crime*. But what else should it be called? To call Brubaker's shack a crime scene would inevitably lead to the wrong conclusion, that the tweaker had been murdered, since only Brubaker's killer knew that what had happened there was not murder but an act of self-defense. Likewise, the fire poker was not exactly a "murder weapon," though it was unquestionably an instrument of death. These distinctions were all-important to Tom. The language and plotting of a detective novel were dangerous because they left him vulnerable to the killer's classic misstep, the essential but ruinous return to *the scene of the incident*.

And yet, as he lay there waiting for Sarah to turn off the lights, and for Ray Jr. to finish his video game and go to sleep so that he could slip away without having to offer an explanation, Tom knew he had no choice but to return to Brubaker's shack. And not out of any latent psychological compulsion to be caught. On the contrary, he was determined to avoid detection, and that's why the fire poker had to be retrieved, though it was a chore he anticipated with mounting dread.

Tom drifted in and out of a light sleep, but in his restlessness, he could not stop reliving the incident with Brubaker, asking himself how it might have gone differently, how he could have avoided it altogether by minding his own business and letting the mystery of Ray Walker go without his investigating it. Or, if his need to investigate led him inevitably to Mark Brubaker, he asked how he might have managed the encounter differently, so that it could end without violence. But as he revisited every step he had taken to Brubaker's door, he found that it always ended the same way: he was standing naked over a dying Brubaker with a bloody fire poker in his hands, which he dropped and left carelessly behind, forcing him now, not three days later, to have to go back in order to dispose of it.

Sarah had long since gone to bed, and Tom gave up the hope that Ray Jr. would stop playing his video game any time before sunrise, so he rolled off the sofa and stood up. Ray was staring at him. Tom put his finger to his lips and gestured in the direction of Sarah's bedroom door, indicating he wanted to avoid waking her up. Ray nodded his complicity. Tom made his way to the door and stepped outside. The night was cold, the sky clear. He was thankful that his car engine turned over immediately, a credit to the missing mechanic who had maintained it and whose sleeping wife was now the beneficiary of his skill. He watched the doublewide recede in the rearview mirror as he pulled away, glad to see that it remained dark.

Fifteen minutes later, he pulled up to Brubaker's equally dark cabin. It looked exactly as it had just days earlier, when he'd fled the scene, the glistening semi parked by the side. Tom sat in his car for a moment, listening intently and hearing only a coyote yelp far in the distance. This will be quick, he thought, imagining he would walk inside, spot the fire poker, grab it, and retreat. He would avoid looking directly at Brubaker's corpse, though he anticipated that he might have to step over it.

Was there anything else he needed to do? Anything he was forgetting? Better to think of it now so he wouldn't have to return again later. Again, he relived the half hour he'd been there, moment by moment, blow by literal blow. Was there anything besides the fire poker he had touched, anything that might retain his fingerprints?

Maybe the bathtub faucet. He would wipe it down. Had he adjusted the showerhead? He didn't remember, so he would wipe that down, too, just in case. After killing Brubaker, did he drink water from a glass?

Steady, Tom told himself. You're going overboard. The fire poker would be enough! With that self-admonition, he purposefully stepped out of the car and pushed open the door of the house, only to have his resolve instantly undone by the stench of Brubaker's death. The odor was a physical force that pushed Tom back on his heels, back outside, where he doubled over and retched.

He covered his mouth and nose with the sleeve of his shirt and pushed his way back inside.

Brubaker's corpse lay just where it had fallen but was so bloated that it looked as if it might explode. The air inside the shack was warm and moist with human decomposition, and there were insects everywhere, mostly houseflies, and their maggots, crawling on the naked body. Brubaker's skin had blackened to the point that his tattoos were barely discernable.

Tom looked for the fire poker but didn't see it where he remembered it falling from his grasp. Now that he was back in the shack, every detail was crisp and perfectly matched his memory of the scene. Only the fire poker wasn't there. It was like one of those games in a children's picture book in which two highly detailed photographs are positioned side-by-side. Can you see what's different in the second picture? Why, the *instrument of death* is missing, of course.

Tom felt sick to his stomach as he stumbled out of the cabin back to his car. Was it the stench? The sight of the rotting corpse? Or was it the shattering discovery that someone had been there and had taken the fire poker?

Tom sat behind the wheel of his car and gazed at the cabin. He had left the door open. So much the better, as it would only hasten the decay of the scene and any incriminating evidence still inside, by letting the coyotes and other vermin in. He thought he could see movement, probably the movement of rodents already on the job, just inside the door.

What an open door could do, broken windows and running water could only help along. Tom walked around the cabin and smashed every window with a stick. Realizing that he had just created another piece of evidence—the stick itself—he tossed it into the ravine. He forced himself to go back inside and using a piece of cloth to avoid planting more fingerprints he opened the tap on the kitchen and bathroom sinks and the shower, plugging the drains so that the water would soon overflow and cause a flood. He opened the refrigerator. He thought about setting the place on fire, but that would only draw attention and ensure a visit from authorities.

Hopefully, nobody would investigate Mark Brubaker's disappearance for months, and by the time anyone did, nature would have cleansed his shack of everything organic, even Brubaker's bones, if Brubaker had been right about the coyotes' diet, leaving it clean and odorless. Like Whispering Jim and like Ray Walker, Brubaker would have vanished. Hopefully, whoever had been there and had discovered the corpse and had taken the fire poker was someone who had no reason or inclination to report what they had found to the law or to look any deeper into what had happened there.

These were admittedly frail hopes, but they were all Tom had.

Chapter 19

NEVER GIVE UP

Tom took refuge in the routine of running the Forum, work that had to be done despite his sense that nothing was or ever could be the same following Brubaker's death at his hands, his deepening anxiety that he would be held to account for it one way or another, and his growing certainty that he would never learn what had happened to Ray Walker. It was work so familiar he could do it by rote and for him to carry on was just another example of a man's ability to adapt to almost any contingency, just as Sarah was making peach pies a few weeks after her husband's disappearance. Yes, Tom now knew from his own experience, you can kill a man one day and be drenched in his blood and return to work the next day as if nothing had happened. Just so, he mused, murderers, rapists and drug dealers easily mix with the rest of humanity, going about their daily lives, utterly undetectable by any sign of their depravity.

The Forum was a one-man band. Tom picked up a folder containing advertising insertion orders. He would spend the morning building ads for clients, faxing proofs, and then making corrections. Tom had enjoyed doing the paper's graphic design work, fully aware that he had no real talent for it, and equally aware that in his market it didn't matter a bit. As a small-town paper, The Forum was entitled to look cheesy, if cheesy was the best Tom could achieve.

There were rarely new ads, virtually never a new customer, just changes to old ads: occasionally a new listing in the ad for Scenic Realty, the week's blue plate special at the Maverick, the sale items at the Merc.

Deciding what to put on the front page was his most important duty. He would flip through the bigger papers from Montrose, Moab, Cortez, and Telluride, to see if there were stories he wanted to reprint: all four papers let him use whatever he wanted, as long as he gave them credit. They in turn were free to republish Tom's stories, as all four did most recently to report Ray Walker's disappearance. He might rewrite a press release from the Division of Wildlife or the State Highway Department or the power company, fleshing the story out with a quick phone interview if necessary. Local residents would drop off photos of newborns or of the newly deceased for publication. For the upcoming paper, Tom had a story prepared about the Naturita Town Board's debate over whether or not to purchase the abandoned former Naturita Elementary School building for a future rec center. Some members of the board saw it as a prudent investment in the future. Others saw it as scarce money down the drain since nobody else was likely to buy the building and the town had no money with which to refurbish it anyway.

"That is exactly why God invented state community development grants," Mayor Denny said.

That was the argument that sealed the deal. Harry Denny was a perfect small-town politician, both sensible and colorful. He and Tom had lunch every couple of weeks, part of Harry's routine of public outreach. In what passed for civic life in Naturita, Tom was a player, a role he had, over the years, come to enjoy.

Denny was one of a dozen acquaintances who called Tom to ask why the paper had been late.

"I was sick and couldn't work," Tom said. "Just couldn't get her done."

"Nothing serious, I hope."

"Just a bad flu."

"You sound a little down."

"Better now."

"So, we can have lunch."

They met an hour later at the Maverick and made small talk until after Sally took their order.

"I've got some good news for you to put in your paper," Denny said. "Highway Department is gonna straighten Dead Man's Curve."

"Good work, Harry."

"Half a dozen people have gone off the road right there, right at that point, and have died in the last twenty, thirty years." Harry dug into his Frito Pie, a ladle of canned chili con carne dumped on a pile of Fritos and topped with grated yellow cheese, raw chopped onions, and shredded iceberg lettuce. "It's a serious health-safety matter. You wouldn't think we'd have had to fight like we did to get it fixed. But highway money always goes to Denver or Telluride first, and to us last."

Tom nodded.

"Here's even better news. I have reason to believe that the Highway Department is gonna give the contract to Brown Construction."

"Is this official?"

"Next week."

"I guess that is pretty big news."

"Big as it gets around here," Harry snorted.

It had only been a couple of weeks, but the mayor had apparently already forgotten about Ray Walker's disappearance.

* * *

Harry hadn't forgotten, but was right, Tom thought, as he walked across the highway back to his office after lunch. A road improvement was far bigger—and far more comprehensible and meaningful to more people—than a man who'd gone missing, and whom nobody wanted to find. So why should Tom bother? The mystery had already cost him far too much, not least his deepening anxiety surrounding the Brubaker episode, which he would now carry with him forever.

"I'm finished," he muttered, resolved that he would not give Ray Walker another moment's consideration.

Lost in his thoughts, he was nearly run down by a vintage 1950s-era jeep executing a U-turn on the highway and lurching to a stop by the Merc. Tom strolled over for a look. The vehicle clearly dated from the uranium boom; it was a prospector's tool as historic as a Geiger counter, and was worthy of closer examination.

Though they had never met, Tom recognized Dick Klein instantly from old photos. The King carefully opened the jeep door and stepped out. He was a small, stout man, stooped and looking every one of his 80-plus years. He seemed confused, an impression that was unavoidable not only because of the terry cloth bathrobe he wore for a jacket and the slippers he wore instead of shoes, but because he was entirely disheveled, unshaven, his hair askew and his shirt untucked beneath the robe.

Klein looked around as if he wasn't sure where he was or why he was there. Tom approached him.

"Mr. Klein," he said. "I'm Tom Austin, publisher of the Forum. What brings you to town?"

No small talk from the King: "I'm looking for miners," he growled. He spoke with a slight, vaguely European burr, most likely a speech impediment he had learned to mask.

"Miners?"

"Yes, indeed. Where's the tavern? Seems to me it was right around here. But I don't remember everything like I used to."

"The tavern shut down some years ago," Tom said.

"That's a shame," Klein said. "We'll have to open it back up. You could always find good men there."

"Why do you want miners? If you don't mind my asking."

"Are you a miner?"

"No, I run the newspaper."

"Oh. You'd make a lot more money as a miner. Good benefits, too. You wanna a job? I'm reopening the Whispering Jim."

Naturita's main street was as deserted as always, and nobody else had spotted Klein yet. Tom wanted him to himself.

"Can I invite you over to my office for a quick talk," Tom asked. "I'd like to hear all about your plans. Maybe I can write about it in the newspaper and help you find the miners you need."

Klein was compliant, apparently accustomed to being led, and he followed Tom to the Forum office.

He stopped when he saw the yellowed poster of Ray Walker in the window. He studied it for a moment as if the image of his son was familiar, but impossible to place.

"That's your son Ray, Mr. Klein," Tom said. "He's gone missing."

"Oh."

"Have you got any idea where he is?"

"No."

Tom ushered Klein inside and showed him to a chair.

"Uranium…." Tom started, pronouncing it like a question.

"Uranium is coming back, of course. I always knew it would come back someday. The price is rising on world markets and the Whispering Jim is not mined out. Not even close."

If the King was confused about where he was and didn't recognize his missing son, he was sharp on the subject of uranium.

"You're not one of them damned radical environmentalists, are you?" Klein asked. "Of course you are! I've got nothing against environmentalists. I've made a lot of money off of 'em, and now I'm gonna make a lot more."

"I'm just a newspaperman."

"The joke is on them, on the Earth Firsters. You know this is a great country, don't you … Who are you again?"

"Tom."

"Tom," Klein nodded. "Yep. First the guv'ment paid us to mine and mill uranium to fight the Japs and the Russians, back in the forties and fifties, and then they turned around and paid us to shut it all down and bury all the tailings. And now we're gonna make more money starting all over again. We'll end up mining the same tailings we buried using new technology to extract what we missed when we processed the ore the first time!"

"You know why uranium is coming back, don't you? Global warming, even if it is a damned hoax. Uranium is the only solution, the only practical solution, if people really want to get away from carbon. Uranium's the only way to generate enough energy to meet the world's demand. I can't tell you that twenty, thirty years ago when the environmentalists shut us down that I knew they'd come up with global warming. I don't think anyone did. But I always knew uranium would come back, somehow, someday, because it's too valuable a source of energy for mankind to ignore it."

"Makes sense."

Tom had grabbed a reporter's notebook and was scribbling notes.

"Plus, oil is running out," Klein continued. "Even if there's plenty of domestic coal and natural gas, there's not enough domestic oil. So, I'm coming out of retirement and we're going to bring the West End back to what it once was. We're going to create good jobs. Real jobs. Meaningful jobs. Jobs a man can support his family on. Not jobs changing the diapers on rich tourists up in Telluride."

"Open the movie drive-in back up."

"Well, yes, we'll do that, too," Klein said.

"I thought uranium mining ended around here because it wasn't economical," Tom said. "Because the ore was too low-grade and too hard to mill."

"Bullshit! The price dropped and the costs of extraction and milling went out of sight due to damned guv'ment regulations that the environmentalists made 'em adopt. People stopped building nuclear power plants and the guv'ment had more bombs than they knew what to do with. But that was all right because we got into the clean-up business. Now the price is back up and it's going higher. Much higher. So, we'll get back in the mining business.

"What a lot of people don't understand is that the foreign ore in Canada and Australia is too damned rich," Klein continued. "It's so damned hot that human beings can't mine it and they have to extract it with robots. And people forget that uranium is a strategic resource, and the United States cannot allow itself to depend on foreign supplies, or we'll end up just like we have with petroleum, dependent on A-rabs and terrorists."

"When do you figure the Whispering Jim will be operating again?"

"It will take a few months to ramp up, that's all. We've kept everything in working order. Mine looks today pretty much the way it did the day we shut 'er down. We'll just pick up where we left off. Turn on the lights and start digging."

"How many people will you be hiring?

"I figure to start with a dozen or so."

"Where are you going to ship the ore?"

"Blanding mill for now," Klein said. "But if it goes as I expect it will, we'll reopen the mill here and create even more good jobs. It only makes sense to mill the ore close to where you mine it. Now I realize that it will take all sorts of guv'ment approvals, and the damned environmentalists will cry about it, so it won't happen overnight...."

"Are you doing all this yourself?"

"I have always operated independently, Mr.... Who are you again?"

"Tom. Newspaper publisher."

Klein leaned back in the chair.

"My son, Albert, wants me to retire," he said. "Says my time is past and I should just let him run everything. Says we have better business opportunities. Better than mining. Says I don't understand that the world has changed. But I'm not ready for that. I'm old, but I still know a thing or two about uranium."

"I've had an interest in the history of uranium mining," Tom said.

"That right?"

"How you found the Whispering Jim..."

"Never give up," Klein said. "That's what I always told my boys. When you know something is right, you stick with it, no matter what anyone else says."

"Dangerous work, prospecting and mining," Tom said. "I can't believe how Whispering Jim cut off his own arm. How do you suppose the two of you got separated out there in Iberia Canyon? Nobody's written down the details of that. It's all kind of vague in the history books."

"He slipped," Klein said. "Jim slipped."

"How do you know?"

"I saw him slip."

"Papers said you just lost him."

"I did lose him. After he slipped."

"Do you remember it all?"

"Like it was yesterday."

"You ever tell anyone the whole story?

"Nope."

Was the old man prepared to confess?

"I tried to imagine what might have happened out there," Tom said. "Tell me if I'm right."

"Maybe."

"I figure maybe it started with an accident, and Jim fell and was injured, got trapped by a boulder and there wasn't anything you could do about it, to save Jim, so you left him to die there. But you didn't want to tell anyone the whole story because you were afraid maybe they wouldn't believe you."

"That's not exactly right."

"No?"

"We got into it," Klein said. "Him and me. We were tired. Discouraged. Sick of each other. It was hard work. We were all alone. We'd been out there, just the two of us, for a whole lot of weeks, for a whole lot of years. Damned drill kept breaking on us. We were about to call it quits. He said I was a damned fool. He wanted out. I told

him that would be fine with me. So he took off. I told him he'd better not try to come back.

"But I didn't quit. I got the drill going and kept digging. And the
next core sample was hot. And the one after that was even hotter.
Hotter than any carnotite anyone around here had ever seen. Geiger
counter was going nuts. And right then, I'll be damned if Jim doesn't
show up again, like nothing had happened, like we were still partners."

"I guess you weren't glad to see him."

"He'd quit. That claim was mine now. It was me, all by myself, I'm
the one that went the full distance. I'm the one who didn't quit. Not
him. You walk away when it's toughest, you're gone. That's always
how it's always been when you're prospecting."

"Is that when he slipped?" Tom asked.

"I told him. We were heading back to town with our samples. I told
him it was my claim. Not his. He'd walked away. I told him he could
have a piece of it, but not half. He gave up his claim to half. And then
he took a swing at me. We were wrassling. That's when he slipped."

"He fell?"

"Yep. Right down into that slot canyon there, right where they
found the bones later."

"Did the fall kill him?"

"Nope. Just banged him up some."

"So, you pushed the rock down there to finish him off?

"It was him or me."

"And you never told anyone what happened?"

"Never did before."

"Why did you just tell me?"

"Don't matter no more, I guess, and somebody ought to know.
It's history."

They sat silently for a moment.

"You know, Mr. Klein, I appreciate hearing the story," Tom said. "I'm glad I'm the one you told it to."

The door opened.

"There you are!" a young woman said. "We've been worried sick!"

She turned to Tom.

"I don't believe we've met," she said. "I'm Melody Anderson. I work for the Kleins, up at the ranch."

"Nice to meet you," Tom said.

"Mr. Klein wanders off sometimes, but he's never gone this far from home," she explained. "He's never gone off in his jeep before. I can't guess where he found the key."

"Mr. Klein seems to be just fine," Tom said. "We've been having a very nice talk about uranium mining."

"That's nice," she smiled. "He likes to remember the olden days. Thank you for taking care of him. Let's go home, Mr. Klein."

The King meekly followed his caretaker out the door.

Chapter 20

HISTORY IS ABOUT US

Tom was used to being handed information. This was his most salient quality, the apparently innate characteristic that made him an effective reporter. He might ask himself why complete strangers so often trusted him and spilled their guts within minutes of first meeting him. Was it because he had an open expression and was good-looking without being so handsome as to be intimidating? Because his build was average, and he didn't appear like a physical threat? Was he so neutral in the way he presented himself that he was perceived as a blank slate upon which the people he interviewed felt safe to inscribe their own versions of reality?

And yet, though he was used to being taken into the confidence of strangers, the confession of the Uranium King staggered him. Was he now called upon to write it down and publish it?

Of what use was the confession if it remained a secret? But the opposite question — of what use would Klein's biography be if it were to be written? — was equally without a clear answer.

The story of how Dick Klein and Whispering Jim came to fatal blows over their strike had the quality of a founding myth, and not just the founding of a family empire that inevitably collapsed in vitriol and bitterness. This was a narrative that suggested that uranium itself was a substance so potent in its destructiveness that it instantly corrupted the men who dug it out of the earth — before it subsequently undid everything else that it touched. But this was mere metaphor, of lyrical interest only, while the notion of justice for Whispering Jim, after all these years, with Klein near the end of his life and obviously suffering from dementia, was even less than that: It was an abstraction.

In addition to an apparently crystal-clear memory of how he found the Whispering Jim a half-century before, and how he had secured sole ownership of it by dispatching his partner, Klein talked knowledgeably about the current state of the world's energy balance. It was an odd trick of the brain that a man so obviously in the grip of senility could be so coherent on selected subjects. There was a basis in reality for Klein's declaration that he was reopening the Whispering Jim. Major mining companies were poking around and making provisional plans to resume mining and milling uranium on the West End, so why not UK Mining? Of course, it was far more likely that Albert Klein, who unquestionably ran the old man's affairs, would have already sold the claim to one of the multinationals with the resources to pay for it handsomely if it truly had remaining value.

More immediately, Tom wondered, why now? Was it just a coincidence that the Uranium King had turned up on Naturita's deserted main street at this moment? Or had something motivated him to bolt the seclusion of his home on North Mountain for the first time in years? Even an old man's dementia might have its reasons.

Tom's options were limited, but he could make a move: he could report in the pages of the Forum the King's announcement that he was planning to reopen the Whispering Jim. From the perspective of a legitimate journalist, it would be wildly irresponsible to publish a story based on nothing more than what Klein had just told him. A responsible editor would consider the reliability of the source and require confirmation that there was substance behind the claim that the Whispering Jim would reopen soon before publishing a story about it. But nobody was holding Tom up to those standards. He could publish the story with impunity; even as an old man's grandiosity talking, nothing more than his valedictory, the story was still of local interest. Klein was a figure of such local importance that his utterances were automatically newsworthy.

And so, that Friday, the Uranium King was back on page one, sharing top billing with the story Tom wrote about the pending reconstruction of Dead Man's Curve.

WHISPERING JIM TO REOPEN

Back to the Future?

By Tom Austin

Dick Klein isn't finished yet. At the age of 82, the Uranium King announced this week that he will reopen the Whispering Jim, the legendary mine that put the West End on the map as one of the world's richest mining districts. The region will be rich again, Klein predicts.

"Uranium is coming back," Klein said this week. The price is up, he explained, and will go higher because uranium is the world's best answer to the threat of global warming.

Klein announced that he is in the process of hiring as

many as a dozen men to work the mine. The ore will be shipped to the mill in Blanding, Klein said, though it is possible that production will be great enough to reopen his shuttered mill here.

Klein is exhibiting the same independence he did fifty years ago, and said he is operating without the backing of one of the major multinational corporations that have come to dominate the uranium business....

* * *

"Whispering Jim to reopen," Molly said cheerfully when she dropped off her history column. She was reading the headline of the paper she was carrying.

"Do you think he's got it in him?"

"At 82? How did he seem to you?"

"Well, apart from the fact he walked in the door wearing a bathrobe and slippers and looked like he'd just wandered away from the Alzheimer's wing of a nursing home, wasn't he always a bit odd?"

She laughed, but then considered the question seriously.

"He wasn't odd so much as he was always very determined," she said. "Whether it turned out he was right or wrong about something. He was right often enough that he could afford to be as odd as he wanted to be. I have to admit I thought we'd seen the last of him. Even Dick Klein can't live forever. But I guess I was wrong. The past is coming back."

"Why, you of all people know that the past isn't even past," Tom rejoined. "Didn't somebody famous say that?"

"I guess Faulkner knew a thing or two."

"It's hard to imagine the West End is quite as twisted as the Deep South," Tom said. "At least, there was no slavery here."

"There was, in a way. We had Utopianists. A lot of people who are still here after the uranium bust are descended from them."

"They weren't slaveholders…."

"Just polygamists. Same difference. Some practiced polygamy well into the 1970s, maybe longer, and that made for some family ties at least as complicated as Faulkner's, I'd say. Of course, nowadays most people don't like to be reminded of it. It's just so much easier for them to be mainstream Mormons. I respect that, which is why I leave it alone. I don't write or talk about it much. Polygamy. It's local history all right, but it's just too painful."

She hesitated, possibly to consider whether to change the subject or risk triggering the pain.

"Did you ever wonder how I ended up in New York, after growing up here?" she asked.

"Not really."

"Seventy years ago, when I was a girl, Center was 100 percent polygamist. It was perfectly normal that when I was 12, I was chosen to be married to my uncle Matthew Taylor, who was in his fifties. I would have been his third wife. The leader of our church, a man named Emerson Redd, made the match over my father's objections."

"At 12?"

"I was the youngest child in my family and my two older sisters had already been married off. My mother died giving birth to me. My father had started to question church teachings when he couldn't remarry and neither of my older brothers could find even one wife between them. The Redds didn't favor the Bufords, and there just weren't enough girls to go around. That's how it goes with polygamy. Too many men and not enough women. When Redd tried to take me, it was the last straw. My father and brothers decided to leave the church. Or they were excommunicated by Redd. I never got clear which came first. Either way, they and a few other unhappy bachelors started an LDS church affiliated with the church in Salt Lake. It was a schism among Mormons that played out in a lot of places after polygamy was outlawed in 1890.

"It took a lot of courage for the Bufords to take the stand that they did. It was difficult enough to be shunned by the community. And there was a risk of violent retribution, too. But they either couldn't or wouldn't leave. They had homesteaded, had built our house, had cleared fields, and most of all, they had spent years digging the ditch, and they had to dig the last quarter mile to our place all by themselves. We were the last place to get water. If you look, you'll see that even today there's nothing cultivated beyond our spread.

"My father and brothers were strong men, prepared to defend themselves. But it was too dangerous for me to stay. They were afraid I would be abducted, that Redd would just take me. So, they sent me back East to live with relatives. For my own protection. They said I could come home when it was safe."

Despite her calm recitation of her story, a tear rolled down Molly's face.

"The years went by and when the day finally came that my father said I could come home, it was too late."

"Too late for what?"

"For me to live a full life. I was already in my thirties by then, which was very old to be single in those years. I was a spinster! I had resisted creating personal ties in New York, never responded to a man's interest in me, thinking every day that I'd be called home."

"This would make a great subject for your next column."

"Now there's a novel idea! At the age of 84, I tell my sob story." She wiped away a tear. "I'm sorry," she said.

"It's never too late," Tom said. "Until you take your last breath. Think how you might feel if you wrote it."

"Maybe I just will." She laughed. "You don't suppose one of Redd's descendants would bother to come after me at this late date, do you?"

"You've been waiting for it to be far enough in the past to feel safe."

"Maybe so. The past isn't past but I'm finally old enough for it to feel safe. Dick Klein has come down from the mountain to mine uranium again, and you got me all rattled by bringing up Faulkner."

"I find it interesting that despite all the trauma, you still wanted to come home, and that you finally did."

"I had to retire somewhere that I could afford. My father died a long time ago, my brothers and sisters all died in the last ten years, but I have a lot of nieces and nephews here. I inherited the old homestead. As harsh as it is, this place speaks to me. The ditch my father and brothers dug still waters the fruit trees, and I've never tasted a better peach than the ones from our orchard. I look to the past and write my column to make sense of it all, but I suppose I've left out the history that's most important, to me, anyway. Until next week, at least. If I'm brave enough to do it, my next history column could be a barnburner! If you are prepared for the blowback."

"You're more than brave enough, and I'll publish it proudly."

"We forget an awful lot, don't we?"

"We do, but what specifically are you thinking about?"

"We forget that history can be so personal. That it's about people. Not only people like us, but us. It shapes our lives, even if we never document it. I often wonder what my life would have been like if I'd been married to Matthew Taylor at 12, instead of being sent away by my father. It might have been richer. I would have had children and grandchildren. I'd be surrounded by great-grandchildren by now."

Chapter 21

'YOU'VE BEEN WARNED.'

There's no fuckin' way uranium's coming back," Oak Winger argued, his voice rising.

"You can't just lock up natural resources," Art Fisher countered sharply.

Tom listened from his usual post at the Maverick counter, where he was eating dinner. The special was pot roast and mashed potatoes with brown gravy, and steamed carrots.

"It costs more to clean up after the uranium is mined than you make mining it, which doesn't make any economic sense," Winger continued. "It ruins the land forever."

"That's bull," Fisher said. "You don't know what the hell you're talking about. The places we mined around here were hot before we mined them. That's how we found them in the first place, with a Geiger counter. And those places where we found carnotite are not as hot now after we mined them out and cleaned them up as they were when we found them in the first place. We miners cleaned up after nature!"

"Naturita's not a mining town anymore and it's never going to be a mining town again. There's a bunch of us who live here for other reasons, and we don't want to see mining come back."

"Now you boys keep it nice," Sally Morgan called out. "We all like a good debate but hold down the cussing. This is a family joint. And no fistfights, neither."

The argument felt to Tom like a return to normalcy after the unwelcome drama of the previous few days and weeks, normalcy he had helped bring about by reporting that the Whispering Jim might soon reopen. The pros and cons of mining could incite strong feelings in the West End, but it was still a safer subject for Tom to investigate than the question of what happened to Ray Walker.

"Where do you stand on mining coming back?" Tom asked Sally, who was resting on her elbows near him.

"I was here when there was mining, and I've been here since it stopped," she shrugged. "Miners are good folk, I'll say that much."

Tom paid his bill and stepped out into the chilly night. Clouds tumbled overhead and a few flakes of snow blew past. He inhaled deeply and was braced by the freezing air that hit his lungs. Back when the town was booming and the mill was crushing and processing tons of uranium ore every hour, 24 hours a day, 364 days a year, a deep breath of air would have been contaminated by radioactive dust. It wasn't enough to cause immediate radiation sickness, and cancer would have been far off in the future. Tom had been told that the constant thump of the mill never annoyed and did not suggest to the populace at the time that they might become ill in the future, but instead was a source of comfort. It meant that people were working, making good money. After the thumping of the mill finally ceased, tens of millions of dollars were spent by the federal government to "reclaim" mined lands in and near Naturita, removing and burying toxic mine and mill tailings, and even the structures, equipment and tools that were rendered radioactive over the years, work that was still not complete. Presumably, under new rules, the government would ensure that new mining would not leave similar waste in need of costly removal.

Lost in his thoughts, Tom realized only later that there was a figure loitering in the shadows. But he had not registered any threat. He had crossed that highway so many times, so routinely, that he did it unconsciously. The sharp blow to his back dropped him to the ground hard, knocking the wind out of him. Gasping for air he rolled over onto his back and his attacker pinned him down with a heavy knee to his chest.

The man who had punched him leaned in so close that Tom's first impression of him was that he reeked of beer. Then he recognized him: his assailant was the same man, in his early twenties, with greasy long blond hair, hollow cheeks and pale blue eyes, who was behind the wheel of the pickup that had almost run him off the road as he fled the scene of his encounter with Brubaker.

"You're a nosey guy, aren't you newsman?" the man sneered, an intentional declaration that Tom was not the victim of a random crime.

"Who are you?"

"That don't matter. The important thing is, you've been warned. Stop messing with other peoples' shit, bro, or you're gonna get hurt. Hurt bad."

The man stood and coolly surveyed the mess he had made of Tom, assessing whether he'd done enough damage to effectively deliver the message. Apparently not quite: He gave Tom a poke in the side of his ribcage with the steel-reinforced toe of his boot, taking aim, followed by a precise, sharp kick. Then he melted back into the darkness.

. . .

After he was able to breathe again, Tom felt almost comfortable lying there on the street in front of his modest business in the center of Naturita, gazing up at the stormy night sky. The slightest movement hurt but the pain was not easy to locate; he hurt everywhere, so he lay as still as he could. He wondered if he'd been so badly injured that he would soon find himself on a stretcher in an ambulance on his way to the clinic, or whether he was just momentarily stunned and would be able to pull himself together. In either case he felt a kind of peace, even a sense of relief that the attack had been endured and the injury sustained, and that he had survived it. His assailant could have as easily killed him but chose not to.

Why?

If it had been a warm summer night, Tom might have lain there until dawn. Instead, growing cold, he hauled himself painfully inside. He pulled off his clothes and examined himself. He was developing an ugly bruise where he'd been kicked, probably had a broken a rib or two, but other than that his injuries looked superficial, a scrape on his hand and on his chin, where he'd broken his fall to the street. He took an Advil and lay down on his bed.

Tom had been warned, but warned about what? And by whom?

What chilled him most is that there were too many possibilities. Was he assaulted by a friend of Brubaker's? He knew his assailant was in the vicinity when Brubaker died and might even have found his still warm corpse, making the connection to Tom. The warning was explicitly to stop nosing around, so did that imply a connection to Ray Walker's disappearance? Was it something to do with Klein and uranium mining? Or meth? Or was it something altogether different, a story he had written or had published whose importance he didn't even recognize?

At that moment, Tom acutely felt his own lack of courage. He resolved to never ask another leading question or take any more confessions. He took the violent warning he had been administered to heart and interpreted it in the broadest possible way. He felt a powerful nostalgia for the simple security that came from publishing the Naturita school lunch menu, the obituaries of old-timers, and the routine news that came out of Naturita Town Board meetings.

He could envision no easy path back to the familiar and secure detachment of an experienced reporter, one who, having been bitten once too often, should have known better than to get personally involved in a story he was covering. But he vowed that if he found the way back to the comfort zone of professional cynicism, if he could somehow turn back the clock, he would never again put himself in the painful position he found himself in now.

Chapter 22

HIGH STAKES POKER

"Looks like you got yourself banged up," Sheriff Trace Martin said to Tom.

"Slipped on a patch of ice," Tom said as blandly as possible. "Last night. Right outside on the highway."

"You gotta watch yourself. That black ice can be dangerous. I fell and broke my collarbone some years back. Still got a pin in there, matter a fact. Doc said there was no point to removing it. Now it's part of me."

"Do you set off the security at airports?"

"Sometimes," the sheriff chuckled.

"I'm pretty bruised, but I don't think I broke anything," Tom said. "I won't need any pins."

"You ought to have it checked out all the same."

"I might just do that."

"But I'll tell you why I come by. We've got a suspicious death here on the West End that I'm investigating."

Tom felt his pulse quicken. For nearly a week he had feared and anticipated precisely this moment, and he had tried to prepare himself for it, imagining how it might unfold and rehearsing what he would do if and when it did. He had worked to supplant dread with something more functional, a steely resolve to do nothing to make the sheriff's job easier. He had remembered some wisdom from a P.D. James novel—in which, of course, every character was a suspect in the murder—to the effect that nothing that is said to an investigator can be unsaid whereas anything withheld can always be revealed later. With that sage advice in mind, he had resolved to act like a reporter by asking more questions than he was asked, a shield against saying too much. As recently as just a few moments earlier, before the sheriff's signature black cowboy hat filled the front doorway, Tom felt he was prepared, or as prepared as anyone in his situation could be. He had been surprisingly calm until the sheriff said the words "suspicious death."

Now he was further unnerved by his strong impression that the sheriff was studying him closely for his reaction to the news he had brought. Or was it only his imagination?

"Anyone I might know?"

Did Tom's voice sound as steady to the sheriff as it did to his own ears? Was he showing enough interest in the sheriff's revelation of a murder nearby? Or, possibly, he would express too much interest as the interview progressed.

"Trucker named Mark Brubaker. Lived alone out on East Bryant Mesa."

Tom shook his head: "Didn't know him, not that I know of anyway."

"Not many people did. And most would run the other way if they run into him."

Tom gave a slight nod.

"I'd like for you to write it up," Martin said. "Believe it or not, the newspaper can actually be of some help in a homicide investigation. Law enforcement wants the perp-a-*traitor* to know that we're after him."

"Well, it sounds like news. And I'm glad to be of service."

"Perp gets nervous, he'll be sure and make a mistake."

Which would be any traitor's just desserts, Tom thought, and especially a perp-a-traitor's, but then he quickly corrected himself. The sheriff had the demeanor of a buffoon, but he was shrewd, and Tom didn't want to make the mistake of underestimating him. So as if to agree with the sheriff and to acknowledge the sure inevitability of the perp's fatal mistake, he again nodded his understanding, trusting that his own case of jittery nerves was, at the moment at least, adequately concealed.

"What else can I report about the victim? Any survivors?"

"Wife. A Russian immigrant named Anya. But he was only married to her a couple of months, and she hasn't been seen in the county since late August or early September. Supposedly, she left him. Whereabouts unknown. Basically, she's an illegal, so she's likely laying low."

"Is she a suspect?"

"Let's just say we'd like to talk to her. If anyone knows where she's at, we'd appreciate it for them to give us a call."

Tom was scribbling notes.

"How did he die? And when?"

"My guess is he's been dead a week or so. Now I can't tell you the details of how he died or that might compromise the investigation."

"Of course."

"You know that cops never show all our cards."

"I guess if you're going to play poker, you'd better know how to bluff."

Tom winced at his unfortunate word choices. What had he killed Brubaker with? Wasn't it … a *poker*. Was he *bluffing* now?

"Why that's exactly right!" Martin exclaimed, grinning. "You play poker?"

"Used to. When I was in college."

"I bet you were good at it."

"I won a few hands. Lost some, too."

"Well, there's always luck involved," Martin allowed. "Luck of the draw, as they say. Nobody can be lucky all the time."

"No."

"You see, Tom, there's plenty of details only the killer knows," Martin explained. "And that can be useful to the investigation, especially when we're interviewing a suspect."

Tom quickly asked a question to make it clear that he, for one, had no such inside knowledge.

"Was Brubaker shot?"

"We're gonna have to wait on an autopsy to know the exact cause of death," the sheriff said. "Corpse was pretty decomposed by the time we got there. But we know the death is suspicious because the killer tried to cover his tracks and made a real mess of it. Flooded the place and broke all the windows. But all he really accomplished is that he left a whole bunch of additional clues. If he hadn't have done that, we might not have looked further. We might have just assumed it was some kind a bloody accident. Probably not, but… maybe."

The sheriff shrugged as if to comment on the general foolishness of the criminal class, and Tom was in no position to disagree because he was silently kicking himself. In his panic, on his second visit to the shack, when he discovered that the fire poker was missing and reacted by flooding Brubaker's shack and breaking all the windows, he had been too clever by half. How many clues had he left?

"Can you keep that last part, how we determined it was a murder, off-the-record?" Martin asked. "I've said too much."

"Sure thing," Tom said, but he wondered if the sheriff had a reason for wanting Tom alone to know about the open taps and broken windows. Off-the-record might be awfully convenient if, in fact, the sheriff had a reason to suspect Tom; he could be using it to tighten the screws and make the perp nervous and more prone to a foolish mistake.

"I'll tell you what," the sheriff continued. "And this is still off-the-record. Just be thankful you're not the one having to analyze the crime scene. It's as nasty and as p.u.-trid as anything I've seen in my near-forty years in law enforcement."

"That bad?"

"You can't imagine," the sheriff said, but of course, with the image of Brubaker's bloated corpse fresh in his mind, Tom could all-too-easily imagine, almost recoiling at his memory of the stench.

"Back on-the-record?" Tom asked, and Martin nodded his assent. "Got any suspects?"

"We've got some ideas. Some good leads to follow."

"Can you say more?"

Martin pushed back in his chair and frowned.

"You can say there is some evidence that it might be related to the meth trade," he said. "That'll reassure the honest public that they've got nothing to fear. We're not dealing with something random here. But I don't want to go into much detail about that. Not yet.

"Back off-the-record, this Brubaker was one nasty cocksucker, if you'll pardon my French. He was mixed up with meth, that much is for sure, like I told you, we've got evidence of that, and God knows what else he did for his jollies. Nothing nice, I promise you. Now, I don't like to speak ill of the dead, but he was about as far from a respectable citizen as a man can get. He was a complete lowlife, to say it plain. And I just hate to spend my time and public resources looking for his killer because the truth is that the world is a better place without him in it. There's no doubt about that. But you see, Tom, I don't have that discretion, not to investigate."

"Of course not."

Was it an accident that of all the French slurs the sheriff might have employed, he called Brubaker a cocksucker? Was he offering Tom some kind of out? Or, to the contrary, by stating that he had no choice but to investigate, was Martin cautioning Tom that there was no way out?

"It doesn't really sound all that complicated, sheriff," Tom said. "Sounds like you've got some kind of drug deal gone bad."

"That'd be a good guess. But it's not the only angle I'm looking at."

Tom felt sure that he knew exactly what the sheriff was suggesting. But he still couldn't tell whether the reference to another angle was intended as a warning. If Martin knew that Tom was involved in Brubaker's death, would he or could he be this subtle? And if he didn't know about the blood on Tom's hands, would he be capable of this much ambiguity? Tom guessed that he was crediting Martin with more in the way of both subtlety and ambiguity than could possibly have been intentional. But how much more? In Tom's mind, he and Martin were sitting across from each other at the poker table. Tom was bluffing, holding a pair of measly deuces, but what about Martin? What was he holding?

Most essentially, Tom knew that both he and Sheriff Martin knew that there were crucial connections between Brubaker and Ray Walker, although neither was admitting it to the other. Tom knew that the sheriff was aware of those connections because Sarah Walker had told him as much. But was the sheriff aware that Tom had investigated the Walker disappearance and that he, too, knew about the ties between Walker and Brubaker? Did Martin assume that Sarah told both of them the same story about the friendship between Ray and Anya? If the sheriff read the paper, he knew Tom had interviewed Sarah, so he certainly knew it was a possibility. But had Sarah asked the reporter to keep her missing husband's awkward relationship with a beautiful foreign woman off-the-record? Or had Tom kept it out of print on his own?

Just a few moments earlier, when the sheriff had asked Tom if he knew Brubaker, Tom had lied, recommitting himself to a strategy of deception. Tom's mind was racing quickly enough that he had time to ask himself if the alternative—if folding his cards and giving up the hand, describing how he had come to kill Brubaker—might not have been the better poker play. Perhaps it would have been, had he reported the incident right after it happened, before more cards were dealt. But it was too late, Tom had calculated, his behavior had been too questionable, making the truth a far riskier proposition. He asked himself: Would he have behaved so questionably if, in the immediate aftermath of Brubaker's death, he had not been tweaking? If the sheriff knew that all-important detail, that Brubaker had forcibly injected him with meth, would it make a difference? Or would Martin prefer to believe, for reasons of his own, that Tom had chosen to mainline the drug?

Tom could guess at least some of what the sheriff had to be thinking. Martin had, according to Sarah, assumed that Ray had run off with Anya. He had almost certainly interviewed Brubaker in the aftermath of Ray's disappearance, and had either satisfied himself that Brubaker had nothing to do with whatever happened to Ray or he had chosen not to investigate that possibility. By the time Tom met him, Brubaker asserted he was happy to be rid of Anya. Even if he told Martin the same thing, it would be logical for the sheriff to theorize now that Walker had subsequently killed Brubaker, which would be precisely the inverse of a theory Tom had nursed (but could still be the truth): that Brubaker killed Walker.

In any case, Martin had a compelling reason to look for Anya Nemerov now, in his investigation of Brubaker's murder. Tom had removed the clues pointing to Anya's location from Ray's file cabinet, but Martin might find other means to track her down. If Martin did find Anya in Albuquerque, he would quickly learn that Ray Walker was not there. Unless, it suddenly occurred to Tom, Ray *was* there, and Anya had deceived him. But that was unlikely. What was much likelier is that Anya would tell the sheriff about her conviction that Brubaker had harmed Ray. That could lead her to describe Tom's visit with her. Then the sheriff would ask himself why Tom had not said anything during this very interview, and he would trace Tom's subsequent move … straight to Brubaker's shack in precisely the time period that Brubaker was killed.

What then, Tom asked himself, should he do? Since Martin chose not to tie Brubaker's death to Ray Walker's disappearance, should he allow it to remain unspoken and off-the-record? Or should he broach the subject himself? To go there would send his interview with the sheriff in a potentially dangerous direction. But if he did not go there now, he would cast himself under an even darker cloud of suspicion if and when the sheriff found Anya and discovered on his own that Tom knew much more than he'd admitted to.

Was there, behind one of these two doors, a lady, and behind the other a tiger? If Tom opened the door to the tiger, he would never know if there was a lady behind the other, because he would be dead. Moreover, it was every bit as likely that there were tigers behind both doors.

That calculation left Tom with no alternative but to push the last of his small pile of chips to the center of the table.

"When you asked me if I knew Brubaker, I said I didn't, and that's true," Tom said. "I never met him. But I've heard of him. Sarah Walker told me that Ray and Brubaker's wife were friends. In fact, she worked for Ray."

"That's right."

The sheriff was squinting, as if he were scrutinizing Tom's poker face for a tell, maybe a quick pulse in his neck or an unnatural movement of his eyes. Tom met Martin's gaze directly.

"She thinks you believe they were having an affair."

"They could have been."

"And she told me that Ray helped Brubaker's wife run away."

"I believe she said something like that."

"She said you figure Ray ran off with her."

"I might."

"But if they were having an affair, then Brubaker could have had something to do with Ray's disappearance. Or Ray with Brubaker's death."

"That sounds pretty good, Tom," Martin said. "It's tight. But maybe it's too tight. Sometimes a coincidence like that leads an investigation astray."

"But you must have your suspicions."

"I'm just gonna have to say 'no comment' on all of that," Martin said. "It's hy-po-thetical, and this investigation is just beginning. I'm sure you can understand. Like you said, a criminal investigation is a lot like a game of *poker*. There's things we know and there's things we think we know and there's things we know we don't know and things we don't know we don't know. Same thing is true for the perp.

"And just like in *poker*, unless somebody gets lucky, the winner is the one who figures all those angles better than the other guy."

Was the sheriff really emphasizing the word poker, Tom wondered. Or was Tom putting it in italics all by himself?

• • •

After the sheriff left, Tom realized that his heart was still pounding. He had given the sheriff something valuable, a hint that he, Tom, was capable of withholding information. He was a player. But to what end? What more might Tom know? The sheriff had to be wondering, if he didn't already know.

There were things Sheriff Martin knew and things the sheriff thought he knew and things the sheriff didn't know, and Tom could not know where the extent of his own investigation of the Walker disappearance and his responsibility for Brubaker's death fit along that spectrum. On the other side of the equation, as the sheriff had further observed, there were things the perp knew, things he thought he knew, and things he didn't know.

Tom breathed deeply to calm himself down. He had escaped the sheriff's inquiry, at least for now. Encouraging Martin's pursuit of the plausible theory that Ray might have killed Brubaker might distract him for a while. By the same token, not telling the sheriff that he had met Anya and knew where she was preserved the possibility, however remote, that he wouldn't be able to find her. If the sheriff did find Anya, Tom would probably find himself in trouble that he couldn't easily talk his way out of, but there was nothing to be done about that now.

Tom was feeling increasingly trapped, the air having become too thick to breathe. In addition to Tom's concern about where the sheriff's investigation might lead, there was the deeply worrisome question of what happened to the incriminating fire poker, which had most likely been taken by the longhaired punk who had mugged him. Did the longhair discover Brubaker's body after he saw Tom fleeing the scene, take the fire poker, and later rough Tom up for good measure, all prior to a blackmail demand that was yet to be presented? But why would anyone blackmail Tom, who was conspicuously close to penniless? More likely, the longhair, who was hardly a law-abiding citizen himself, had reported Brubaker's death to the sheriff, which would suggest not only that Martin himself might have the fire poker by now, but that he was corrupt and up to his fat, red neck in whatever treachery Tom had stumbled into.

If not from the longhair, how else would the sheriff have learned about the suspicious death of a hermit nobody knew? Tom could imagine only one other possibility. He found himself hoping that Brubaker was not as friendless as he had imagined, but that someone had stopped by to visit or check in on him, not having heard from him in a while, and had discovered him dead. Then the sheriff could be legitimately investigating Brubaker's death. In that case, though, Tom could still find himself in Martin's crosshairs.

Wherever he looked, Tom could find little solace. In any case, his next move was both clear and unavoidable. It was only Friday, but he started writing a story for publication in the next Thursday's paper. Writing it early would allow him plenty of time to read and reread the article before it was printed, fine-tuning it to make certain he reported enough about Brubaker's death for the story to seem complete but not so much that it revealed more than it should; to ensure, according to an increasingly complex calculus, that he faithfully reported what should be on-the-record and omitted what should not.

Saying too little could be as risky as saying too much, and the slightest miscalculation either way could be disastrous, leading to his arrest, trial, and imprisonment, maybe even to the death penalty. With so much at stake, Tom was uncomfortably reminded of his lost career in big city journalism, a humiliation that he hoped he had put far in his past. His failing then had been a sloppy disregard for the truth, as if the accuracy of details didn't matter in writing stories of mere human interest, like the story of a home-schooled whiz kid's university scholarship offers, as opposed to hard news, like a murder investigation. Now he was writing a fabrication out of a deep regard in his own mind for the distinction between hard facts that may be misleading—that he had killed Brubaker, for example—and some species of deeper truth that may be difficult for any outside observer to fully comprehend, namely that he had killed Brubaker in self-defense and was wise, for a host of reasons, not to report it to the authorities.

Of course, Tom might well be justifying his own self-interest. Truth might be a noble ideal, incapable of corruption or taint, a pure virtue that sometimes demands nothing less than self-sacrifice. If so, then deception must always be wrong; and a lie is always a lie. Someday, but not now, Tom told himself, he would wrestle with those vexing philosophical questions, which could be reduced to one overarching question: Was Tom a good man, overall, in the larger scheme of things? Or was he just another cheat?

If not sooner, Tom vowed to take the matter up on his deathbed.

Now, he just worked to get the story of a man's suspicious demise ready for publication in a small-town newspaper. He was so skilled at his craft that in some respects it was easy, despite the fact that the purported mystery at the story's center—so far as the man writing it was concerned—was not mysterious at all.

SHERIFF REPORTS SUSPICIOUS DEATH

By Tom Austin

The death of a West End resident last week appears to be suspicious in nature, according to Montrose County Sheriff Trace Martin.

The body of Mark L. Brubaker was discovered on Wednesday in his remote home on East Bryant Mesa. Brubaker, 34, was a loner, and had virtually no contacts with his neighbors, the sheriff said. He worked as a long-distance truck driver.

Brubaker had been dead about a week when his body was found, Martin said. Martin said he could not state a cause of death, pending an autopsy, but that Brubaker's home appeared to be the scene of a violent encounter. Though he was unable to reveal details, he did suggest that one line of investigation involves the possibility that the incident could be related to the region's methamphetamine trade.

In what the sheriff cautioned could be a mere coincidence, Brubaker's wife, Anya Nemerov-Brubaker, a Russian immigrant, was employed by Ray Walker, the Naturita auto mechanic who disappeared without a trace three weeks ago. Nemerov-Brubaker last drew a paycheck from Walker Auto Repair approximately three weeks prior to that, the sheriff said, and her current whereabouts are unknown.

"We would like to talk to her," the sheriff said, and he asked that if anyone knows where Nemerov-Brubaker might be, they should call his office at 970 355-3333.

Martin declined detailed comment when asked if he believes the disappearance of Ray Walker, the absence of Anya Nemerov-Brubaker, and the suspicious death of Mark Brubaker could in any way be related.

"Sometimes a coincidence leads an investigation astray," the sheriff said. "This investigation is just beginning."

Clearly the story could not be published as Tom had written it. Despite his best efforts at obfuscation, rereading his own first draft, Tom saw that it would very likely serve as his obituary it if were published. When you put something into writing, he mused, and especially if it is published, it becomes part of the material world and is impossible to erase. So it was with the unavoidable truth that the misfortunes of Ray Walker, Anya Nemerov and Mark Brubaker must be inextricably related. It would have to be revealed, eventually, one way or another, that he, Tom Austin, was the missing link.

Tom might not die peacefully of old age at the West End Clinic after all, as he had once imagined, or at the Manor Nursing Home in Cortez, possibly in the same room now occupied by Elizabeth Walker. Instead, he now seemed destined to be swept up in the vortex of a West End conspiracy whose dimensions he could just barely discern. He might well meet a violent end in the next five minutes, five hours, or five days, or he might die in prison.

As consolation, there was time for Tom to find a way to rewrite the story before he was forced to publish it—if he could only figure out how. There might yet be a way out of the devious trap he had managed to set for himself. But his escape would require not only more ingenuity, but also a dramatic turn of events that Tom could neither foresee nor imagine. He had only a few precious days' time to work things out, or for fate to lend a hand, with nothing less routine than his own impending newspaper deadline ticking away the minutes and hours to his probable doom.

Chapter 23

ANOTHER TWEAKER CRASHES

S arah was out of breath, having run to the Forum office as fast as she could from the school, where she had just finished work. She was preoccupied but stopped short when she saw Tom's bandaged chin.

"What happened to you?"

"Tripped and fell."

"Oh."

"Last night, outside. Patch of ice."

She didn't ask a further question because the subject on her mind was so much more pressing.

"Angie is in jail," she said. "I need to go up to Telluride."

Tom didn't move. He had been deeply immersed in his own troubles since the visit from the sheriff that morning and had no need of somebody else's. The temptation was strong to push Sarah away, or to turn the tables and ask her to help him, to plead weakness, exhaustion, indifference, or ordinary selfishness. Even as his life was collapsing in on him, putting him under pressure that was becoming more unbearable the more he dwelled on it, Sarah's life was clearly proceeding on its own catastrophic course. There seemed to be no stopping it.

"The baby's been taken by social services," Sarah said. "They'll put him in foster care if I don't go now and he'll be there all weekend."

She answered his silence by adding, "I thought maybe you could come with me. I don't know who else to ask."

"OK," he said, feeling instantly lighter. "Let's go."

Movement, he realized, would be an improvement over sitting in his office waiting for the other shoe to drop. At the same time, to become re-engaged with Sarah at this moment, putting his own misery on the back burner in order to tend to hers, would serve as a respite.

Topping the hill as they drove up and out of the San Miguel River valley to Wright's Mesa, Tom and Sarah could not see the San Miguel Mountains ahead; they were wrapped in thick clouds. The previous evening's storm had moved east from Naturita. It was snowing in the high country.

Sarah needed him, Tom thought. She could have gone alone to bail her daughter out of jail and rescue her grandson, but she felt the need for support and wasn't afraid to ask him for it. Or he was the only alternative. He might have imagined given all the concern voiced in the first week after Ray disappeared, with the community rallying around so vocally and devoting itself to the search, that there would be plenty of other people Sarah could lean on. But he remembered how desolate things got just a few weeks after his father's death, when for a time he was his mother's primary source of emotional support. After the official mourning is over and daily life returns for everyone else, the family's real sense of loss sets in for a long winter.

And yet, Tom wondered, why him? When had he and Sarah

bonded to the point that she turned to him first when faced with a new crisis? Admittedly, the two of them shared something profound. She must have sensed, particularly after Brubaker's death, that Ray Walker's disappearance had become almost as deeply personal for him as it was for her. By insistently looking for Ray over her objections, Tom had forced himself into her life. He had become deeply entangled. Now, in a sharp reversal, as if it were a matter of establishing some basic physical equilibrium, she had asked for his help, and he had agreed. Their unusual courtship included full- and half-steps forward, backward, and to the side—by both of them.

Turning his thoughts over, Tom asked himself why he didn't tell her immediately, as she sat next to him in the car, about Brubaker's death; she would hear about it soon enough, certainly no later than the next Thursday, when the paper was published. He understood that to bring it up would lead to a discussion he was not yet prepared to have. What would he say when she speculated about who might have killed Brubaker? That her missing husband was the sheriff's preferred suspect? Or that he, Tom, was the guilty party? Neither option was palatable, and the only other possibility, that Brubaker's killing was completely unrelated to Ray's disappearance, would surely seem incredible to Sarah. Tom resorted to misdirection.

"What about Craig?"

"I can't reach him."

After traversing the mesa, the road began the climb to Telluride and there the snow began, an abrupt transition to an entirely different climatic zone. Just as the snow on the road forced Tom to slow down to a crawl, Sarah began talking again.

"She got fired from her job. They accused her of taking some jewelry from a guest's room and called the cops. And when the cops got there, she started cursing at them. They charged her with resisting arrest and found the jewelry in her pocket."

"Jesus."

"Then because she was in jail, she couldn't get Tyler from daycare, and social services got involved. A social worker called me and told me the whole thing."

Telluride was not in Montrose County; they were outside Sheriff Martin's domain, in a much richer county. The San Miguel County Jail was a modern fortress of steel and concrete, its high walls capped by concertina wire, to Tom's eye far more formidable than a resort area jail needed to have been. It was set off by itself on a side road where tourists would never see it.

"I'm here about Angela Pellison," Sarah told the deputy sitting at the front desk. "And her baby."

"Have a seat," the woman said.

"How many prisoners can this jail hold?" Tom asked.

The deputy looked at him quizzically.

"Professional curiosity," Tom explained, handing her a business card. "I publish the Forum down in Naturita."

"Forty," the jailer said. "Thirty men, ten women."

"A lot of crime around here?"

"More than people know."

"DUIs?"

"Not only. I'd say about as much domestic abuse and a lot of dis-orderlies after the bars close. You'd be surprised what goes on after one a.m…"

Tom silently completed her thought: …after all the decent people have gone to bed. Only the cops and the miscreants themselves fully experience life in society's underbelly.

A crying baby announced the arrival of the woman carrying him. Sarah jumped to take Tyler from her.

"I'm Rachel Smith," the woman said. "I'm with San Miguel County Social Services. There's a room in the back where we can talk."

She looked over at Tom.

"Friend of the family. Tom Austin."

"Would you like Tom to join us?" Rachel asked Sarah, who nodded.

"Thank you for coming so quickly," Rachel said when they reached the barren room, harshly lit, and furnished with nothing more than a card table and metal folding chairs. Apart from saving taxpayer dollars, the sheriff apparently had no interest in making people feel comfortable there.

"The baby, his name is Tyler, isn't it? I'm afraid he may not be right. Colic or something worse. He'll need to see a doctor as soon as possible for a complete evaluation. He's more than fussy. He's impossible to comfort."

Indeed, Tyler was still wailing.

"He's just been away from his mother too long," Sarah said. "He's probably just hungry. I've got a bottle for him."

She rocked Tyler in her arms as she rummaged through her bag for the bottle.

"My job is to protect the child. I'm not confident he'll be safe with his mother," the social worker said.

"He'll be safe with me. I'm his grandmother."

"We much prefer to place a child with a close family member when we can," the woman said, with a warm smile. "But once a child is referred to us, it can get tricky. I can release Tyler to you because you are his grandmother, and you have a clean record. I checked because I was hoping we wouldn't have to place him in foster care. But if you take him, you'll have to agree to certain conditions. And we'll have to follow up and make sure he's being properly cared for."

"Angie can take care of him."

"I can't take that chance. We see many cases of child neglect like this stemming from methamphetamine addiction. We don't see many… let me correct myself … we *never* see this sort of situation improve quickly."

Sarah gasped. "What do you mean addiction?"

"Tyler was probably born with meth in his system."

"That's just not possible."

"Angie's only been charged with felony theft and resisting arrest," Rachel persisted. "The police didn't find any drugs on her, or they would have charged her with possession, too. But it seems clear she was high on meth, or she wouldn't have been so belligerent. She exhibits all of the symptoms. Her moodiness is quite striking. You need to get her some help."

Sarah was having such a difficult time absorbing what she was being told that the social worker turned to Tom for help in getting through.

"We can refer you to several good drug rehabilitation programs. And if you need financial assistance, the state might be able to help out some."

"I'm just a friend," Tom said, his hands raised in a defensive posture.

"Thank you," Sarah said. "We'll do whatever we have to do."

"You can bond Angie out now if you're prepared to take responsibility for her."

"Of course. She's my daughter."

"But I need absolute assurances from you that you will protect the baby. You can't leave him alone with her. Not even for a few minutes. You have to agree to wean him immediately, if he's still breastfeeding. And more than assurances, we'll need to schedule a home visit for Monday to evaluate the conditions at your home and we'll need to devise an appropriate monitoring plan. You need to assume legal responsibility, at least temporarily. Are you prepared to do all that?"

Sarah sighed. "If I have to," she said.

As Tom witnessed this exchange between Sarah and the social worker to the sound of Tyler's anguished cries, he wondered when he could make his escape.

Maybe, he thought darkly, Ray had fled after all. Anyone would want to run from the train wreck that Angie presented. So how exactly had he been sucked in?

. . .

Angie wasn't tweaking by the time they saw her; she had crashed. Dressed in an orange jumpsuit, there was none of her normal air of defiance; she looked defeated and afraid. Her face was flushed, and she shuddered involuntarily every twenty or thirty seconds.

"Mommy," she said, when she saw Sarah, and she grabbed Tyler, who had finally fallen asleep in his grandmother's arms. She gazed into his face with an unnatural intensity and held him too tightly, waking him up. He started bawling again.

"Let me, honey," Sarah said, taking Tyler back.

Rachel explained that she was releasing Tyler not to Angie, but to Sarah, adding that Angie could be with Tyler only when Sarah was present, until there was time to do a thorough evaluation.

"Do I have to agree?" Angie asked.

"If you don't, I'll put Tyler in foster care."

Angie made a show of trying to read the document Rachel put before her, as a conspicuous demonstration that she was a responsible adult, but she gave up quickly.

"Where do I sign?" she asked, with plain irritation.

Tom could see that the social worker was unsure if she was making the right call by releasing the baby to Sarah. He felt she was looking to him for reassurance when she glanced in his direction. He nodded slightly, hoping that she would read his deep misgivings—and not his acquiescence, much less his endorsement—in his admittedly subtle expression. *Please*, he was thinking, as if thinking it hard enough could transmit his strong advice telepathically to the social worker without his having to say it out loud, as if prayer might actually work sometimes, *please put the baby in foster care.*

No such luck. A half hour later he was back in his car, driving down the canyon, with Sarah, Angie, and Tyler riding in the back seat.

"I've already lost Ray," he heard Sarah say. "I can't stand the thought of losing you, too. But Angie, I want you to know that I absolutely refuse to lose Tyler."

"Don't fucking start in. Not now." Angie's voice was hoarse. "I just got out of fuckin' jail."

"Where is Craig?"

"I don't know."

"You're a mother now. You have a duty, not just to yourself. You have your baby, another human being, to think about."

No reply.

"You promised you'd stop taking meth."

No reply.

"The social worker thinks that Tyler has meth in his system. She says you can't breastfeed him anymore."

"Fuck her! She's full of shit. He's just a cranky baby. You even told me some babies are difficult.... You said it's colic. Plus, I hate breastfeeding anyway."

"Meth…."

"Will you stop fucking talking about meth? You don't know any-thing about it!"

"*Something* changed you, Angie. And if it's not meth, I don't know what it is. What happened to my sweet little girl?"

"She fuckin' grew up. It happens."

"You didn't just promise me. You promised Ray…."

"Well Ray isn't exactly here, is he?" Angie said coldly. "He gave up and he left. So, I guess you'll just have to figure out how to han-dle me all by yourself."

"She's not by herself," Tom interjected, rising to Sarah's defense, rejecting the cruel insinuation that Ray Walker had given up on his wife. He would have to admit, if he kept talking, that he wouldn't have blamed Ray for giving up on his daughter. So he shut up.

"Oh great," Angie groaned. "Now this one wants to play daddy."

With that, she started sobbing theatrically, as if her father's aban-donment of her, or the mere mention of it, or more pointedly Tom's gall in trying to assume Ray's role in her life, entitled her to every bit of the trauma she was suffering. Clearly there had been strong words exchanged about Angie's meth habit before Ray disappeared. Had Ray been able to keep his daughter off drugs while he was around, making her current relapse a consequence of his not being around? Or had Angie's addiction somehow exposed her father to risk? Could that explain Sarah's evasiveness, a concern that to uncover what had happened to Ray could pose a similar risk to her daughter?

But Ray had not been able to keep his daughter away from meth in the first place, and Craig clearly exerted a strong contrary influ-ence. Angie would probably be going through exactly the same his-trionics now if it had been Ray and not Tom who had driven with

Sarah to Telluride to bail their daughter out of jail and rescue their grandchild. If Ray's disappearance and Angie's dissolution were tied together, the link did not need to be so direct as cause-and-effect. It was as likely to be something in the water they both drank and the forbidding landscape they shared.

"Oh, honey, it will be all right," Sarah said reassuringly. "Somehow…."

But neither Angie nor Tyler stopped bawling, and Tom was confident that Angie wouldn't be all right, at least not anytime soon. He was impressed by Sarah's devotion to her broken daughter, which so easily transcended their current misery. He could only assume that a parent easily remembers back to when the child was still malleable and full of promise, another example of how the past can trump the present. He thought back to his one previous encounter with Angie, when she was an adolescent, and how, then, talking about the mountain lion she had bagged, she had struck him only as unformed, more a vessel for Ray's hopes than a teenager with meaningful aspirations or interests of her own. Now she was totally debauched by meth, but beneath her crystalline armor there must be a warm-blooded person who once had the capacity to be molded into somebody with a soul. One thing she clearly did not lack for was the love of her parents. So, what had gone so terribly wrong? As Sarah had suggested, meth was a sufficient explanation, even though a drug counselor would surely insist that there was something more, something deeply psychological, behind the addiction.

Not another word was spoken on the rest of the drive to Naturita, and when they reached the doublewide, Angie dragged herself to the room she had shared with her brother before she had moved out to live with Craig, and she slammed the door behind her.

"What's wrong with her?" asked Ray Jr., who was sitting at the kitchen table doing homework.

"She got herself arrested," Sarah said dully.

"Arrested? Like jail arrested? Whoa…."

He was already on her way to the bedroom to learn the glamorous details for himself.

"What do I do now?" Sarah asked, the whimpering baby in her arms.

If only out of necessity, because Ray was gone, she had flung open the door to the chaos of her life. For multiple reasons of his own, not least the simple circumstance of his being there, he had walked in.

"Maybe I can help," he found himself saying.

Chapter 24

NOBODY CHOOSES WHO THEY'RE BORN TO

Craig was too big for Sarah's doublewide. They were watching a Broncos' game. Craig sat on the sofa, tapping his foot, looming over the jar of Picante salsa and bag of Doritos on the coffee table. Angie and Sarah were in the kitchen washing up. The baby was finally sleeping in a bassinette. Ray Jr. was outside, shooting hoops.

Craig had turned up on Saturday morning, the day after Angie was arrested, with a tall tale of having lost his cell phone and his truck getting stuck in the snow because he didn't expect snow so early and forgot his tire chains at home. He had quickly taken charge.

No fuckin' way was he gonna allow his wife to lose custody of their kid, he proclaimed. He'd hire a lawyer on Monday, and they'd prove it was all a gigantic misunderstanding.

What meth? His wife didn't do meth, he asserted. They couldn't prove a thing. End of discussion.

He only reluctantly agreed to leave Tyler at Sarah's house until the entire mess was straightened out, but just to avoid any more complications. They would all stay there together.

Sarah seemed to buy it wholesale, grateful that someone was taking charge, and though Tom was skeptical he was also happy to cede authority to the blowhard. He wasn't even sure why he'd accepted Sarah's invitation to a Sunday afternoon barbecue.

"You could really do something with that paper," Craig said.

"What do you think?" Tom asked.

"Running a paper, you like, run the town. You probably never have to pay for anything. Just trade it all out. Trade favors. Trade for ads."

"Not quite. The printer requires cash."

"I might like to run a newspaper someday," Craig said. "I could see myself doing that. Writing stories. Write down what happens. That can't be hard. But not here. This goddamn town is too fuckin' small... Shit!" he exclaimed as Champ Bailey failed to deflect a pass. "What the fuck is wrong with that guy? For the millions they pay him, fuck! I could have picked that fucker off myself. Goddamn donkeys!"

He leaned around to shout at Angie in the kitchen.

"Hey hon, could you bring me another Bud? I think Tom here could use another one, too."

"I'm good."

"I'm working on this house up near Telluride, twenty-fucking-thousand-square-feet," Craig said. "*Plus* a caretaker unit. Guy started up some cable channel or something. We're doing this *media* room, fuck, it's like a movie theater, a private movie theater, with a row of those seats they have at the movies that rock back, except bigger. And there's a room just for wine. A wine *cellar*. It's got a hot tub on this deck in the back, and we're building a pond, you know, their own private *trout* pond or something. It's up at about 10,000 feet with this view of the San Miguels."

He sucked on his beer, and looked off into the distance as if he were formulating a thought. Then he slapped Tom on the knee.

"What the hell is wrong with us, huh, Tom?" He laughed. "How come you and me don't have a *media* room and a *wine* cellar?"

"Good question."

"We've got to finish the house by Christmas because they're coming up for the holidays. These rich assholes are gonna come up from sea level for Christmas and they're gonna find out that they can't fuckin' breathe at that altitude. Ha! Serves 'em right."

His attention was suddenly diverted by the television.

"Wooo-hoo! Donkeys score! D'you see that, Angie? Great fuckin' interception! Champ Bailey! What a stud!"

Angie set a bag of Oreos on the table and sat across from Craig.

"Get your sweet butt over here," Craig said, patting the empty space on the sofa next to him. Angie obeyed and Sarah took Angie's place on a tattered armchair.

"Well, I guess Angie and I don't need to ask if we can leave Tyler with you and go catch a movie in Junction," he grinned. "You signed a fuckin' paper taking responsibility for him!"

* * *

Thump. Thump. Thump. Pling. The sound of Ray Jr. outside, shooting hoops. *Thump, thump....*

"Craig's got no idea what kind of trouble he's in," Tom said. "And you are gonna end up raising the baby."

"I can't think about that right now. I'm just glad Angie's out of jail."

As they sat there quietly, Tom's thoughts were leaping ahead. Sarah couldn't think her newlywed drug-addicted teenage daughter was going to suddenly turn into a responsible mother. He felt like he knew too much, and the walls of the doublewide were closing in on him.

"I need to get out of here," he said.

Sarah nodded. "I can't blame you, I guess."

"Fresh air."

But he didn't move.

Thump. Thump. Pling. Thump. Swish.

"She was probably doing meth when she was pregnant with him. The social worker is right. That's what's wrong with him. Not colic. He was born addicted to meth. He's probably disabled. He'll have all kinds of learning disabilities, and that's if he's lucky."

"He'll be fine."

"Foster care might not be such a bad thing."

"That's not right."

"What's not right?"

"He's my grandson. I can't give him to someone else. And anyway, Angie is going to raise him."

"Angie is a drug addict who got herself pregnant by her drug-addict boyfriend. The two of them couldn't take care of a puppy! What kind of life will their baby have?"

"They are *not* addicts."

"They are."

"I wasn't much older than Angie when I had her," Sarah said.

"And look how well that turned out," he muttered.

"What did you say?" Tears sprang to her eyes. "I can't believe you said that."

"I'm sorry. I'm sorry," Tom said. "I didn't mean anything by it."

"Oh, yeah, you did."

"What the fuck am I doing here? I should go."

"Yes, you should."

He stood but still couldn't move. He had hurt her with the truth, and he felt terrible about it.

"All right then," he said.

He headed for the door.

"I don't understand you," Sarah said. "Nobody chooses who they're born to."

"No, but people sure as hell can choose whether or not to have a baby."

"Are you sure about that?"

Thump. Thump. Thump. Pling.

People should choose, Tom thought, his hand on the door, but perhaps Sarah was right. Maybe in real life, certainly in real life as it was lived on the West End, they don't. They just have sex out of boredom or lust, the women get married off and pregnant young, the men are trapped in dead-end jobs, and it all seems inevitable, as if they have no idea how babies are made. The condoms discreetly on display at the Merc are probably covered in dust, having long since passed the expiration date.

"Maybe that's how you were born, and how Ray and Angie and Tyler were born," Tom said. "Some bored kids went to a movie at the Uranium Drive-In and nine months later a baby just sort of happened. But it doesn't have to be that way, does it? Not for Tyler, anyway. Or even for Ray Jr. Not yet. Maybe they still have a chance."

"*Angie* still has a chance. She can be a *good* mother."

"She won't be. She can't be. You'll end up raising her baby. How will you manage that? How will you keep your job? Who'll watch him when you're at work?"

"I guess none of that's any of your business."

He felt lightheaded and knew he really had to leave.

"I'm going," he said. And he walked out, firmly closing the door behind him.

Tom nodded to Ray Jr. as he walked toward his car.

The boy stopped dribbling and rested the basketball on his hip. Surely, he had heard their raised voices.

"Hey," he said hopefully, as Tom climbed into his car.

Tom sat behind the wheel for a few minutes but did not turn the key. He and Ray Jr. stared at each other, neither one moving. For a moment, Tom felt as if he was looking back in time, at himself when he was Ray's age. Was their transaction reciprocal? Did Ray, in Tom, see himself twenty years into the future? That was doubtful. Instead, Tom thought that Ray must be praying for his own reasons, transmitting his hope to Tom, begging him *to go back inside*, just as Tom had recently prayed to the social worker.

Tom expressed receiving the message in the form of a frown, and slowly got back out of the car.

"You're right," he said to Ray.

The kid nodded sagely.

If Tom was going to walk out of Sarah's life, there were things he had to say to her first.

Chapter 25

FRIEND OF THE FAMILY

Sarah had not moved from the corner of the sofa, right where he had left her.

"I haven't been honest with you," he said.

"You've been honest about Angie," Sarah said. "She is an addict. I don't know why I couldn't admit it. Or even see it. My blindness has been costly."

"She can get better. I did."

"You?"

"I was going down, just like Angie is now. It's the first thing I haven't told you, that I haven't been honest about. I haven't told you where I came from, and that I came to Naturita to get better, to go straight."

"You came here? To the meth capital? To go straight?" She laughed bitterly. "Well, that was one big fucking wrong turn, wasn't it?"

He sat next to her.

"Maybe not. Because I met you here."

"Me?"

"The second thing I haven't told you, Sarah, is that I have feelings for you…."

"You have feelings for me? Since when?"

"Since I don't know when. Maybe since the first time I saw you at the Merc and you smiled at me, before I knew who you were."

"And why?"

He shrugged. He knew she was worthy of his love, but not nearly so confident that he was worthy of hers.

"That had better be all," she said, taking a deep breath. "Because I'm not sure I can take any more honesty right now."

"Well, there's more. Mark Brubaker is dead."

"Dead?"

"It will be in Thursday's paper."

"I don't understand what...."

"I don't want you to learn about it by reading it in the paper. That's why I'm telling you now. The sheriff suspects that maybe Ray killed him."

"Ray? That's impossible!"

"I know."

"Ray would never hurt anyone."

"I know. But if the sheriff thinks Ray is with Anya, you can see why he would suspect he might have had it in for Brubaker. He'd have a strong motive."

"You can tell him. You can just tell the sheriff that Ray is not with Anya. There's no motive."

"I can't do that."

"Why not?"

"Because I went to see Brubaker after I met Anya. To talk to him. To try to understand what happened to Ray."

Tom was studying Sarah's reaction. Was she worthy of his trust? Clearly not, but the impulse had come over him when he was outside in his car, prepared to turn the key and drive away forever. Ray Jr., or what-ever he symbolized, had demanded nothing less of him than to unbur-den himself, to let go of a weight he could no longer carry alone, to trust her in the hope that she might reciprocate and trust him back. Some-how, he had concluded under the boy's steady gaze that he had nothing to lose because to lose Sarah now would be to lose everything anyway.

Tom had not calculated how much to tell her. He was winging it. But with the floodgates now open, he continued.

"And Brubaker attacked me, and I defended myself and I killed him."

"My God," Sarah said.

"And then I made things worse. I should have reported it, but I didn't. I thought nobody would ever find him and I wouldn't ever have to answer for it. Now I don't really know what I should do."

Does everyone need a confessor? Was it a measure of Tom's weak-ness or of his strength that he rashly opened himself up to Sarah? Probably it was both, he thought, as he sat beside her fully exposed. He did not feel more vulnerable than he had before he blurted out the truth, but he did feel less alone, even knowing that she now had the means with which to betray him. The risk Tom had taken had not been properly calculated, and this might well have been the perp's fateful mistake, as prophesied by Sheriff Martin. How well did Tom know Sarah, really? Hardly at all.

He could see in her expression that she was struggling to pro-cess everything he had told her, and yet her response was not what he expected.

"It's all my fault," she said.

"How could it be your fault?"

"I told you about Anya. If I hadn't done that, you wouldn't even have known about Brubaker."

"I asked. You didn't tell me to go looking for her. In fact, you told me that Anya had nothing to do with Ray's disappearance, and that turned out to be the truth. Or at least, right now, I think it's the truth. Anyway, it's not your fault that I tracked her down. I went looking for her all on my own. And I went out to Brubaker's on my own, too."

Tom was once again presented with the question of why he had so insistently pursued a story nobody else seemed to care about.

"I had my own reasons," he said.

She was watching him intently.

"I was a reporter, Sarah," he said, opening up the most painful chapter of his past to her. Sparing himself nothing, he told her how he had lost his career in Boston, and how he had abandoned Miranda, leading him, eventually, to Naturita.

"I was a good reporter before I got messed up," he concluded. "I used to care about the truth, just because it was the truth. That used to be reason enough to care about a story, because it was true. But then I lost that, and I think maybe I've been trying to get it back."

"So, what happened to me, and what happened to Ray, whatever it is, you've made it all about yourself. You've been using us."

"I'm sorry."

"Don't be. I'm glad, actually."

"Glad?"

"Because it brought us together."

"What do we do now?"

"I don't know. I guess we just figure it out."

They sat quietly for a few moments.

"Do you realize that this is the first time we've ever talked about you," Sarah said. "Always before, whenever we talk, it's been all about me."

Lying in her bed later—after they tended to Tyler, after making and eating dinner, acting out normalcy, after Ray uncharacteristically went to his bedroom early to allow them some privacy, and after they had made love, with Sarah breathing softly by his side in seemingly untroubled sleep—Tom retraced the steps that had drawn him so deeply into a situation that was so utterly hopeless. When had the journey begun? When he first met Miranda? Or when his career crashed, and he left her? In Marathon? When he bought the Forum? With the news of Ray Walker's disappearance? His being drawn into investigating it? The death of Brubaker?

Or was it only now that he was irretrievably committed, with the realization that he was in love with Sarah?

He couldn't say. But whatever it was that brought him to Sarah's bed, he didn't want to leave, not ever. He had made promises to Sarah, but wondered how he could fulfill them. Even if he managed to save himself, how could he possibly save Sarah and Tyler and Ray Jr., and maybe Angie, but not Craig, who was far beyond salvation? He knew that Angie would only hate him for getting involved and Sarah would blame him when Angie crashed. Angie would break her mother's heart and Craig would be breathing down his neck.

Ray Jr. was almost certainly doomed, too, but there might be hope for the baby, if he got away from the West End soon enough.

This frail family, these broken people, were now, somehow, his responsibility—because their true and faithful patriarch had gone missing.

Sarah stirred next to him.

"You were right not to tell the sheriff," she said, sounding as if she was talking out of a dream.

"Why?"

She didn't answer because she'd already fallen back asleep.

Tom despised the painful reminder of his own past addiction in the form of the selfishness and raw greed of a teenaged waif. He knew it was sheer arrogance to think he could help Angie. But there he was just the same, eating a burger with her at lunchtime at the Maverick.

He and Sarah had agreed that he would talk to Angie before the social worker arrived later that afternoon, hopefully to coach her in what to say and how to behave to improve her chances of regaining custody of Tyler as soon as possible. Sarah, meanwhile, had taken another day off work in order to take care of her grandson. Obviously, better arrangements would have to be made quickly, which was precisely the reality Tom hoped to impress on Angie.

Tom knew she would never cop to her addiction, not easily, not in a first meeting, and probably not without being forced to, but had also calculated that nothing would be gained by small talk.

"I know you and your family are going through hell," Tom said. "And I'd like to help. I told your mom I'd try to help."

"What can you do? Are you gonna bring my dad back?" She rolled her eyes and snorted to air her doubts. "Can you get the cops to drop the charges against me? Or get me custody of my baby? I know! Maybe you could just write me a big fat check."

"No big check," he said, smiling despite himself. The girl was not as dull-witted as she had often appeared. "But I can listen and maybe I can help you figure things out. I might be able to suggest a good move or two."

"Doubtful," she said. "But I guess I would appreciate it if you'd keep fucking my mom. That's a big help, actually. It keeps her busy and off my case."

Tom was stung, not by the jab but by the surge of rage it produced in him.

"Actually, I'm not *fucking* your mom" he said mildly, masking his anger, thinking to himself that this was not a lie because what he had done the night before was to *make love* to Sarah. What's more, he had done it only once. "What makes you think I am?"

"She told me."

Had she? Tom doubted it, but it was at least possible, and it reminded him that he'd been rash to make himself so vulnerable to her. Angie clearly thought she could wound him with it.

"I don't really care," she said. "She can fuck anyone she wants. She's still married to my dad, so I guess that makes it cheating if you want to get all technical about it. But I think you're safe. He's not coming back."

"How do you know that?"

"He finally got away. Why would he come back?"

"You think he just left. No reason?"

"I think he probably had a lot of reasons."

"Like what?"

"Like maybe *he* was fucking somebody he wasn't supposed to," she said. "Or maybe he was sick of us. Maybe he realized he couldn't handle his daughter. But what's it to you?"

"I like your dad. It's not like we're great friends or anything, but I care about what happened to him. Now that I've gotten to know your mom, I like her, too."

"That's just so sweet. Isn't that what they call 'a friend of the family'?"

"Something like that."

"So ... the great friend of the family fucks the missing husband's wife. That's nice."

She smiled primly. Tom replied with a hard look.

"Who the fuck are you anyway?" she continued, pressing her advantage. "Just because you're screwing my mom doesn't mean you're anything to me." She stopped herself for effect and added, as if the question had just occurred to her: "But you might as well tell me this much. Is she a good lay?"

Now Tom shook his head sadly.

"She says you're great," Angie added, but the forcefulness of her delivery had been blunted, as if she realized too late that she had done enough damage and wanted to stop digging the hole deeper.

"I can see this was a waste of time," Tom said. "I'm sorry. It was a big mistake. There's really nothing I can say to you."

"Nope."

She had not intended to so successfully push Tom away.

"Let's finish lunch and go our separate ways," he said.

The two of them sat quietly for a few minutes, Tom gazing out the plate glass window at the empty highway and Angie staring down at her plate. She twirled a soggy French fry in a pool of ketchup, drawing the pattern of her tangled thoughts.

"I'm sorry," she finally said, chastened, her tone dramatically softer. "I know you're just trying to help."

"If there's any way that I can," he shrugged.

"I just don't see what you or anyone else can do. I think I'm a hopeless case."

"Well, you're a hard case for sure. Maybe not quite hopeless, but hard as hell."

She started to tear up.

"Do you even know what the problem is?" he asked.

"It's everything," she said, the tears flowing freely. "Everything is all fucked up. My dad disappeared and the baby won't stop crying and Craig doesn't help at all. And my mom is on my case all the time. Then I got busted. It's every fucking last thing."

Tom anticipated that at some later juncture, if they proceeded that far together, he would broach the problem she had conspicuously not cited: her painfully obvious meth habit.

"I understand," he said.

She swallowed a sob and put her head down on the table. "It's not like I want to be like this," she cried. "This is not who I want to be. This is not who I am! But what can I do?"

"You can come work for me at the paper," Tom said gently. "Maybe I can help you figure out a way to start over."

She agreed and they arranged for her to report for work the next day, on Tuesday.

Chapter 26

OPEN SECRETS

After lunch with Angie and after processing invoices so that he would get paid—a task he could no longer afford to put off—Tom called Sarah at home to make plans to see her. He wanted to know how the social worker's visit had gone and tell Sarah about his talk with her daughter. He hoped the social worker had helped devise a plan for someone to watch Tyler during the working day. Otherwise, he worried, that responsibility would somehow fall on him, too. Angie would probably ask if she could bring him to work with her, and the social worker would allow it if he agreed. That would be all he needed: an endlessly crying inconsolable meth baby at the office.

"It went well," Sarah said, when he asked her how the home visit had gone. But she sounded distracted and offered no details.

"I thought I could come over and cook dinner for you and Ray tonight," he said, improvising. "It's time you sampled my famous spaghetti."

"Why, that would be so nice," she said, "but…."

"But?"

"It's been a long day, that's all. Can we do it tomorrow?"

"Tomorrow."

"And I have a headache," she added.

"So let me come over and I'll watch Tyler for you."

"He's sleeping."

"Angie and I had a good talk."

"Yeah, she told me."

"Tomorrow?"

"It would be better."

"All right then," he said cheerfully. "I'll see you tomorrow."

But her evasiveness was infuriating. Hadn't they moved beyond this point? He had come clean with her, *had confessed to murder*, had helped bail her daughter out of jail, they had made love, and she was still playing games? She hadn't hesitated to call on him for help when she needed it but was blowing him off now when it wasn't convenient, and for reasons she didn't bother to explain. Was it a mother and daughter talk that he would be interrupting? Impossible. Or was she suddenly self-conscious about the chaos of her life, which she'd rashly opened up to him, and so she was tactically pulling back? Equally doubtful.

Something else was obviously going on.

Tom drove out to Sarah's doublewide and parked a short distance away. He retrieved his binoculars from the glove compartment and watched Ray Jr. shooting hoops. His suspicion that she had some kind of secret engagement was confirmed when Sarah emerged from the doublewide carrying the baby. She strapped Tyler into a child seat in the back seat of her car and got behind the wheel. Her sense of purpose was palpable.

When she drove past where Tom had parked behind some cottonwoods, he turned to follow her, leaving his headlights off. Before reaching town, at the battered marquee for the Uranium Drive-In, she turned off the highway. Tom knew that this was her preferred meeting place. But who was she meeting? He parked where he found the most inconspicuous vantage point for observing the intersection of the drive-in entrance and the highway.

Only a few minutes passed before another car turned into the drive-in. Tom's heart skipped a beat. It was a car he'd seen less than a week before: Albert Klein's polished black Hummer.

Tom's sense of betrayal was complete. Not only was the Uranium Drive-In his place, his and Sarah's place, now violated, but she was in some sort of league with Albert Klein, her missing husband's half-brother, who had professed absolutely no interest in Ray Walker's disappearance when Tom had asked him about it; the same Albert Klein whose name meant something sinister to Mark Brubaker, and whose brothers were convinced was a sociopath.

Tom had already constructed a mental image of the West End with Albert Klein operating at the center of it, pulling all the strings. But not Sarah, too, he thought morosely. He knew that Sarah had often been less than forthright with him, but until this moment had not seriously considered that her underlying motives might be corrupt. Now he felt that he had too easily chalked her dissembling up to fear or embarrassment.

Tom couldn't readily identify the stitch in his side, a tight knot that reminded him of what it felt like when he ran too hard for too long as a child. Was it jealousy? Paranoia? A sense of impending doom? The anxiety only mounted while he waited for Sarah to finish her assignation with Klein. They must be fucking. Why else would they take so long?

It was only half an hour before the black Hummer drove down

the driveway and turned to the north. Tom was prepared to follow him, planning to confront Klein and ask him point blank why he was meeting secretly with Sarah Walker, a reckless course of action that at the moment seemed necessary. But then Sarah's car emerged and turned south, back toward her home. He wanted to confront her, too, and Tom turned his wheel to follow her as he pulled onto the highway. Then he swerved back north and followed Klein from a safe distance. He would deal with Sarah later.

Speeding down the highway, it occurred to Tom that his own behavior was every bit as suspicious as Klein's or Sarah's. What was he doing? He could easily be tagged a stalker. He imagined his interrogation by Sheriff Martin, upon being investigated for spying on Sarah Walker, a woman who had already suffered so much, a married woman whose missing husband might still be found. Would the sheriff accept his explanation that he was a journalist pursuing a story? Would the sheriff accuse him of playing detective? Or would the sheriff simply conclude from the abundant evidence that Tom Austin had lost his bearings?

Tom parked a short distance from the gas station where Klein had stopped to fill his tank, watching this most unremarkable activity through his binoculars, transfixed. Klein nodded to an acquaintance at the next pump.

Why had Klein met with Sarah Walker? It might be expected that Albert and Sarah knew each other; they were in-laws, after all, except that there was no openly acknowledged relationship between Ray Walker and the Klein family. The secrecy could only mean something nefarious. Otherwise, why wouldn't Sarah meet Albert Klein in public at the Maverick? Or at her home? Or at his? Why would they choose to meet at the Uranium Drive-In? She had, after all, chosen the same location to meet with Tom precisely because it was discreet.

Obviously, Tom concluded, as he resumed following Klein down the highway, it was because Sarah was the one having the affair; she and Albert, not Ray and Anya, were the threat to the Walkers' marriage. Either she or her lover or both of them were responsible for her husband's disappearance. That would give them every reason to keep their relationship secret, for at least a reasonable time, which was why she had leaned on Tom and had not asked Albert for support when she needed someone to help her with Angie. The fact that her lover was her husband's stepbrother only made it all the more unsavory, more dangerous, and more likely to have ended, as it apparently had, in violence.

Tom tailed the Hummer all the way to the gate to the Uranium King Ranch, where Klein turned off the highway and Tom turned around to go back home.

He was heartsick.

* * *

After another restless night, polluted with images of Sarah and Albert plotting against him, making him the dupe in their scheme and having sex in the back seat of the Hummer, Tom went to the Maverick for breakfast and took his customary seat at the counter next to Dave Best. Sally quickly delivered two eggs over easy with hash browns, crisp bacon, and sourdough toast. The eggs had hit the griddle when she saw him across the street, heading her way. If, one day, he felt like scrambled eggs for a change, it would be too late.

"Do you know Albert Klein?" Tom asked Dave as casually as he could. "Did he play ball with you as a kid?"

"He wasn't much of an athlete, and he was a few years older. He was in Denver for years. Now that he's been back, he pretty much keeps to himself up there on North Mountain. He was always the fuck-up. You know, the spoiled rich kid constantly getting in trouble. He fell off his bike when he was about ten and was never the same after that. It was hard on him because his big brothers were such Eagle Scouts."

"Now he's the one in the old man's good graces and the brothers are out of favor."

"Could be." Dave shrugged. "I think I heard something like that."

"Do you think he and Ray Walker were friendly? Did they know each other? I mean, how does that work? You knew that Ray was Dick's son, so did Albert Klein know they were half-brothers? Did you all know when you were kids?"

"I guess we did. But maybe not. Who remembers?"

"There are all these open secrets on the West End. Everyone knows everyone else's personal shit, but they also know who they can tell and who they can't tell. And I guess I'm the guy you can't tell anything."

"Nah, you're the guy who knows more than anyone else. You're the newspaper guy, always asking questions."

"I'm the guy who can't tell the truth from a hole in the wall."

"Well, you're still pretty new here. Haven't even been here ten years and you haven't married in, so no family ties."

"Can you blame me?"

"We'll find you a wife sooner or later," Dave laughed. "I guess it's pretty messy. Maybe that's why we protect each other. Isn't every-place like that?"

"No," Tom said. "Not like this."

"Huh. I guess I wouldn't know. I've never lived anywhere else."

"Molly says it has to do with the Utopianists, and the fact that they were the first ones here. What do you think about that?"

"Makes sense. For most of the last hundred years and even today you don't practice polygamy out in the open. People around here know to keep their family lives private."

"What do you mean today? How many people are there who still practice polygamy? There can't be more than a few families."

"It's actually coming back. Kind of a trend. There's more pligs now than there were. More than you think."

"What did you call them?"

"Pligs. You know, polygamists. Pligs."

"Do I know them?"

Dave just grinned at him.

"People I know are in plural marriages? Is that what you're telling me? But they're able to keep it secret?"

"Sure."

"Have you got more than one wife, Dave? Another wife besides Ginger? Or two more wives, maybe? Are you supporting three families by selling groceries and supplies at the Merc? Or have you got secret businesses, too? Are you selling meth along with the bread and milk?"

"Now Tom, you know if I told you that, I'd have to kill ya."

Dave was so deadpan that Tom wasn't sure how to react until Dave punched him in the shoulder.

"Hey man, lighten up," Dave said. "I'm just kidding ya. Ginger would kill *me*."

"But you are LDS?"

"Well, yeah, everyone's LDS, pretty much. Some are just more hypocritical than others."

"But they're not all pligs. Is that what you call them? Some kind of slur like nigger or spick or kike."

"Yeah, pligs. And it's not a slur, exactly. It's what they call themselves. And no, not all. Most are mainstream."

"I'm starting to feel like the town fool," Tom said, "the last guy to know something that's obvious to everyone else. I think that maybe everyone in town knows what happened to Ray Walker except for me. The sheriff knows, Sarah Walker knows, Albert Klein knows, even you know. And the big search was just a show you all staged to keep me in the dark."

"No." Dave shook his head sadly. "Ray's really gone. That one's a true mystery. Nobody knows."

"You really don't know?"

"I wish I did."

* * *

Tom tried to work, but it was difficult to stop thinking about Sarah and Albert Klein having sex. When he did manage to chase that image away, it was replaced by the thought that Sheriff Trace Martin was closing in on him. Or he imagined that the odor of Mark Brubaker's death was trapped in his sinuses, that the smell would be there forever, and he found himself trying to guess who had the bloody fire poker. He still had not figured out how to report Brubaker's murder in the Forum.

Worst of all, he dreaded having to make good on his offer to hire Angie Walker, but she showed up as planned, only a few minutes past 10 a.m.

"How is Tyler doing?" he asked.

"He's good," she replied dully, and explained that the social worker had arranged for daycare from a certified foster care provider so that she and Sarah could both go to work.

"The social worker doesn't want us to lose our jobs and have to go on any more public assistance. If she's gonna pay for daycare, I don't see why she can't just give the money to me instead so I can stay home and take care of my own kid. It really sucks how she's ordering us around."

"Yeah."

"It's stupid."

"Yeah."

Now Angie sat across the room painfully pecking at the computer keyboard to type the school lunch menu. She'd been at that one menial task for an hour, a chore he could finish himself in five minutes. The slow *click, click* of her finger tapping out words like pizza, one … letter … at … a … time, was a source of irritation that ratcheted up as the morning wore on.

He had an overwhelming desire to confront Sarah, to demand that she tell him everything. He was convinced that only the truth could quiet his monkey mind and restore any sense of peace. Ray Walker's disappearance had grown into an obsession, a glaring symbol of everything he couldn't begin to comprehend, not just the hidden meanings behind uranium mining and meth abuse and polygamy as a way of life and the rest of the antique mores of life on the West End, but the riddle of life itself: inchoate human yearnings, duplicity, and evanescence. His impulse was to hunt Sarah down and take her by the shoulders and physically shake sense into her, to speak forcefully and insist that she confess to her affair with Albert Klein and tell him exactly what happened to Ray. He would promise that her secrets were safe with him, but then would use the information to blackmail her:

Drop Albert Klein for me and I won't report that you murdered your husband.

Then she would be unable to use his confession that he had killed Mark Brubaker against him.

It all fit so perfectly. Sarah was the guilty party, she was the unreliable witness, she was source of every red herring, each one designed to throw him off the trail. It was symptomatic of his own tortured psyche that he had fallen in love with her. How else could he explain his raging hurt?

At noon, he gave in to his obsession and finally called her. Unaccountably, she sounded happy to hear from him and agreed to meet him after work. They could have met at her place, but he suggested another spot instead: the drive-in.

SARAH'S WARNING

Despite his intention to play it cool, Tom blurted it out just as soon as Sarah slid next to him in the passenger seat of his car: "Why didn't you tell me you're having an affair?"

She was stung. "Because I'm not," she said.

"Come on, Sarah!" His voice rose quickly. "Stop lying to me. I know that you are. I saw you with him."

"Who did you see me with?"

"With Albert Klein." It pained him to say his rival's name, so he repeated himself sorrowfully and with deep disgust, for double the effect. "I saw you with Albert Klein."

"I am *not* having an affair with Albert Klein."

Her indignation ramped up the emotion, further justifying his anger: "You were too tired to see me last night but not too tired meet him up here," he said with too much anger in his voice. "You were fucking him, weren't you? Didn't you tell me this is the fucking field?"

"Who the hell are you to be talking to me this way, to be asking me questions like this? My relationship with Albert Klein is none of your fucking business. And what were you doing spying on me?"

"Maybe Sheriff Martin would like to hear about this. He thought it was Ray who was having an affair, so he figured that maybe Ray left you and that's that. No crime and nothing to investigate. But if it was you having the affair, he might just draw a different conclusion. Maybe there is a crime to investigate after all."

"Are you threatening me? After you killed Mark Brubaker? I don't think so."

She reached for the door handle, but he grabbed her arm.

"I have a good defense," he said coldly. "What's yours?"

"Keep your hands off of me!"

"I'm sorry."

But he didn't relax his grip.

"You're hurting me."

He let go and she rubbed her arm.

"What has gotten into you?" she said. "I thought you had *feelings* for me?"

"I did. I do. But you lied to me."

"I did not. I just didn't tell you everything… yet."

"Goddamn it, Sarah! It's the same thing."

"Albert is not my lover. Albert was…"

"Albert was what?"

"Albert was my husband. A long time ago. Before I met Ray. Before Angie was born. Albert is Angie's father."

"I thought Ray…"

"Ray adopted her and took care of us. I told you that Ray was very kind and that's the truth. He took care of me the same way he helped Anya."

"He was kind, but maybe you didn't love him."

"Stop," she said, and she started to cry. "You aren't this cruel."

"I'm sorry," he said again, but this time he meant it.

They sat quietly for a moment.

"Maybe it's time for you to come clean and tell me everything," Tom said. "And start at the beginning."

"I was born in the church and was engaged to Albert when I was just 14," she said.

"The Kleins are pligs?"

"Just Albert. He converted because he liked the idea of having multiple wives. And Victor Redd, who was head of the church at that time, was happy to have him because he was prominent and rich. Albert gave a lot of money to the church, which was just like giving it to the Redds. Redd paid him back by making me Albert's first wife."

"Your parents allowed this?"

"They were honored. There's a room in the temple where new marriages are consummated. The whole thing is very ceremonial, the deflowering. I was only 14 and I didn't like it. I got pregnant right away, but before I started showing, and before Albert knew about it, I decided to run away. It was the middle of the night. I was hitchhiking and Ray picked me up. He hid me until the baby, until Angie, was born. Then he went and told Victor Redd and Albert that he had me and the baby and told them that I didn't want to go back to them and that he was going to protect me."

"They let him get away with this?"

"He was smart about it. And he was tough. We had gone to a lawyer in Denver where we made up these sworn statements and he gave copies of the statements to Victor and Albert and told them that the lawyer had instructions to share the information with the authorities if anything happened to either one of us. That was enough to keep them quiet. It worked for almost twenty years."

"You think they did something to Ray?"

"Victor Redd died a few years ago. But Albert is capable of anything."

"Why didn't you and Ray just leave and get away from here?"

"Ray didn't want to go. Sometimes we talked about leaving, but then we just never figured out how we could pay for it, or where we would go, we had a place to live, and he had his business, and the years went by, Angie grew up, Ray Jr. came along, and somehow the memory of how we started out just faded away into the background. It didn't seem all that strange around here. It actually seemed kind of normal. Just how things happen. Albert moved away so he wasn't a problem and Victor died and life went on. But then Albert came back."

Sarah stopped talking and Tom sat back to absorb all she'd told him. Without looking over at her, he grabbed her hand, and he squeezed it to reassure her that he was there for her and to ask her forgiveness, a lot to express, he realized, from a hand squeeze. She squeezed his hand back.

"After Albert came back, supposedly to take care of the old man and run the family business, he looked for Angie and he told her that he was her real father. She confronted us about it. I've never seen Ray so pissed off. Angie said we lied to her for her whole life and that we were keeping her from her inheritance. Ray was so hurt when she turned on him like that, after they were so close…."

"What did he do?"

"He wanted to have it out with Albert, to tell him to stay away from Angie. I begged him not to and made him promise me that he wouldn't. But he did it anyway."

"And then?"

"And then Angie and Ray started fighting all the time and Angie got pregnant and engaged to Craig, and we planned a wedding for them, and it seemed like maybe we'd weathered the crisis. Then Ray disappeared."

"None of this explains what you were doing with Albert yesterday."

"It's because of you. When you told me Angie is an addict, the reason that was so hard for me to hear is because Ray tried to tell me the same thing, and I wouldn't listen to him, either. I kept making excuses for her and that was wrong. It was like I was reliving the same argument I had with Ray all over again with you. Then you got mad and walked out of the house. I realized that I was doing the exact same thing when I told you that I didn't know what happened to Ray. I wasn't telling you the truth, and I was putting you in danger, just like I put Ray in danger.

"That first time we met here, at the drive-in, I called you because Albert warned me. He said it was my fault that you were nosing around, my fault that you went to meet Elizabeth at the nursing home and that you went to North Mountain to ask him about Ray. He was positive I put you up to it, or why else would you bother, and why would you suspect him? He said if I knew what was good for myself, I'd make you stop. I asked you to stop but you wouldn't listen, so I got the smart idea to tell you about Anya. I didn't think you could ever find her. You would just think that she was the reason for Ray's disappearance, that it was obvious that he'd run off with her, and you'd stop looking. But you did find Anya, and then you almost got yourself killed when you went out to Brubaker's place. I didn't think anyone could be that… I don't know, that *stupid*, to tell you the truth, to go out there to try to talk to him.

"And then the other day we went to bed and made love and afterwards I thought to myself, 'Sarah Walker, it's time you found your backbone. You can't keep running from Albert Klein your whole life.'

I called Albert and told him that I had something to tell him, in person. I needed to look him in the eye and tell it to him to his face. I wanted him to know that he can't hurt me anymore. I wanted him to know that I'm ready to fight back. I don't have Ray anymore to fight for Angie so it's up to me. I told him to leave Angie alone because he's already hurt her enough. And…"

"And what?"

"I told him that he might get away with whatever it is he did to Ray, because even though I know damn well that he's responsible for whatever happened to him I can't prove it and he's got the sheriff in his back pocket. I told him that if anything happens to you, then he'd better be prepared to deal with me, too. I told him that he'll have to kill you and me both because if he does something to you and lets me get away, I'll come after him."

"You told him that?"

"I did," she said grimly.

"What did he say?"

"He looked at me and said I was always about half crazy, and now I've gone all the way off the deep end. I laughed and said, 'Maybe so, but I'm also dead serious about this.' And that was it. Who knows what he's going to do now?"

Finally, she lost control of her emotions and allowed a full sob to escape. She leaned into him, and he put his arm around her.

"You are giving me way too much credit," Tom said. "You didn't get the courage to confront Albert like that from me. You found it by yourself."

"You know what's really weird about it is that I don't really know that Albert did anything to Ray," she said. "I suppose Ray could have run off to Vegas. But I'm pretty sure Ray threatened Albert, and that's not something Albert would take lightly. If Albert did do something to Ray, then you know he's going to come after you next. That's why I had to tell him: He'd better not dare. But I fucked up. Now he'll come after both of us."

Sarah sounded resigned, and Tom should have felt threatened. But what he felt was the opposite of vulnerability. Sarah's desire to protect him was all the more impressive given that the only weapon she had at her disposal was bluster. The toxic entanglement of depression, pain, anger, and jealousy that had been consuming him suddenly unknotted itself to be replaced by something lucid and pure.

Tom knew then, finally and with absolute certainty, just as Sarah had always known, that Ray Walker had not abandoned his family, he had not run off to Vegas. An accident having been ruled out by the exhaustive search, only foul play could have kept Ray from returning home to Sarah and Angie and Ray Jr.

Tom knew that he would never abandon Sarah, either. Somehow, he had come to occupy the void left by Ray.

Chapter 28

ILLUSIONS

They had run though their emotions, so they just sat quietly at the drive-in, watching the lights come on in the town below, until it was dark. Naturita didn't cast much of a glow and the sky was full of bright stars, another quality of life on the West End that Tom appreciated more fully than the natives, having come from places where the Milky Way and even the brightest planets were washed out.

"I have to go," Sarah said. "I have to get Tyler from the sitter. I'm already late. If I'm not careful, they'll take him away from me, too."

"I'll go with you."

The foster home was yet another minimally rehabilitated miner's shack on the edge of town, but with a rusty swing set in the yard and broken toys strewn about. To be a certified foster care home compensated by the state was undoubtedly one of best business opportunities on the West End.

Nobody answered when Sarah knocked on the door. She shouted, "Hello?" No answer. She pushed the door open.

The place was unremarkable, furnished in the usual assortment of hand-me-downs, Wal-Mart merchandise, and domestic clutter, but there was nobody there. A crib was empty.

"Where's Tyler?" Sarah asked, fighting back panic.

"Maybe the sitter went to look for you."

"She wouldn't. I'm not that late coming to get him. And her car is here."

Tom stepped to the window, pulled back the curtain, and looked out at the car. A tumbleweed rolled past. He surveyed the kitchen. Then he heard Sarah gasp. She was standing in the door to a bedroom.

The babysitter, a heavy woman with her hair pulled back by a dirty rubber band into a ponytail, dressed in a faded T-shirt and baggy sweatpants, was bound to a chair and gagged. Her eyes rolled as she struggled against the tape.

She inhaled wheezily when Tom loosened the gag.

"I told them I have trouble breathing," she cried.

"Who?" Tom asked, working to free her.

"I almost died," the woman sobbed.

"Where's Tyler?" Sarah interjected.

But the woman was hyperventilating, still gasping for air, and having difficulty getting more words out.

"What happened to Tyler?" Sarah asked again.

"They took him," the woman finally said.

"Who took him?"

"Your daughter and her husband. I couldn't stop them. He had a gun."

Sarah was slow to understand.

"Angie?" she asked.

"I'm going to lose my license," the woman gasped. "I told them I could only give him to you. But they were crazy, all hopped up. The husband was cussing and said he was going to kill me, and the baby was crying…"

"Did they say where they were going?" Tom asked.

"I don't know, I don't know." She was still struggling for air, wailing, and Sarah grabbed her hand to calm her down.

"It's OK, you're OK now," Sarah said. "They didn't hurt you."

"But I'll lose my license. I won't get any more children. How will I survive?"

"They'll understand that it's not your fault," Sarah said. "We'll tell them it's not."

"I couldn't protect him," she wailed.

"We've got to find them," Tom said. "Are you sure they didn't say anything?"

"North Mountain," the sitter said. "I think they said North Mountain."

It seemed painfully obvious, after she said it. Tom could have guessed. All roads circled back to the Kleins, sooner or later.

* * *

They raced through town down the highway to the entrance to the Uranium King Ranch as fast as Tom's Corolla could go. Deputy Pederson rarely stopped anyone for speeding, but if by chance he were to stop them now, his help in rescuing Tyler would be welcome.

"They'll know we're coming," Tom said as he turned into the ranch entrance. He pointed to a camera mounted on a tree. "There's plenty of surveillance."

Up the winding mountain road, deeper into a mature ponderosa forest, pealing around sharp curves that forced Sarah to cling to the dashboard. Tom was prepared to race past the guard at the gatehouse, but it wasn't necessary because it was unmanned. They reached the resort complex at the mountain's summit in ten minutes.

Tom pulled into the main parking lot, even emptier than usual, and shut off the car engine. They were enveloped in silence. Apart from the fact that it was illuminated, the place appeared deserted. There were no attendants at the entrance to the main lodge. Birds chirped. Everything appeared peaceful. There were even a few elk grazing nearby.

"What now?" Sarah whispered.

"I don't know." He was whispering, too.

They sat for a moment, unnaturally becalmed at the eye of an emotional storm, and then a golf cart approached from the direction of the historic ranch house, Albert Klein behind the wheel. Tom and Sarah stepped out of their car to meet him.

"I've been expecting you," he said in a strong voice, breaking the air of silence.

"Where's the baby?" Sarah said. "Where's Tyler?"

"He's perfectly safe, with his parents," Klein said. "Hop in. I was just enjoying a cocktail. And we have a lot to talk about."

As he shuttled them the hundred yards to the family residence, he assumed a conversational air, as if they were any other resort guests.

"We've shut down the lodge for a couple of weeks, just during this slow season," he explained, as he pulled to a stop in front of the expansive front porch. "It's very quiet. Our peak season is in the summer."

He led them into the living room. Tom had a strong sense, more powerful than déjà vu, that he had been there before, in that same room, though it seemed smaller and more intimate than he remembered it. Had the photographs he'd studied when he was in Denver just a week earlier etched themselves into his then-meth-addled brain?

Or was it that the house had been maintained like a museum and the room was utterly unchanged from the way it had been furnished a half-century before, hunting trophies alternating with undistinguished Old European paintings on the walls, and the same cowhide sofa positioned before the mantle where Dick and Betty Klein had long ago posed for the portrait Tom had found at the library? The mid-twentieth century ranch-style elegance was intact but musty, and somehow disconcerting, and Tom felt the impulse that must have led Albert Klein to want to update it all, even if his own sense of more modern elegance in the new resort structures was every bit as off-kilter.

Klein led them to a picture window overlooking the back patio. His excessively calm demeanor cut sharply against Tom's and Sarah's sense of urgency, deliberately, Tom thought, as a way of controlling of the situation.

"The view from here in the daytime is something to see," Klein said.

Right where he would have expected to find it, Tom noted the enormous flagstone patio where the King had once grilled hamburgers and hot dogs for the citizens of Naturita on the Fourth of July. Even the utensils hanging on hooks were vintage. All that was missing from the scene was the King in his apron.

"You can see almost fifty miles," Albert Klein said. "The town of Naturita is that tiny cluster of lights right over there." He pointed to the concentrated lights of the town. There was another smaller cluster, Nucla, just beyond, with fainter, more scattered lights surrounding it. Beyond those lights, there was a vast sea of darkness.

"And that way," Klein pointed the other direction, "are the lights of Telluride. On a dark night, you can make out the glow in the sky."

"Your kingdom," Tom said. "When the old man goes."

As if on cue, the Uranium King emerged from the shadows at the back of the living room, dressed in his bathrobe and slippers. His son barely acknowledged him as he sat nearby, seemingly absorbed in his own world.

"I do have a family legacy to protect," Albert said. "My father built an empire. Much of the land you can see from here and quite a bit more that you can't see from this particular vantage point, all told almost a half million acres, all belongs to the Klein family. Most of the residents either worked for dad or worked for people who worked for him or for businesses that depended on his businesses. Even now, while uranium mining hasn't geared back up yet, we're providing jobs, with the resort here. And we have interests in Telluride, and many people from Naturita commute to them."

"I heard you had lost most of it," Tom said. "That you've poured too much money into the resort up here and it hasn't exactly worked out."

"Oh, no, no," he chuckled. "You shouldn't listen to Frank and Richard. They don't know what they're talking about. Neither one of them has a mind for business and neither one has done anything productive with his life. They've grown bitter and vindictive as a result. My parents really had no choice but to disinherit them. It's pathetic, really, how they've squandered their advantages."

"I want to see the baby," Sarah said impatiently, oblivious to Albert's jab at Tom, the implication that Albert knew Tom had spoken with Frank and Richard. Despite their mutual antagonisms, were the brothers in touch with each other? The family was more than twisted enough for that to be a real possibility. Or did Albert simply assume his affairs were a subject of speculation and that Frank and Richard were the probable source of any trash talk about him? In any case, Tom's own sense of paranoia was every bit as unsettling as any intention by

Albert to threaten him, and the only reasonable response to feeling so endangered was for Tom to maintain his composure.

"The police will be here soon," he said, lobbing a grenade back. "The babysitter will have reported the kidnapping."

"Yes, Sheriff Martin is on his way. I've explained the situation to him," Albert said. "And we've spoken to San Miguel County Social Services about Tyler, as well. I told them that I'm as much of a blood relative as Sarah is, and much better able to provide for a baby."

Tom's earlier supposition that the Kleins controlled the Montrose County sheriff was confirmed. And it was no surprise that his influence extended to the next county over. That specific fear was not paranoia at all. At the same time, it was clear that he and Sarah had almost certainly failed to help Tyler, and had only put themselves at risk by rushing heedlessly to North Mountain. They should have been less impulsive or should have sought help, Tom thought, but from whom? In the Uranium Kingdom, was there was no recourse other than to the royal family? If that was the case, they had their audience now.

Tom caught the eye of the older Klein, wondering how closely he was following the conversation, how much of it he understood, and whether he exercised any influence at all. Could Dick still sense clearly what other men couldn't see, the very structures that lay hidden beneath the surface of things, and not least the earth itself? Or was he so enfeebled by dementia that he was firmly under his son's thumb? Tom wasn't sure but thought that the King was possibly looking back at him kindly.

"What do you want from me?" Tom asked Albert, a little too sharply.

"Shouldn't I be asking you that question?"

"I'm just interested in the truth."

"Somehow I imagined that you, of all people, understood that truth is not something to be possessed or apprehended," Klein said. "You can't *know* the truth. Truth, like any ideal, can only be approached."

"Is that right?"

"We all need our illusions," Klein shrugged, as if his dictum was self-evident. "To encounter the full truth would destroy any of us."

Sarah was growing more impatient, either unaware of Albert's gamesmanship or bored by it. "I want to see Tyler and Angie, Albert," she interrupted.

"Yes, of course," Klein said, "but first, if you'll excuse us for a moment, there's something I want to show Tom."

He gestured for Tom to join him, and put his arm on Tom's shoulder, the better to share confidences as they walked outside onto the patio. There in a corner under an eave, resting on spread-out newspaper—pages from old issues of The Forum—lay the fire poker with which Tom had killed Brubaker, still covered in Brubaker's dried blood and Tom's fingerprints.

"I wanted you to know I have this," Klein said. "I know it's yours, but I don't want you to worry about it. If you want me to, I'll keep it safe for you. You know, Mark Brubaker was a piece of shit, but he was useful to me and it will cost me to replace him. So, I figure that you owe me, know what I mean?"

It felt like a blow to the solar plexus, though Tom had half expected it, and he was at a loss for words.

"I've got something else that's maybe not quite as valuable, but I like it," Klein said, and he turned over a newspaper to reveal the edition of The Boston Mail with the headline *Mail Reporter Fabricated Articles* emblazoned on the front page, illustrated with Tom's mug.

Klein clearly believed that this was the knockout blow, that he now owned Tom fully, and maybe he did. His worst fears were fully justified.

"What's that you were saying about the truth?"

Tom opened his mouth to respond, but stopped short after uttering the word, "How…"

"Everyone has secrets," Klein said with a shrug. "I hired someone to find yours. It wasn't hard. I knew you were running from something bad. Why else would you have shown up in Naturita? You call yourself Tom Austin, but never got proper paperwork? Or should I say, forged documents?" He stepped close to Tom and with a jocular punch to the shoulder offered some friendly advice: "If you're going to be a scoundrel, man, you have to be all-in. You can't be signing a notarized document using a Massachusetts driver's license with a different name on it, sticking an AKA in the agreement!"

Tom hadn't really been trying to hide his identity when he signed the purchase agreement for the Forum. He had buried his birth name along with the rest of his past. The assumed name and a fresh start were one and the same thing.

"It's just a pen name," Tom said. "There's nothing illegal."

Klein just shook his head sadly.

"Is that right?" he asked. "That might be true. But hiding your identity makes you look, I don't know, *deceitful.* It will make you so much easier to convict. I think of it as a bit of insurance. I've got the murder weapon for evidence. Not to mention poor Anya's testimony."

As he clearly intended, to Klein, Tom must have appeared to be in checkmate, with no alternative, stunned but not quite ready to concede, shattered but not yet his willing vassal.

"I can see you need a little time to think this over," Klein said, almost kindly, "so here's what I'm going to do. There's something else I'd like you and Sarah to see, and it will take just about half an hour to show it to you, and that's right about when I expect Sheriff Martin to arrive. He may want to question you. Or he might not. It's really up to you."

Chapter 29

ROYAL FIREWORKS

Dick Klein was smiling benevolently at Sarah, as if they had been talking, when Tom and Albert walked back inside.

"Tom has asked to see the house," Albert proclaimed. "And Sarah wants to see Angie and Tyler, so let's go."

They strolled through the living room, Albert carefully shepherding Tom, Sarah to one side, and Dick shuffling behind.

"You see, Tom, it wasn't easy for my father to create all this, but the next generation has challenges of its own. Uranium was a beautiful business back in Dick's day, when the government guaranteed the price. Now of course, uranium is subject to fluctuations in the price of commodities, not to mention all the political uncertainty over whether it will be used for energy production and all of the new environmental regulations and permits that are required. That makes it only prudent for the family to seek out new opportunities."

As they walked through the ranch house kitchen and out a back door toward one of the outbuildings, a baby's painful wail could be heard.

"We've developed a much more lucrative business, one with far better margins."

Albert opened the door to the small cabin and an odor of ammonia wafted out. Albert ushered them inside.

There were drums of chemicals along the walls and propane tanks hooked up to burners. Glass and plastic tubes connected glass jars to one another. On one of the burners a vat of chemicals bubbled away. A large fan set in a rear door failed to keep up with the prodigious production of fumes. Craig and Angie, along with another young couple, were absorbed in the business of operating the lab, oblivious to Tyler's loud cries. He lay in a baby carrier in the middle of the room.

"Angie, how could you?" Sarah cried, rushing to pick Tyler up.

Angie sat a table where she was measuring out quantities of the lab's finished product, crystal meth, and carefully funneling it into the narrow blue plastic zip-lock bags that Tom had seen before: at Brubaker's place and in Denver, when he scored a bag of it. By Angie's side there were cartons full of the trademark baggies, ready for shipment out to the market.

Was the resort just a front for a meth lab? Meth was pervasive, but ordinarily associated with cheap motels and abandoned buildings and the operation was out of context on North Mountain.

"Oh, hi mom," Angie said, looking up without any hint of surprise, as if she'd been interrupted while making fruit preserves, or lavender soap, for a 4-H project.

"You come with me right now," Sarah commanded, and Angie responded with an adolescent roll of her eyes. But she obediently followed Sarah outside.

"I'm sure they have some mother-and-daughter issues to work through," Albert said. "You know my son-in-law, Craig, of course. A fine young man. A real entrepreneur. With his help, we'll soon double, or triple, our production."

Craig looked up from his work with a broad grin. In another context, his easy warmth would have made him instantly likeable.

"Hey, how's it going?" he asked.

"And I believe you've met both Randy and Melody."

Tom recognized both of them: Melody had introduced herself when she had come to his office a few days earlier to retrieve the Uranium King. Randy was the longhaired thug who had roughed him up and the discoverer of Brubaker's still-warm corpse. It was Randy, clearly, who had retrieved the incriminating fire poker for Klein.

Randy nodded in Tom's direction, but his pale eyes were devoid of any particular interest. Mugging Tom had just been part of a day's work.

"Yeah," Tom said. "Why'd you send Randy to mess me up?"

"You know, Tom, that story you published about my father, that was a real cheap shot," Albert said. "You knew he wasn't going to open the Whispering Jim, not at his age, so I wonder why you'd do a thing like that? Hold an old man up to public ridicule? Did you do it just to piss me off?"

Tom frowned and shook head, not to reject the assertion as absurd, as much as he would have liked to, but to acknowledge, painfully to himself, that Klein saw through him so easily and was probably correct about his motives. Called out, it was clear that Tom had, in effect, taunted Albert and invited Randy's assault.

The meth cooks had clearly quality tested the product and were so intent on what they were doing that they paid virtually no attention to Tom and Albert.

"It's quite an operation, isn't it?" Albert said. "Just a few workers and it's highly profitable. Of course, you wrecked my distribution network."

"Sorry about that," Tom muttered.

"It's OK. You'll make up for it."

The two men surveyed the operation for a moment, Albert with an air of pride and Tom seemingly puzzled.

"You figure I'll make a good courier? That I can replace Brubaker?"

"Why that's a great offer, Tom. A fine opening bid in our negotiation."

"Tell me why," Tom said. "With everything you have, the Klein inheritance and the ability to do anything you want. With all you've put into the resort, and all the land that's still left, why do you need this?"

"We're diverse, Tom! Successful families adapt to changing times. There's the next generation to consider, my daughter Angie and my new son-in-law, they need opportunities, not to mention that I'm a grandfather and there's another generation to be planning for. The old man thought we should get back into uranium, and he may be right that uranium is coming back, but not for the Kleins."

"The Uranium King is dead, long live the Meth King?"

"That's good, Tom," Albert laughed. "I like that."

"I still don't get it. You say you're doing it for Angie and Craig, but you've turned them into crank heads."

Hearing himself dissed, Craig glanced up, looking vaguely annoyed.

"That's a little harsh, don't you think?" Albert said.

Tom shrugged.

"People in Europe in the 1920s thought that absinthe was a diabolical drink. In the fifties and sixties they made up similar stories about heroin and 'reefer madness.' Then it was crack. So much hysteria…" He chuckled at the sheer absurdity of it. "Craig and Angie are adults, and they make their own choices."

Tom might have argued that Tyler didn't choose to be a born tweaker, but there was no point.

"You've explained everything, or almost everything," Tom said.

"Almost?"

"What happened to Ray?"

Albert grimaced. "You never want to be forced to take extreme measures," he said. "But Ray left us no alternative. He allowed his troubled relationship with his daughter, with Angie, who is my daughter and only his stepdaughter, after all, to interfere with common sense. He threatened to expose all this...."

"Just like he did twenty years ago, when he protected Sarah."

"I have a different perspective."

"She was a child."

"We're back to philosophy," Albert smirked. "You have your illusions and I have mine."

Maybe so, but they're not equal, Tom thought to himself, but said, instead, "That's true."

"Ray always had a chip on his shoulder," Albert said. "Even though dad took good care of him and his mother, he thought he should have more. It never pays to yield to blackmail."

"So you had Randy take care of him?"

"You'd agree that Randy does good work."

"Clearly, it's not smart to cross the Kleins."

"Like other powerful families, we have interests to protect."

Albert didn't see or didn't care that his father had slipped in past them. The elder Klein caught Tom's eye, held his gaze, and nodded to confirm his full understanding of the situation. More precisely, Dick Klein was enlisting Tom as an eyewitness to his son's gargantuan megalomania, which resembled nothing so much as a nuclear reaction racing out of control. The son made the father's greed, and his hunger for control over the power of the atom, seem quaint, as if the cataclysm that meth visited on its victims was a modern variant on an atomic weapon, albeit one that exploded within the individual and wreaked its devastation on the landscape of the psyche. Dick Klein had not turned up at Tom's office randomly to proclaim he was re-entering the uranium business, which was eminently respectable compared to the tawdriness of a meth lab, but in a valiant if vain attempt to reassert himself against the incomprehensible depredations of his son.

But the Uranium King wasn't dead yet. He angled his head to indicate the flames beneath the boiling cauldron of chemicals. Tom took the cue and repositioned himself, as if he were further inspecting the premises, so that Albert unwittingly turned his back to his father in order to continue talking to Tom. At the same time, Tom was close to the door for a quick exit.

"So where does this leave us? You and me?"

"You're my kind of guy, Tom. You're a fraud and a killer. I can use a man like you."

"You might just be right," Tom nodded. "I've been looking for the right opportunity."

"I'm glad you see it that way because," Albert glanced at his watch, "Sheriff Martin will be here soon and…"

Before he could complete his sentence Tom lunged at him and shoved him forcefully toward the center of the room. Simultaneously there was a loud whoosh. Dick Klein had thrown himself against the vat of boiling chemicals, spilling the contents onto the flames below and setting off an explosion, the force of which blew Tom back, right out the door.

He picked himself up and ran backwards, away from the rapidly exploding blaze. From a short distance away, Angie and Sarah were watching in horror, the baby in Sarah's arms.

There was another explosion and flames leapt higher out of the building's roof, which collapsed inward. Nearby trees were starting to smolder, and a neighboring shed had already caught fire.

Tom pushed Sarah and Angie further away from the burning building.

"We have to get out of here fast," he shouted. He was beginning to be overcome by the smoke.

Sarah grabbed Angie by the arm, and they ran the hundred yards to where the car was parked. Tom revved the engine, pulled the car around, and headed for the road. The forest had ignited, and the fire was racing almost faster than Tom could drive them to safety. Angie and the baby were both shrieking, and then, thankfully, the fire was visible only in the rear-view mirror. Tom hit the brakes. The three of them looked back to see that the main ranch house was engulfed in flames. They watched for just a moment as the fire quickly spread to the new resort structures, and then Tom lifted his foot off the brake, and they headed down the mountain.

Halfway down, they passed a Montrose County Sheriff's vehicle, Sheriff Martin himself behind the wheel, heading up. Both cars slowed down and Martin and Tom exchanged a look, an acknowledgment that they'd seen each other. However the story would play out in the coming days, they were witnesses to one another's deep involvement in it.

"When you were on the patio with Albert, Dick told me that Albert was going to take us to the lab," Sarah said. "He told me to grab the baby and run outside with him. He was going to fix everything. What did he do?"

"He warned me, too," Tom said. "Told me with his eyes to move close to the door. Then he threw himself into fire and set off the explosion."

Tom didn't stop until they reached the Forum office and Tom's adjoining house, just as the town's single fire engine was pulling out of the station. The Naturita Volunteer Fire Department would be no match for the conflagration.

As they climbed out of their car, a terrified but relieved Ray Jr. stepped out of the shadows to join them. He had biked into town to look for them when his mother had failed to return home after work a few hours earlier.

"I thought something bad must have happened," he said to Tom.

"Something bad did," Tom answered, putting his arm on the boy's shoulders. "I'll tell you all about it later."

The entire population of Naturita, Tom and the Walker family among them, stood silently on the highway beneath the brilliantly illuminated night sky, watching the spectacle of Dick Klein's ultimate fireworks display, as smoke, embers and ash drifted down on them.

The fire would burn hot all night, all the next day, and all the following night, until there was nothing left to burn on North Mountain.

Chapter 30

DETOX

Sheriff Martin was covered in soot and smelled of smoke when he stopped by the Forum office three days after the blaze had started. The fire was still burning, he told Tom, but it had spread to remote areas where no structures were threatened and where it could be allowed to burn itself out.

"I'm thinking maybe it's time for me to retire, Tom," he said. "I'm getting too old for this shit."

"Have you got any idea what caused the fire, Sheriff?"

"It was a meth lab explosion. It's hard to believe the Kleins could have come to that. But the evidence is overwhelming. And we've been in a drought for five years. So that's why the fire spread so fast and burnt everything."

"You were close to Dick Klein, weren't you?"

"Well, I was. I knew him for almost forty years. The Dick I knew pretty much faded away ten, fifteen years ago. I believe it was the son, Albert Klein, that got the family mixed up in illicit drugs. Dick never would have done anything like that."

"That sounds right," Tom said. As the only living witness to Dick Klein's final act, he knew without question that the sheriff was correct.

"Yep," Martin said sadly. "But if you write it like that, you have to say it's just my feeling, knowing the family as I did. I've got no real evidence. But Albert was something of a bully. Worse than that, he was a so-cee-o-pathic personality. And I could see he wasn't treating his father right."

"Did Albert Klein try to bully you?"

"I'll admit he might have tried a few times. But I'm pretty ornery myself."

Tom nodded.

"You see, Tom, this has always been rough country. Only tough men, men like Dick Klein, can survive here for long."

"Men like Klein and like you, sheriff?"

"Why, that's exactly right, Tom! I'm glad you see that. In fact, I've been impressed by your toughness, too."

"Is that right?"

"We know each other pretty well by now, don't we Tom? Know a lot about each other. In a small community, the newspaper and law enforcement have got to work closely together. You and me, we've got no need to say anymore what's on the record and what's off when we talk."

"I'd say that's right, sheriff."

"Yes, indeed," Martin said. "For example, I understand you've been in some tough scrapes, met up with at least one rough hombre, and you come out smelling like a rose."

"I imagine you have quite a number of open cases, unsolved crimes, like the Ray Walker disappearance and the death of Mark Brubaker, where you never do know for sure what happened."

"In the Brubaker case, I believe we do know. I'm hoping we can put that one in our closed case file. We know Brubaker was mixed up with the Klein operation. We found boxes of meth in his rig. He was the Klein's courier. Seems plain that he got himself crosswise with Albert Klein and he was executed. He was probably stealing from them. His killer most likely died in the fire. I'm figuring it was the kid, Randy Wagner, who was the tough guy of the operation, as best as I can tell. He had a police record, a bunch of disorderlies, a few drug busts, and an assault or two."

Tom nodded, a sense of relief washing over him at being exonerated by the sheriff. With Martin off his case, the only solid piece of evidence linking him to the Brubaker death was now lost in the ashes of the Klein homestead. Even assuming he knew about the fire poker, the sheriff wasn't planning to look for it, and even if someone else were to find it, it would raise no suspicions because it would be found among Dick Klein's many vintage barbecue tools. Any burned blood on it would look like it came from a steak. Possibly, after a few months, Tom himself would go to the site of the fire to look for it; he would perhaps take the fire poker home and keep it, not as a trophy or memento, but as a talisman whose power to hurt him was gone.

"What about Ray Walker?"

"That one's not so easy to figure. Because I'll tell you what, from everything I know, Ray Walker really was a good man. But I sure as heck wouldn't be surprised if Albert Klein had something to do with it, considering their blood tie and all."

"I think that's probably right, too," Tom said.

"I expect that we'll only ever know what happened to Ray if he turns up alive one day to tell us about it, or if we find his body."

"There are things we know, and things we think we know and things we don't know," Tom muttered, repeating the sheriff's wisdom as if it had become a personal aphorism.

"That's right, Tom. And sometimes we don't know which is which, because we don't always know what we don't know. And sometimes it really is best, and not just for the people directly involved, but for the public interest, to look the other way."

"Can I quote you on that sheriff?"

Martin put his fist to his chin and made a show of thinking through his answer.

"Well, you can," he said carefully. "But, of course, I'll have to arrest you if you do."

The newsman and the lawman had reached their understanding. They could easily destroy each other, but neither was of a mind to do any such thing. It was as if the fire on North Mountain had been so cleansing that no further action by either of them was warranted.

. . .

In a period of a few weeks Angie had lost the father who lovingly raised her, her newly discovered biological father, whom she had imagined would be her salvation, her new husband, and custody of her baby—but it was losing easy access to unlimited quantities of high-quality meth that hurt most, or most urgently. To Tom, Angie's pain—her pounding head, unquenchable thirst, nausea, and twitchy limbs—was palpable, almost contagious, as he and Sarah drove her to a detox center in Grand Junction.

"Mommy," she cried. "I really, really, really can't do this."

"I know, baby," Sarah said.

"I just want to be dead.

"This is the worst of it," Tom said. "We'll be there in an hour and there will be help for you."

"I don't care," she cried. "I can't wait that long. Please, shoot me now!"

Out of the fog of her catatonia in the days after the fire, Angie revealed enough for Tom and Sarah to fill in the last few gaps in their understanding of what had happened to Ray. Despite Sarah's denials, Ray had not been blind to Angie's deepening addiction. Craig had prevailed upon Angie, over Ray's objections, to take advantage of everything she stood to gain from her relationship to the Kleins, not least the business opportunity for them to join Albert's criminal enterprise. As stepfather and fiancé fought over Angie—which for Ray was a losing proposition—Craig was callow enough to boast about his new job, working with his father-in-law in the meth trade. That revelation gave Ray the leverage he needed to threaten Albert with exposure if he didn't cut ties to Angie.

Ray may have been overconfident that standing up to Albert to save Angie would work as well as it had twenty years before, when the Meth King was engaged in a different crime, of child abuse masquerading as polygamy, and Ray had saved Sarah. Or Ray may have seen no alternative other than to try.

Though a half-Klein, Ray had for decades stubbornly refused to toe the Klein family line, and so he was finally dealt with.

* * *

FINAL TOLL OF NORTH MOUNTAIN BLAZE MAY NEVER BE KNOWN

Fire Was Ignited by Meth Lab Explosion

By Tom Austin

Montrose County Sheriff Trace Martin said this week that last week's fire on North Mountain was caused by the explosion of a meth lab. The blaze burned so hot, and the devastation is so complete, that it may never be possible to determine how many people died there.

At least five individuals are believed to have perished in the fire: Dick Klein, 82; his son Albert Klein, 45; the recently married Craig Pellison, 21; Randy Wagner, 25; and Melody Anderson, 22; all of Naturita. The fire burned so hot that it will certainly be impossible to identify human remains amid the ashes, the sheriff said.

"The victims were as good as cremated," Martin said. "Someone might find a tooth if they looked long enough."

The tally would have been much higher, the sheriff added, if the UK Ranch Resort had not been closed for the off-season. But no other persons are reported missing.

Martin said that the nature of the meth operation housed at the resort remains under investigation. But early indications are that it was a large volume operation that supplied methamphetamine to a regional market.

"It is almost impossible to believe that the Klein family would sink so low as to operate a meth lab," Martin said. He himself has been sheriff for almost forty years, he added, and has vivid memories of the family at the height of its wealth and prestige. The sheriff expressed his opinion, emphasizing it was only speculation, that the elder Klein was not at the center of the operation, but that it was headed by his son, Albert Klein.

The tragedy has plunged the community of Naturita into a state of shock and mourning. Every one of the victims had deep roots here. Dick Klein was the region's most prominent citizen, discoverer of the famous Whispering Jim uranium mine and founder of the Uranium King Mining Co., which was the region's biggest employer for a generation. Klein had recently announced plans to reopen the Whispering Jim.

One of the victims, Craig Pellison, was married just three weeks ago to Angie Walker, the daughter of Ray Walker, the Naturita auto mechanic who disappeared without a trace four days prior to his daughter's wedding. The Pellisons' son, Tyler Pellison, is six weeks old.

Wagner and Anderson were both employed by the Kleins. Each is survived by parents and siblings in Naturita. There are two surviving Klein brothers, Frank and Richard, both married, who live in Denver. Dick Klein's wife, Betty Klein, preceded him in death by five years.

Sheriff Martin said his office is investigating a related homicide, the apparent murder of long-distance trucker Mark Brubaker, whose body was found last week at his remote East Bryant Mesa home. There is strong evidence that Brubaker, 34, was working with the Klein methamphetamine operation, the sheriff said, and that his death may have come at the hands of one of the deceased on North Mountain.

A schedule of memorial services appears on page 5. Obituaries of each of the victims start on page 6.

Chapter 31

KARMIC JUSTICE

As soon as Tom wrote his story and got the paper out, he put new laces in a pair of old sneakers, pulled on a pair of sweat-pants and a T-shirt, and made his way to the Walkers' house. As he expected, he found Ray Jr. on the court, shooting hoops.

Ray greeted him with a grin and by passing him the ball. The two of them played for half an hour without saying much until Tom, winded, held the ball to take a time-out.

"You know your dad was a hero," he said. "He died because he was trying to help Angie."

Tom and Sarah had earlier told Ray everything they knew, and all they had surmised, about what had happened to his father.

"I hate Angie," Ray said.

"I know."

"I hope she never comes back."

Tom arced the ball toward the hoop, Ray rebounded, and the two of them dribbled, defended, and shot baskets for another five min-utes, until Tom stopped again.

"I told your mom that you and I would cook dinner tonight."

"I don't know how to cook."

"I was planning to teach you."

Inside, Tom set out ingredients he'd brought from the Merc, from left to right on the counter, a package of spaghetti, a couple of onions, ground beef, a large can of tomatoes, tomato paste, dried Italian herbs, chili powder, a container of grated parmesan, yellow cheddar cheese, and finally a can of pinto beans.

"This is a trick every man must know," he said to Ray. "Right here are all the ingredients you need for two staples of the manly diet: spaghetti and chili."

Ray eyed him skeptically.

"Any woman will think it's the best meal she ever ate if you cook it."

Ray nodded.

"Which do you feel like tonight?

"Spaghetti."

Tom set the chili powder, pinto beans, and cheddar to the side.

"We'll put those away. But if you'd said chili, we would have put these away." He indicated the spaghetti, Parmesan, and herbs.

Tom set Ray up with a cutting board, peeling and chopping the onions, while he rinsed lettuce for a salad.

"It's late and your mom and Tyler will be home in an hour. Some day when we have more time, I'll show you how to dress the spaghetti sauce up and make it fancier. You can use Italian sausage and add other stuff, like peppers or mushrooms."

"I don't like mushrooms."

"We'll leave those out, then. You start the chili exactly the same way, chopping onions and browning ground beef, but you just use the chili powder instead of the herbs and add pinto beans."

Ray nodded, but his thoughts were elsewhere.

"I just don't get why Angie did it," he said.

Tom didn't answer quickly, allowing Ray's question to hang in the air.

Ray had been the odd man out since his father's disappearance. Angie and her meth baby had commanded all of Sarah's attention, and Ray's stoicism had made him easy to overlook, as if he were adequately caring for his own broken heart by shooting hoops for hours on end and could be tended to later, if it proved necessary and when it would be more convenient. But Tom had known, from his own experience, that Ray was silently bleeding.

"Picture a track athlete running hurdles," Tom said. "One of the highest hurdles on the course is drugs and some people just sail over that hurdle and hardly notice it and go on to the next hurdles. Others get tripped up just a little bit but still continue with the race and then they do just fine. Others fall down hard but pick themselves up and still manage to finish. And some fall down and can't finish."

"Why?"

"Nobody knows. It's like how some athletes are born with talent and some have to work harder. Some have more drive than others. Some get good coaching, and some are naturals. Think about Tyler. He was born addicted. That huge hurdle of having to survive drugs was in front of him before he could crawl, even before he took his first breath. That's just horrible bad luck. It's nothing he did to himself."

"Yeah."

"But he has some good luck too."

"Like what?"

"He has you for an uncle and Sarah for a grandmother," Tom said. "Looks like those onions are ready to put in the pan."

Ray handed Tom the cutting board.

"Tyler is lucky that he has you, too," he said.

. . .

Six weeks later, after she got out of detox, Angie returned home. She looked worse than she had in the throes of addiction, not only her face but her torso and limbs broken out in acne, her eyes vacant; she was more sullen than ever, her affect was flat.

"They say I've broken the physical addiction," she explained to Sarah, plainly reciting a script she'd been taught. "But I won't feel good again for a long time. They say I'll need lots of emotional support or I could slip back."

Mother and daughter hugged tearfully.

But it was no surprise to Tom when Angie disappeared after a few days, leaving Tyler behind.

Sarah received a post card, postmarked Los Angeles, the next week.

"I couldn't stay in Naturita," Angie had scrawled on the back. "I'm going to beautician's school. Take care of Tyler. I'm sorry."

Sarah was devastated by the loss of her daughter, which revived all of the pain of losing Ray. The noblest purpose of Ray's life, protecting Angie from her malevolent father, had failed, but there was some meager consolation that Angie wasn't entirely lost and might someday return. Closure was at least within sight.

Tom had imagined that closure for him would arrive when he finally learned what had happened to Ray Walker and he could break the story in the pages of the Forum. That had been his ostensible purpose, after all, and presumably the source of his drive: his need to affirm his profession. He sat down several times to start but found himself blocked.

The problem, in a large sense, was that the tale of Ray's disappearance wasn't his to write, at least not as journalism. He had lost all objectivity, and his perspective was too personal. He couldn't report the truth, and certainly not the whole truth, without exposing himself as Mark Brubaker's killer. To tell a partial truth, withholding the potentially self-incriminating crux of the matter, which was precisely how the truth had been uncovered, seemed impossible because the story wasn't easily parsed to include what was safe to report and in the public interest and to exclude what wasn't safe and was nobody's business because it was deeply personal.

There was an added challenge of sourcing the information, since so much of what he knew was based on his own observations and actions, or on what he was told by the woman he loved, with no other substantiation. There were no living witnesses to support a story Tom might publish asserting that Ray had been killed by Klein's henchman, Randy Wagner. Ray's motive for trying to blackmail Klein was equally without supporting evidence, without revealing the details of Angie's birth, which would be a betrayal of both Sarah and Ray Walker and their marriage.

Tom might have been able to write his way around all of those problems. But what could he do with Sheriff Trace Martin's complicity, up to and including turning a blind eye to the North Mountain meth operation? At the very least. He was more likely taking kickbacks or was a full partner. Martin had agreed to let Tom off the hook with regard to the Brubaker killing; the obvious quid pro quo was that Tom would not look into the sheriff's relationship with Albert Klein. Martin had strongly hinted that he knew exactly what happened to Ray Walker, just as he knew exactly what happened to Mark Brubaker. In both cases he had his own reasons, admittedly venal, for looking the other way.

In short, if Tom tried to report any aspect of the story, he would surely "end up with a big ole mess," just as Martin had warned him could happen during an early interview after Ray first disappeared. "You don't always report every detail you know, now do you?" Martin had asked then. And, of course, the answer was that no reporter ever reports all he knows. Along with information he may deem irrelevant, there are facts that can't be verified and sources to protect. In this case, the primary source in need of protection was Tom himself. Nor did Tom see any percentage in either provoking or exposing Martin, however deserving he was of a prison cell. Their truce was fragile and could too easily be undone.

Neither truth nor justice is always best served in the public sphere, Tom reasoned. Sometimes newspapers unwittingly publish fictions and sometimes truths are best kept confidential. Even more frequently, the truth is misapprehended by people in the grip of fear or confusion or by those whose selfish motives cloud their perceptions. A good lie can have a half-life far longer than several human lifetimes, and when a secret is well kept the truth may be lost to human memory. By way of example, Tom was now the only living person who knew how Whispering Jim died. Unlike Ray's disappearance, Jim's was a story he could write and publish, and without compromise. Indeed, he felt a compulsion to write it and redeem Jim from the dust. There was no risk of betrayal in a story that began: "The week before he died in the North Mountain fire, Dick Klein, the West End's legendary Uranium King, revealed the previously unreported details of how his partner, Whispering Jim Stewart, disappeared in Iberia Canyon almost fifty years ago. That story can now be told."

As Klein had allowed, Jim was "history," and so was Klein himself, immune to betrayal or retribution. But when the truth is irretrievable or unprintable, the only compensation may be karmic justice. Just so, in the public record, what happened to Ray Walker would forever remain a mystery.

At the same time, with the mystery of Ray's disappearance solved to their own satisfaction, and with this truth as the basis of their bond, Tom and Sarah had affirmed their love for one another. They lived as a couple in the doublewide that Dick Klein had originally purchased for his mistress, Elizabeth Walker, and his bastard son. He and Sarah had become the parents to Tyler and Ray Jr. Soon, Tom thought, he would take his new family back East to meet his mother and sister. Someday, he and Sarah would quietly get married.

In all of this, although it had come at a high cost and was undoubtedly imperfect, there was a deeply satisfying sense of equilibrium having been achieved and of justice having been served.

Circumstance—sometimes thought of as history, as Molly Buford observed—was the most powerful force in most people's lives, Tom concluded, far more of a factor than their ambition or talent or will. That was as true of a kid growing up in suburban Boston who unaccountably found himself running a community newspaper on the West End as it was of the daughter of polygamists who was born there and never left, but the native West Ender had the advantage of never indulging any other conceit. Character was crucial, too, but Tom could never explain where Sarah got hers, or Ray Walker his, for that matter, making character largely a matter of circumstance, too.

In a world of unyielding moral ambiguity, each accommodation Tom had made seemed to him to have been his best option when it was presented to him. The choices, if they were real choices, added up to the quality of his character. Of course, he might have rejected the messy compromises the West End had presented him with and fled, just as he had fled Boston, and he could have gone back to the Keys or maybe in the opposite direction, to Baja. But flight hadn't worked then, and even when he'd felt the most trapped in Naturita, he retained the awareness, however subconsciously, that running away wouldn't have worked any better if he'd tried it a second time. Tom's grip on his new life on the West End was tenuous, but it was all he had. With foresight, he might have chosen somewhere less harsh to make his stand, someplace like Ireland, under a blanket of green moss, or San Francisco, wrapped in silky fog.

But at some point, and he couldn't say when, it had become too late for that, and he had resolved to stay and fight.

EPILOGUE

Six months after the North Mountain fire, Tom received a call from Mayor Denny.

"We've found something at the Dead Man's Curve work-site," Denny said. "You might want to come down, and be sure to bring your camera."

By the time Tom arrived, a crowd had gathered. Word had spread quickly that the road construction crew had found a vehicle in the San Miguel River, and a crowd had gathered to watch. Deputy Billy Pedersen was supervising. Tom was standing with Dave Best when the winch started up and, to gasps but no real surprise, Ray Walker's bright red truck slowly emerged from the muddy water.

For a brief moment, to the onlookers for whom the mystery had never been solved, a resolution appeared at hand. Like so many others before him, Walker had apparently gone off the road at Dead Man's Curve. He had not been found during the extensive search for him because his truck had come to rest in the deepest spot in the river.

The crowd fully expected that Ray's body would be found trapped in the cab of the truck.

But the truck was empty and the mystery was not so easily resolved. It could have been that there had indeed been an accident and Ray's body had later floated out of the truck cab and had been carried downriver, probably during the spring runoff when the current was strongest. That possibility was quickly ruled out, though, by the simple fact that the truck windows were rolled up tight. Even more perplexing, the truck showed no signs of having been damaged in a wreck, which it would have been if it had flown off the road with enough velocity to reach the spot where it was found. Moreover, if there was anyone who knew not to speed on Dead Man's Curve, it was Ray Walker. The stretch of highway was famous for claiming victims, but they were almost always the unwary.

Somebody had carefully placed the vehicle in the river, choosing the one spot in the San Miguel that was deep enough to keep it hidden for years. It was easy to see how it was done. The truck would have been positioned above the river, put into neutral, and given a shove. It could have been Ray himself who did it, or someone else.

"Walker Disappearance Deepens," was the headline Tom wrote for the Forum. In the story he wrote he quoted Billy Pederson saying, "I reckon we'll never know exactly what happened to Ray."

We will truly never know, Tom mused, as he prepared the story for publication. Not with any certainty. More to the point, the deeper mystery in the end was not what happened to Ray Walker. The deeper mystery was how anyone else—some who drifted to the West End and some who were born there—managed to beat the odds and survive.

Tom had often wondered how people endured the pitilessness of life on the West End, how they inhabited this beautiful but forbidding place where human nature is rubbed as raw as a rock spire eroded over the millennia by the forces of wind, rain and frost. Now he was one of them, living out his brief moment of existence on the same implacable landscape.

AUTHOR'S NOTE

The Uranium Drive-In is a work of fiction inspired by a true story. On May 27, 1999, 42-year-old Dale Williams, an auto-mechanic in Nucla, Colorado, disappeared after he responded to a call from a stranded motorist. His Ford pickup truck was found two months later, submerged in the San Miguel River. Thirty-five years later, the mystery remains unsolved.

Some weeks following the disappearance, I saw the MISSING posters with Dale Williams's face on them posted all over the West End. Any resemblance between Dale Williams and the fictional Ray Walker ends with their profession, their disappearance, and the discovery of their vehicles in the San Miguel.

The character of Dick Klein is very loosely inspired by Charles Steen, a geologist who was known as the Uranium King, who lived not on the West End of Montrose County, but in Moab, Utah. All of the other characters in this book are fictional inventions and any resemblance they may bear to any person living or dead is coincidence.

ABOUT THE AUTHOR

Seth Cagin and his wife Marta Tarbell founded The Telluride Watch newspaper in 1996, selling it in 2014. Seth is the co-author of three books of non-fiction, *Hollywood Films of the Seventies: Sex, Drugs, Violence, Rock 'n' Roll and Politics* (Harper & Row, 1984); *We Are Not Afraid: The Story of Goodman, Schwerner and Chaney and the Civil Rights Campaign for Mississippi* (Macmillan, 1988) and *Between Earth and Sky: How CFCs Threatened the Ozone Layer* (Pantheon, 1993).

If you enjoyed *The Uranium Drive-In*, you'll want to follow Tom Austin to Telluride, where, four years later, in 2008, he has become the publisher of The San Miguel Examiner newspaper.

The Examiner is also available at Amazon Books. Here's a head start:

1. EYEBALLS

Tom was sitting in Erica Ortiz's office when he learned that Jay Cluff had been killed.

Erica was Tom's biggest advertiser in The San Miguel Examiner and his friend.

They were talking about the collapsing economy and what to do about it.

"We kept telling ourselves that the market would pick up," Erica said. "And it just kept getting worse. Now it's as bad as it can get. It's dead."

Erica had a television mounted high on the wall in a corner of her office, where she could keep an eye on it. It was perpetually tuned to a cable business channel. Tom glanced up at it. Crashing stock prices scrolled across the bottom of the screen while a reporter standing on the floor of the New York Stock Exchange talked.

Wall Street was only confirming what Erica and Tom already knew. The decade-long boom in Telluride real estate had started to tail off a year earlier. In March, real estate sales had come to a total halt. Six months later, Tom's biggest customers, including Erica, had fallen behind in paying for their ads. Tom was falling behind with his print-ing bills. The outlines of what would be called the Great Recession were in clear sight.

"Lehman is going down and nobody's gonna save it," Erica said. "Nobody can, except the federal government, and Bush is too chickenshit to try."

"Maybe Obama," Tom ventured.

"Fuck Obama. Nothing but a lot of pain will fix it. The slow economy was bad enough. We could have survived that. But now we're facing a total collapse of the financial system. You know that Lehman was the lender for the Mountain Village hotel project, right?"

"No."

But Tom should have known. The hotel was his biggest advertiser's biggest client, its luxury condos offered for sale at pre-construction prices in a full-page ad on the back page of every edition of The Examiner. Erica paid Tom $65,000 a year for that ad alone. It was beyond lucrative, it was essential, but it was also such a constant that Tom had come to take it for granted.

"I'm what's wrong with Lehman," Erica said. "I can't sell the condos, which a year ago would have sold overnight, which means Lehman can't recover what they've put into the project. And it also means I can't keep up with my own debt or pay you for my ads. I'm not the only realtor who's fallen behind with his advertising bills, am I? Properties are falling out of contract like drunks in a flop house falling out of bed. Nothing's closing. Or haven't you noticed?"

"I assumed that you and all the other realtors were telling me the truth," Tom said. "That this year's slow sales were just a normal part of the real estate cycle, and they'd bounce back bigger than ever next year."

"I can't blame you for falling for our bullshit since we fell for it ourselves."

"Film Festival is coming up in three weeks. Got $40,000 in ads booked."

"We're all hoping some Hollywood fat cat will fall in love with Telluride, decide to buy a mountain retreat and save our ass. It won't happen. Even movie stars are paralyzed because they have no idea where their money's safe. There sure as hell won't be a truckload of them making an impulse purchase this week. Maybe one of us might get lucky. Or two."

"Ever the optimist."

"It might be me who makes the sale to Brad and Angelina."

"They're coming?"

"Who the fuck knows?"

Erica's sharp tone was startling. Tom had spent countless hours with her, conducting business in this very office and socializing over dinner with their spouses in one of Telluride's fine dining establishments or at one of their homes. He had witnessed her speak in public and interact with others in both professional and personal settings, engaging with colleagues, clients, and her two young daughters. He had never seen Erica lose her cool before, not even under pressure, not for a moment. Along with her good looks, Erica's polish offered reassurance and was the foundation of her personality and her business success. Now, cracks were showing, and Tom could observe her struggle, if only momentarily, to regain her composure.

"It doesn't take a psychic to see what's going to happen," Erica said, her tone reined back to a sympathetic register. "You'll publish a big fat paper full of all those ads we've booked. Then you'll owe a huge fucking printing bill, and you'll find yourself sitting on your hands waiting for the realtors who placed all those ads to pay their bills."

"What do we do?"

"Cut expenses to the bone and try to ride it out."

Erica had deep pockets. If she was scared, what was Tom feeling? Was it the first tremor of panic threatening to undo his equanimity?

That's when Tom's phone beeped.

He glanced at the screen. It was a text message from his senior reporter, Peter Barnard.

Tom read it out loud: "Jay Cluff found shot dead in Bear Creek."

Erica flinched and looked confused; the change of subject too quick to process.

"Cluff dead? Are you sure?"

"It's from Peter, so, yeah."

"Fuck."

"Well, the paper's not dead yet. I'd better go deal with it."

"The collapse of the economy will just have to wait, huh?"

Erica was reaching for the light irony she favored. But the subject was too big for that and there was a trace of something darker and more bitter in her voice.